Confessional

'What have we here?' asked Father Sterling as he nudged Faren's small scarlet panties with the toe of his shoe. He flipped them carelessly to his companion, Father Drew, who expertly caught the feminine items. 'Go on, Edmonds,' said Sterling, 'you know you want to.'

Drew Edmonds needed no further urging. He lifted the gossamer panties to his face and inhaled deeply of their scent.

'What are you doing in the showers?' squealed Faren. 'You shouldn't be in here!' She took a step forward but her foot slid from beneath her, and her slick body landed on the floor, legs splaying in a most unladylike fashion, giving the two priests an unimpeded view of her most intimate self. It was too late for modesty.

Confessional

JUDITH ROYCROFT

Black Lace novels contain sexual fantasies.
In real life, make sure you practise safe sex.

First published in 1999 by
Black Lace
Thames Wharf Studios,
Rainville Road, London W6 9HT

Typeset by SetSystems Ltd, Saffron Walden, Essex
Printed and bound by Mackays of Chatham PLC

ISBN 0 352 33421 5

Chapter One

'You did say, Miss Lonsdale, that you wish to become a priest?'

Faren watched the priest's expression tousle with a mixture of amusement and interest. His sharp hazel eyes assessed her coolly, and Faren doubted he was taking her the least bit seriously. She squared her shoulders. She would just have to show him that she meant business. 'Yes, Father. I've always wanted to be a priest.'

'Always, Miss Lonsdale? It is very unusual for a young person to be so certain.'

Faren flushed. In the stifling heat of this airless room, Faren marvelled that the priest could bear to be wrapped in neck-to-ankle black robes. But then she knew the choice of attire would not be his; this was the age-old habit of men of the cloth. Fleetingly, she wondered what Father Murray was wearing beneath his garment. Nothing, if he had any sense.

'There are some men here who take their vows because of family tradition. Others are beckoned by the mystique of the priesthood. Now, can you honestly tell me this has been your wish for as long as you can remember?'

'Perhaps I exaggerated, Father,' Faren admitted.

1

The priest smiled. A kindly expression, and somewhat knowing, more like one would expect from an elderly man. 'Now that we have that out of the way, we can proceed.'

'Yes, Father,' Faren murmured. Calmly seated in the sturdy visitor's chair, Faren settled her elbows on the armrests before opening her legs a fraction. In the heat, her thighs had stuck together, and now with her subtle movement she was feeling more comfortable as the air rode and circulated around her skin, drying the clamminess that had deposited there.

The priest went on to ask, 'What would you say is your main avenue of interest here, Miss Lonsdale?'

Faren was suddenly brought back to the scene she had to perform. She stared at the man behind the desk. 'I'm sorry, I don't quite know what you mean, Father.'

Father Murray took a deep breath, as though he were merely humouring her. 'If you gain admission to St Peter's, what would you wish to do eventually? Are you good with children? Or, if you are a ready listener, then perhaps counselling would be a good line to follow.'

'Oh, I see, Father!' Faren shifted in the chair and silently cursed the cracked vinyl that pricked her through the thin fabric of her dress. She wished this dreary interview were over. She would give anything to be outside, soaking up the summer day, feeling the sea breeze on her skin. But first things first. 'I consider myself a very sympathetic listener. And yes, I would enjoy a role in counselling.'

'Right. Of course, your specialisation would be deferred for a few years yet, but it helps to have some notion ahead of time. We can then guide you into the right area of study.' Father Murray tapped his pencil on his thumbnail. 'A very important question is: how does your family feel about this?'

'There's no problem there, Father. I'm from a large family and my parents are very happy to have one less at home. My brothers drifted off to the city as soon as they left school.' She shrugged. 'I couldn't wait to follow. My mother has her hands full with the three girls left at home.'

'Well then, all that seems satisfactory. You're used to sharing and living with a number of people. Life in the seminary is certainly not isolated.' Simon Murray's hand strayed to his hair and then, as if realising it was vanity for a priest to preen, he hastily withdrew it. He glanced down at her papers. 'You did your commerce degree part time, I see. Commendable, Miss Lonsdale.'

'Thank you, Father. I did have plans to attend university full time but I was offered an excellent office position soon after I arrived in Sydney. The money I earned helped me to get through.' She spoke the truth. What Faren was omitting was the fact that she was employed by the controversial Sydney magazine, *Splash!*

'Right. Now, most important of all, I need to ask why you wish to become a priest.'

Father Murray was regarding her steadily, perhaps wondering just what her objective was, how serious her intent. Whatever she might convey during this interview, she must not give him cause to doubt her sincerity. Above all, she must refrain from presenting herself as a sensual woman. That would come later. With this in mind, Faren clamped together her heated thighs. 'It's all rather embarrassing, Father.' She took a deep breath. 'I would like to enter this order because – oh, how can I tell you?' She fiddled with the hemline of her dress, smoothing it across her knees.

'Come now, Miss Lonsdale. Surely you are exaggerating? How can your reason for wanting this life possibly be embarrassing?' When Faren failed to respond, he lumbered on. 'It's something we ask all applicants. I've surged ahead of myself in my questioning, though this is the time to tell you; this is a male domain.'

'I've been following the news reports, Father. And I

3

know the Church has yet to make a decision on whether to allow women into the priesthood. I also know the day will come, and I believe it is not far off, despite the majority of men wishing to block progress. Someone has to make the first move, Father. Why not St Peter's?'

The priest's hazel eyes narrowed to little more than amber shards. But she had him thinking. He nodded, as if agreeing to whatever thoughts were playing through his mind.

'If I accept your challenge – and I do believe that is what you have presented here – it would be for a probationary period only.' He shifted slightly in his chair, studying Faren. 'Even as we speak, my superiors are paving the way to admit a small handful of women into seminaries around the world. Many priests have registered their displeasure. But I'm an open-minded man, Miss Lonsdale, and I know the world has to change. I know the Church has to change.' He tapped his pencil on the edge of his desk. Then he sought her gaze once more. 'What is your honest opinion? Do you believe the world is ready for women priests?'

'We won't know until we try, will we, Father?' A safe answer, she thought. It was obvious that priests deemed themselves far superior to women. But as the priest frowned, Faren hurriedly added, 'I'd give it my best shot, Father. Women do want to be represented in the priesthood. I won't let them down.'

'If – and it is a mighty big "if", young lady – I can persuade the governing board to support your proposal, I would trust you to do your utmost to ensure my faith in you is warranted.'

'Of course, Father.' Her hands resting in her lap, Faren crossed her fingers.

'All those chosen to enter St Peter's are exceptional young people. Yes, indeed. Exceptional.'

'Oh yes, Father, I do know this.' What was one more lie amongst many? But exceptional at what? 'And as to why, well –' she took a deep breath, aware as never before of her breasts rising and falling, and she shrunk inwardly, ineffectively drawing in the ripe fullness of which she had always been so proud, trying in desperation to appear unflirtatious '– I was to have been married next week and my – my fiancé jilted me.'

While preparing for this assignment Faren had decided the jilted bride-to-be would appear a genuine reason for her lost faith in romance. That for a time she had allowed her religious aspirations to be forgotten in favour of love should strengthen her case. She had tried romance and found it wanting. Therefore, she now knew her own mind; she was back on track. She sighed, peeping out at him from beneath her lashes.

The priest was giving her his full attention, concern clouding his eyes. 'Did he offer you a reason, child?'

Faren was about to launch into her prepared spiel when there was a sharp rap at the door. Both occupants turned as the door swung open.

'Your coffee, Father.'

As, complete with laden tray, the woman nudged the door wider to accommodate her ample girth, Father Murray jumped to his feet. The perfect gentleman, Faren noted wryly, a consideration he had failed to afford her.

'Thank you, Mrs Cheaters. We can manage now,' he added, as the woman picked up the silver coffeepot to pour. He missed the uneasy glance his housekeeper shot Faren. However, the moment the woman's attention swept back to the priest, she was all graciousness again. Faren was perplexed at the sudden wariness directed towards her. Surely the woman did not think she was about to be usurped?

With the priest's focus on the older woman, Faren was able to study Simon Murray more fully. She had been informed at the outset that his mentor, a Father Cossly, normally interviewed potential recruits, and although he had agreed to see her, he had been called away to read the last rites to one of his flock at the local hospital, therefore leaving this meeting in the capable hands of Father Murray. Relatively new to the parish, and, at thirty-six, many years younger than his predecessor, Simon Murray was attractive in a devil-may-care way that piqued Faren's interest. A waste of prime male flesh, she observed. Then wondered if it were so. Knowing men as highly sexual animals, Faren refused to believe the code of ethics, that of abstinence in the priesthood. Occasionally a maverick priest – even a bishop – would feature in the tabloids, betrayed by an unhappy or spurned mistress. Less common – but wielding no less impact – was a contented mistress sharing her secret love with the world. And a small number of priests had fathered children. Now, taking in the tanned, handsome man smiling animatedly at the housekeeper, Faren found it difficult to believe that female parishioners would allow this man to escape their greedy libidos. The older woman was obviously affected by the priest's charms, as she wore a rosy flush. Her blue eyes were almost feverish as she gazed up at Father Murray.

'Sugar?'

Faren blinked, so caught up in her appraisal of the priest that she had failed to witness the woman's departure. 'No. No, thank you, Father,' she said breathily, wiggling in the chair to shift its hard flap of protruding vinyl from one tender part of her anatomy to another, while veiling her movement to prevent drawing attention to her bare legs. If she failed this interview it would mean an end to her project. She intuitively knew it could be the scoop of the decade. And if she was to gain a place for herself in this seminary, she needed to be extremely careful; her request must seem to be genuine. The man was endeavouring to keep things on a normal footing but things were far from normal. They were holding each other's gaze for far too long; even his wonderful tan failed to hide his blush when he stared at her. And his tan puzzled her. Surely it was a vanity? Would a priest sunbathe? It seemed inconceivable that he would seek out the sun on the local golden beaches like laymen of his age. And, she mused, with a tingle of sexual anticipation, was the tan confined solely to his face? Or did it dip down beneath the black fabric of his cassock, bronzing his entire body? The aroma of coffee was in the air and Faren, grateful to be yanked back from her dangerous musings, busied herself with a sip. It was imperative that she present herself as serene, intellectual, and, above all, ladylike. By the time she glanced up, Father Murray had himself fully in control. If indeed he had lapsed at all.

'You were about to explain why you wish to enter the priesthood.'

'Quite simply, Father, after the letdown by my fiancé, I've had enough of men.' Her sober gaze locked on to his. 'In a romantic context that is.'

'Oh, come now, Miss Lonsdale. Because one man has let you down is no just cause to give up.' Father Murray leaned back in his chair, his gaze fixed on hers. When she remained silent he cleared his throat. 'Give yourself time to recover from your shock. There'll be someone else out there.' He followed his advice with a smile.

Faren remained serious, feeling her nipples beginning to push at the cotton cups of her bra as she responded to the warmth in his voice. Steady, she urged silently. This is the only way to play it. Though she wanted to smile with him, to prolong the enjoyment of watching his generous mouth curve, the toss of his wayward hair. 'I've made up my mind, Father. I see the priesthood as a wonderful means to serve people. Particularly women. It's what I want to do; take my vows and forget all about the games men and women play. They are not for me. I see it clearly now.' She saw him watching her thoughtfully, and Faren knew he was framing his next question, but still, it took her by surprise.

7

'Did your fiancé explain why he had a change of heart?'

'We weren't compatible. So he said.'

'But you are not convinced?'

'In the beginning, no, I didn't agree with him.' She gave a tight smile. She pleated the hem of her dress. Then looked up at him. He was smiling.

'What I am endeavouring to establish is: do you realise what you will be relinquishing? It's a lot to give up. And before you ask, yes; I give the same talk to the young men who sit right where you are sitting and tell me tales of their disillusionment with life.'

She kept her gaze steady and waited for him to continue.

'And so I must ask you again, Miss Lonsdale.' He looked over to the letter outlining Faren's personal details on his desk. 'Do you realise what you are giving up?'

Without the slightest hesitation, Faren moved into her answer. 'Most definitely. My fiancé told me I was useless. And though I consider he was incorrect in his assumption, even cruel, my eyes have been opened. I want to help women. Jilted women. Women who have been made to feel inadequate in a relationship. I believe I could make a good job of it.'

'With such determination, I'm apt to believe you could. I've long since thought that some of those poor souls need a woman to confide in. We help them to the best of our ability. But undoubtedly they would respond well to a woman. Having been in a similar situation yourself, your services would be of immeasurable value. However, your proposal must be put before the Council. The young priests of today are more liberal; already they question the old system. And because I have had this opportunity to interview you, I can see for myself your determination, your potential for leadership.'

Unable to contain her excitement, she leaned across the desk, her elbow knocking his calendar to the floor. 'Oh!

8

Excuse me, Father.' Bending to retrieve it, her hands curled around the smooth wooden base of the desk as she glanced towards the pair of shiny black shoes, then allowed her gaze to trail up along black-clad legs. His cassock was scrunched up around his waist, yielding an excellent view of his lower body, and what was holding Faren's intense interest was the enticing bulge cradled between his thighs. She fisted her itching hands and took a long breath.

Smiling, she popped up and placed the calendar, all askew, on the desk. 'Sorry, Father,' she demurred. Privately satisfied that she had viewed the true response from the man, now she was prepared to consolidate her position. 'It is true I have such skills. If you take a look at my high-school records, you'll see I was captain of the debating team. And twice voted class president.' She toyed with her skirt, then, realising how he might interpret that action, her hands stilled and she looked straight up at the priest. Briefly, he returned her regard.

'Quite so, Miss Lonsdale,' he agreed, mopping a film of perspiration from his brow. He shifted about in his chair, his hands every bit as restless, while his discomfort grew. Twice already he had stuck his index finger down his clerical collar, as though the action would loosen it and allow a breath of air to circulate, but he managed only to pull the stiff material momentarily from his neck. Faren watched the priest swallow. Surely it was only the humidity of the room that made him restless?

From the beginning of this interview, Faren knew she was here on an assignment. She hadn't expected to be attracted to the priest. But she was. Her nipples were straining against her bra. The cotton felt abrasive on her sensitive skin. The tight buds ached, yearning for a man's caress. A man's moist mouth. The warmth between her thighs was building up to an almost intolerable level, an unbearable aching, and Faren crossed her legs to intensify the pleasurable feeling. The gusset of her panties grazed the swollen lips of her sex, and, if she moved slightly, she could create a satisfying friction. She fancied she was releasing the first note of her arousal, a delicate scent, ever so faint, but tangible nonetheless. She must resist the urge to inhale deeply and savour it, if indeed her imagination was not playing tricks. Instead, Faren schooled herself to concentrate. There would be time enough for pleasure later. Self-gratification must not be allowed to swamp her and this interview, and all it could mean to the advancement of her career. Watching the priest's mouth as he continued to preach, Faren concentrated on banishing the sensuous heat that threatened to overtake her as she visualised what that sexy mouth could do to her.

'As you pointed out earlier, we play no "games". We have no personal problems to distract us. Therefore we are able to give ourselves entirely to advising young courting couples, counselling married folk, and working to keep people together in their relationships. Now, is there a chance you will get back with your fiancé? No? Right then, my advice is to put this behind you.'

Surely he was not suggesting she get out there and meet someone else? Faren thought she was losing it, the exposé she had placed all her hopes on relegated to the backburner, never making the big time. She blamed herself of course. She had allowed herself to be swept away by self-confidence, and the obvious attraction the priest felt for her. This scheme, this story, could rocket her to the top. There had to be another way. She needed admission into St Peter's. Instead of focusing entirely on that objective, she had been playing eye games.

Conceding she had nothing to lose, Faren crossed her legs, her tight skirt sliding along her thighs. Earlier she had moved away from the large desk which had hidden her legs. This was more effective. The priest's gaze was pinned on to the expanse of naked skin. Pleased now she had shucked her stockings in deference to the heat,

Faren watched Father Murray. So, he's not as immune to me as he pretends! she thought. She could almost smell his desire for her.

Just then the telephone on the wall behind Father Murray shrilled. He jumped. No doubt his mind was taking the same evocative path as her own, and the outside sound had pierced his meditative state. Tearing his eyes from her – almost reluctantly, she guessed – he spoke quietly into the receiver. 'Can I help you?'

Faren studied the hand clutching the black Bakelite. The nails were clean and clipped short, very masculine. How would those fingers feel on her skin which was now highly sensitised with her daydreaming? Would they have the power to light her senses, scorch her skin? Already her sex ached and throbbed for their touch, and the thick hardness of him. Firmly she admonished herself for those wanderings. She was not here to seduce or be seduced, though her secret place continued to send out frantic signals to the contrary. She squeezed her thighs tightly, feeling the muscles of her sex contract in pleasurable anticipation. Not for a moment did she think seduction was on the agenda; she was here merely to procure, by observation, a highly evocative magazine piece, and it was imperative that she did not lose sight of her objective.

The one-sided telephone conversation droned on, and Faren, paying little attention to the words and concentrating more on the warmth of her sex, was bent on studying the man behind the desk. Why would an attractive man like Father Murray – or any young man for that matter – choose to walk this barren path? It seemed ludicrous to relinquish all the fun that life had to offer and settle for this unbelievably austere existence. Faren shrugged. People were different, with different tastes and desires in life and, on reflection, perhaps this was just as well. It made for an interesting life. Lifting her gaze to the masculine face, Faren liked Simon Murray; she liked the hazel eyes that darkened when he stared at her. She liked the seductive curve of his mouth when he smiled. He gazed at her intently as he listened to his caller, the stubby receiver cradled in those tapered fingers, and, as they flexed, Faren sighed, asking herself if they had touched a woman's smooth skin, caressed a woman's soft breast, stroked the satiny, most intimate folds of a female. Surely, in his teens, exploring his adolescent awakenings before aspiring to this life, he would have fondled the moist pout of a woman's sex. She was aware of her own sex, the dampness between her legs, as she pulled herself up sharply. Here she was, a dedicated journalist, drifting off into an evocative daydream, ruled by the throb between her legs, instead of eavesdropping. And who knew what morsel of information might be revealed in this room? But it was such a mundane conversation that Faren's attention soon wandered again, her gaze drifting to the priest's inviting lips. They were firm, luscious in their fullness. So vivid was the picture of his mouth crushing hers that she could almost feel his kiss. But she would never get to confirm its texture, its taste, the excitement Faren sensed that mouth would evoke. Sadly, this man was out of bounds.

Suddenly, Faren tensed, sitting rigid in her chair, her ears perking, and tuned into a conversation that by its very tone had subliminally sent signals to alert her brain.

'That's exactly what I said. Two or three years. That is the very earliest. We have a lengthy waiting list of new entrants to St Peter's.' The priest grimaced. 'Oh? If you knew this, why did you ring?' In the silence, Faren hardly dared to breathe. Then Father Murray spoke again. 'An interview would not be granted before that time, you understand? It would be pointless. There are several equally fine establishments throughout the country. I suggest it would be prudent to try one of them.' There was a pause while the priest pursed his lips, obviously frustrated at his inability to get through to his caller.

Once again Faren found her imagination rioting at that small, sexless gesture. Exactly the right shape to suckle and tease. She groaned as her aching nipples responded to the fantasy, thankful Father Murray's attention was reined to his call. 'I'm not surprised to hear they can take you now. Several people on our waiting list have told us of this. My advice to you is to go ahead.'

From the gist of this speech, Faren finally began to realise how very fortunate she was at having been granted this interview. Obviously they were turning away recruits. This conversation set to tingling Faren's acute journalistic nose; she was on to something here. Something more important than she had originally opted for. Unless, she thought, her neck hairs beginning to prickle, they were connected. Despite hearing only segments of the conversation, it appeared glaringly obvious to Faren that the caller wanted to enter this seminary. After being informed he could not take up his training for several years, still he persisted in waiting. What was so special about this particular institution? To Faren, St Peter's appeared like any other, though she could hardly be labelled an expert. After a cursory research into seminary life she had assumed that one was much like another. From this side of the line there was little doubt that the caller was adamant about waiting; there was something intriguing to ferret out here. Faren's bloodhound instincts just knew it. Thoughts of a promotion that could stem from a blockbuster story had Faren hanging on every word. There was no more daydreaming about the luscious male body going to waste. To Faren, her career meant everything.

Chapter Two

'*S*he's gone then?'

Simon Murray glanced up as his housekeeper let herself quietly into the study. Mildly annoyed with the woman's intrusion, he sighed, realising he felt this way purely because her presence superseded his memory of the young woman he had recently escorted from his office. 'You know she's gone, Rosemary.' He had seen her lurking in the hall. Then, as a rosy flush spread across the woman's anxious face, Simon relented. 'You have served me well all these months, Rosemary. Nothing will change.' But he struggled to meet his housekeeper's eyes, knowing it was hardly her fault his loins were aching for the slim, tight flesh of the woman who was to be St Peter's newest entrant.

'You want her, don't you?' Rosemary Cheaters accused, thrusting a dull blonde curl behind her ear.

Simon held out his hand. 'Come here.'

The housekeeper turned the lock in the solid oak door, a smug smile playing across her face where moments before there had been fear. She walked towards him, her fingers already working loose the buttons of her blouse. Simon forestalled her. His desire for quick release of his pent-up passion did not allow for the divesting of clothes. He'd had a permanent erection almost from the moment Faren Lonsdale had walked into his office. The effort of banishing sharp images of sinking himself to the hilt into Faren's yielding flesh had almost brought him to an explosive climax there and then. Seated opposite him, she had seemed so innocent, demurely crossing those long, naked legs, sitting so primly it was difficult to imagine her giving herself to any man. An ex-fiancé, and the man had announced her frigid! Or at least that was the way Simon read it. He refused to believe it. The man was a fool. An experienced lover could awaken the sweet promise of her youthful body. He knew he should not have these lustful thoughts, but did he not pray for his soul every day? His sins were many, and the Good Lord would not renounce him.

'Simon!'

Rosemary's strident tone recalled Simon from his reverie, which was a pity, he thought, as his mind's eye had been readying to plunge his cock into the delectable Miss Lonsdale. Now he must attend his lover. He sighed, then pushed the woman to her knees. He watched her burrow eagerly beneath his cassock and felt her fumble for his zip. His penis leapt from the confines of his trousers and encountered Rosemary's warm breath. Work-roughened hands roamed his flat belly, particles of callused skin snagging his arrow of dark hair, inflaming him. Her thumb and forefinger stroked his aching, impatient flesh, and then he was immersed in her mouth. Simon groaned. Her eager tongue was prodding his small slit as she sucked strongly on his cock. Simon placed his hands on the woman's shoulders, steadying himself as he thrust into her mouth. As he pulled out, the tips of her teeth scraped the soft, helmeted head. He moaned with the sweet, sharp torture and plunged in again. When Rosemary gripped the base of his shaft to control his strokes, he shuddered, knowing she would

15

start the strong sucking action once she found her rhythm. He felt so thick and hard in the wet softness of her mouth that he thought he would come at any moment, but he managed to control it. It took yet more restraint as feminine nails scratched lightly across his flat belly, the thumbs tickling his pubic hair before dropping to gently press his scrotum. Expertly she fingered his balls. Simon arched in an endeavour to convey his desire to be swallowed whole. His buttocks clenched. Then there was only coolness surrounding his aching flesh. Simon looked into Rosemary's blue eyes as she rocked back on her heels. Strange, he had never thought them cold before, but now, after Faren's stirring green gaze, Simon knew he was seeing his housekeeper with the eyes of an employer. Or a priest. But certainly not as a lover.

Then Rosemary wheedled, 'Please, Simon! I want you inside me.' And despite his full-blown arousal, the voice grated. He clenched his hands to resist shoving her away.

She got up and moved across the room. Having heaved herself up on to the priest's desk, Rosemary was already wiggling her bottom across the polished teak as Simon, his hard cock bouncing, stalked towards her. The grey pleated skirt was bunched around her waist. In anticipation, she had worn no panties.

Simon gazed at the tangle of hair that shielded her sex. He smiled for the first time since ushering Faren out into the sunlit courtyard. 'Tell me; are you hot and juicy? Do you want my cock? Tell me you want it.'

'I want it,' she said, her breath coming in short gasps.

She parted her legs. Simon could see the glistening dampness in the crease of her thighs. He nudged his straining penis at her pussy. 'You want my cock. Say it!'

'I want your cock, Simon. Your hard, beautiful cock!'

He groaned as his aching flesh lightly touched the dark tuft between her thighs. He pushed her back so that she sprawled across the desk, unmindful of his papers fluttering to the floor. With his hands at the back of her knees, he pulled her forward until her bottom rested near the overhang, then pushed her knees hard back to meet her shoulders, exposing her sex completely. He always enjoyed seeing a woman so open to him. It conveyed absolute trust, he thought. With his thumb and finger he spread the lips, peering at her before his finger dipped inside. She moaned, then protested loudly when he withdrew. When he penetrated her with two fingers, she grunted, pushing herself down to meet the rhythmic strokes. He pumped into her, deliberately steering clear of her clitoris; she thrived on a little torture. As soon as he withdrew his fingers, he wiped them across his mouth, then gripped his cock. Expertly he manoeuvred it between the plump sex lips and wiggled in the dampness he found there, rubbing against her clitoris once, twice, before plunging inside her. Immersed in her heat, he gave a deep, guttural cry, his head thrown back, his buttocks tightening on each thrust, his cock pulsating as he stroked easily in and out. Several times her sex clenched around him, and he revelled in the strong, dragging sensation as he partially withdrew. His hands clutched Rosemary's hips, helping his thrusts, and she slid effortlessly back and forth across the polished tabletop, impaled on his cock. Her grunts delighted him. Simon closed his eyes and fantasised that he was pleasuring Faren Lonsdale. He felt no guilt. In all his couplings with his housekeeper, this was the first time he had been with her only in body. She could hardly lay claim to his mind; he was giving her what she wanted.

As he slapped hard against her, his balls touched skin which was wet with her juices, firing him on to greater heights than he'd ever thought possible of achieving with this woman. 'I'm not going to last long,' he grunted. Certainly not while imagining Faren's soft, young body. She would be tight. Her flesh would clamp his; he would probably disgrace himself and spurt his seed the moment the sensitive head of his cock touched her moist sex. The image, far too powerful for Simon, ignited a groan deep in his throat. He tightened his buttocks as he reached the most sensational orgasm he had ever experienced. As he shuddered inside the woman, strong spasms shaking his body, Simon congratulated himself on approving Faren Lonsdale's application to enter St Peter's. Rosemary was not going to like it. But that was just too bad. And he would convince the High Council they needed fresh young blood. It should not be too difficult, not when he pointed out the advantages. St Peter's, nurturing an intelligent and desirable young female novice, would lead the Church into the twenty-first century.

'Get out, Rosemary,' Simon said, tucking his flaccid penis into his trousers as he turned his back. Not from any false sense of modesty; he just did not like himself very much at this moment. And he should not be acting like this because it would only put the woman on her guard.

Glowering at the priest, Rosemary said, 'It's that girl, isn't it?' She slipped off the table and straightened her skirt. 'Don't think you can toss me aside for her, Simon. I'm warning you.'

'And who are you to warn anyone, Mrs Cheaters?' Simon asked coldly, as he rounded on her. He was satisfied only when she dropped her aggressive stance, and she patted at her hair as she shifted away from him. 'You've gone too far. If you want to continue housekeeping here, I suggest you watch your tongue.'

'Simon, there's never been anyone to threaten our relationship before. I couldn't bear it if I lost you,' Rosemary whined.

'I was unaware we had a relationship.' He spoke the truth. As far as Simon knew, their coupling was merely a mutual pleasuring between two consenting adults. Obviously the foolish woman had read more into it than he had intended. Then he softened; his latest novice might not wish to have anything to do with him outside of professional matters, so until he found out to the contrary, it would be unwise to antagonise Rosemary. He could fantasise all he wished and it wouldn't hurt her; in fact, it was likely to enhance their lovemaking. His recent sensational orgasm was testimony to that.

Having asserted his position, Simon could now afford to be generous. 'Don't you worry yourself. I'll always want you, Rosemary.'

'Will you?' she asked.

He could see that she was struggling to believe him. Simon hoped that he spoke the truth; he certainly balked at the idea of making an enemy of his lover. A woman scorned. She could blow the whole set up. The bishop would spirit him off to some dust bowl in the outback to atone for his sins. He would live in a shantytown and inhale dust and grit, perhaps forsaking forever the sharp saltiness of the Pacific Ocean. He reached out for Rosemary and she snuggled against him before placing her hand over his flaccid penis, pouting up at him when she failed to arouse him.

'You didn't get much pleasure out of that, my dear,' Simon said. Then he added charitably, 'I was too fast.' He kissed the top of her head, inhaling a spicy mix of herbs, the aroma from the kitchens where she spent a good part of her day.

'It's okay.' Rosemary shrugged.

'Look,' he said, anxious to keep her sweet, but just as anxious to be rid of her, wanting to work on his strategy for tonight's council meeting. 'How about a quick finger fuck?' His hand was already under her skirt, his fingers fiddling between the fleshy lips. He found the hard bud and flicked it a few times, grinning to himself when he heard Rosemary suck in her breath. He rolled the bud with thumb and finger, then squeezed. As Rosemary writhed against his hand, he slid a finger alongside her clitoris and started up a rhythm. The faster he rubbed, the more she arched into him, grinding her hips. He loved the wetness of her, the sloppy noise his hand made. He wouldn't mind shoving it into her again. Just as he was tiring, he felt Rosemary stiffen beneath his hand. He worked his fingers harder, keeping the stimulation going even as she shuddered and cried out her release. As she collapsed against him he gave one last stroke along the length of her wet cleft, then withdrew his hand. 'Give me an hour or so to get some of this paperwork out of the way, then come back, eh?' Rosemary rewarded him with a broad smile. The happiness reflected in her eyes buoyed his old feelings towards her. 'It's the least I can do for you, my dear.' Having used her so callously, Simon meant every word.

Gently, he pushed her away, but she was reluctant to take the hint, her eager gaze on his crotch again. His former agitation returned. 'I have work to do,' he said, striding to the door in an effort to be rid of the woman.

As Simon's fingers hooked the key, ready to turn it, Rosemary seemed to forget his generosity of minutes before. 'That woman's application. Will you pass it?'

'I'm working on it,' Simon replied, knowing unquestionably what the outcome would be. Never before had he wanted anything – or anyone – as much as he wanted Faren. So she was a star-struck novice right now. He did not want to disillusion the young woman, but he could make her incarceration at St Peter's so much more pleasurable. If only she would allow it.

His housekeeper's voice snapped Simon from his thoughts. 'You know, you're going to have trouble with that Lonsdale girl,' she said with an air of impatience.

'What do you know about her?' he asked, his eyes narrowed at the woman.

'I was thinking of Father Karl.'

'Ah, Karl Sterling.' A man he knew would never be interested in a woman like Rosemary, despite her ill-concealed desire for the priest. 'You haven't had him, then?' he said, not believing for one moment that she

20

had, but unable to resist a dig at her, since she had clearly shown her distrust of the young woman.

'Of course not,' Rosemary protested, and, as a faint blush coloured her cheeks, Simon realised for the first time just how heartily she lusted after the young priest.

'Don't you worry yourself about Father Karl. Or Miss Lonsdale, for that matter,' Simon said as he unlocked the door and yanked it open.

Down on his knees in front of the Virgin Mary, Simon sought forgiveness for his sins. 'Our Lady have mercy upon my soul. Show me the way so that I may follow.' He spent the next fifteen minutes at prayer, the rosary clicking through his fingers. When he was done, he raised the crucifix to his lips and then lay it back on his breast. He made a promise to attend chapel later. It would do no harm to ask for guidance again.

Later the next morning Faren could barely contain her excitement. 'I did it, Martine, infiltrated the hallowed ranks!' she crowed to her editor. Faren had come bursting into Martine Danson's office only to be met with a glare at her unprofessional entrance. But her words had soon changed the glare to a smile. 'I received word from Father Murray just as I was leaving home.'

'Well, well. That was certainly quick. Congratulations! I must admit I didn't think you would accomplish it, knowing how the average man feels about womanpower. I thought it was a crazy scheme to begin with, but you have proved me wrong,' Martine announced magnanimously. 'You'll be my star reporter yet.'

Faren glowed. 'It's what I'm aiming for. And considering you never admit to being wrong, it's very big of you,' she joked.

'Less of your cheek.' But Martine smiled. She waved in the direction of a chair. 'Sit down. I'm all ears.'

In the privacy of the office, Faren related to her editor how well her interview had flowed once the priest terminated the telephone call. 'He suggested special training – whatever that means – might be in order before I commit myself. So, I take it I'm on trial.'

'That's understandable. It all sounds very intriguing.'

'I can't believe my luck!'

'Luck may have played a small part. But I'm sure it was your arguments that convinced him. What else?'

'Well, then he said, "It's a life of deprivation for a young, vibrant woman."'

'And any young, virile man.'

'Absolutely,' Faren agreed. 'But I guess he was just trying to prepare me. He wanted me to be very sure about it. I gathered he didn't want to stick his neck out for me unless he thought I was sincere.'

'Then you gave a convincing performance.'

Faren shrugged. She was just doing her job. Then she lowered her voice for full dramatic effect. 'There is definitely something going on behind those walls, Martine, believe me, and I won't rest until I uncover it.' She leaned forward in her chair; it had been months since she'd had her editor's avid attention and she was not about to let go of it now. 'As for Father Murray, you should have seen the way he ogled me!' Faren decided to pass on mentioning she had done much of the ogling herself.

'That has got to be a positive sign.'

'I enjoyed playing a part and pulling it off.' In fact, she had been so immersed in her role that at times she felt as though she was genuinely seeking a place at St Peter's.

'Never had a man of the cloth eye me before,' Martine grumbled good-naturedly, 'but then I don't suppose there are many men who could resist you when you pin them with those cat's eyes. And that long hair probably had his imagination working overtime.'

Secretly pleased with Martine's compliments, Faren basked in their warmth. Martine valued the efforts of her loyal staff but only occasionally remembered to voice her appreciation. As Faren gathered a strand of her chestnut hair and tucked it behind her ear, she visualised how it could be used to turn on a male. Preferably a male in the seminary.

'OK, Faren, what happens next?'

'I pack my bags and move in next Thursday.' Faren grimaced. 'Not that it looks as though there are any mod cons in that place. Still, it is wall-to-wall with gorgeous hunks, and I'm the only female, bar the inhospitable housekeeper. So it should prove very interesting.'

Martine tapped her pencil against her perfect teeth. In her late thirties, the editor of *Splash!* magazine was impeccably dressed in a navy, classic line suit. Faren thought that with her dark eyes, red-slash mouth and jaw-length ebony hair, she looked stunning.

'Do you expect this housekeeper to give you any trouble?' Martine asked.

Faren shrugged, refocusing her attention on the conversation. 'Who knows? But I can handle her.'

'Maybe the woman enjoys the monopoly.'

Faren pulled a face. 'Perhaps. Don't worry about me; I'll get my scoop.'

'Don't go stepping on her toes. Cultivate her if you can.' The editor frowned. 'What's your gut feeling about the priests? Content, daring, or desperate?'

Faren smiled. 'I only got to see Father Murray. But who knows how desperate any one of us would be if we were deprived of openly seeking sex? They are men, after all.'

Martine responded with a wry grin then relaxed back in her chair. 'It shouldn't be too difficult to ferret out what we need to know. They're not on to you. Otherwise you wouldn't have been admitted to the house. So, when you move in, they shouldn't suspect a thing. Over the years they have been rather insulated from the outside world, I should imagine, and if anything, they are probably too complacent.' Martine lined up her pencil with the others on her desk, then steepled her hands. 'How do you plan to keep in touch?'

'Haven't given a thought to that yet, though I'll hardly be a prisoner. Then again, those men get leave only once every few weeks, I believe. More than likely I'll be expected to abide by the same rules. After all, my cover is my desire to become a priest. Frankly, I can't imagine anything worse.' Faren laughed. 'My desires run along other channels, I assure you.'

Martine smiled as she lazed back in her chair. 'Depends. My horniest fantasy is to be ravished by a man with a dog collar.'

'You do mean a man of the cloth, I take it?'

'What else?' But Martine's grin widened.

'Well, I'll pass on voicing mine, thank you.' In the four years Martine Danson had been her boss, they had discussed many subjects, but the revelation of the woman's fantasy held an element of intimacy. Faren was unprepared to go that far.

As if her editor sensed this, she narrowed her dark eyes and leant across the desk. 'I don't expect you to hold out on anything you come up with, Faren.'

'Have I ever?'

Martine shrugged. 'As long as you understand the rules.'

Faren got to her feet and prodded the chair aside. She ran her hands over her hips to straighten her skirt and turned to leave. 'Whatever else I get out of this research, it should prove interesting. By tomorrow I'll have wound up my interview with General Parkinson's widow; I'll have it written up before I leave.' Faren paused with her hand on the door. 'I wonder how long I'll need to come up with something?'

'Not too long, I shouldn't think,' Martine said. 'If they accept you as they would any novice, they won't hide behind their cloaks. Besides, I doubt you would want to be in there any longer than absolutely necessary. Think what you'll be missing.'

Chapter Three

*I*n the late afternoon sun, Faren shivered. She cast her gaze over the brooding structure of the monastery, wondering what secrets it concealed. She stood contemplating the stone building across the street which would be her home for the next couple of weeks. Longer, if she failed to come up with what she wanted in that time. If she were legitimate in her desire to embrace her vows – and nothing could be further from the truth, she reminded herself – she would spend the next few years here, not weeks. Despite the warmth of the day, a shiver raced along her spine. She trusted that her self-imposed deprivation of life's comforts would last only long enough for her to obtain her story. Of course, she would have preferred to remain in her comfortable flat and report daily. However, to maintain her cover, staying here was her sole option.

She could imagine Father Murray's astonishment if she had suggested that she live at home and report daily for lectures. He would have seen through that ruse. Just because he had paved the way for her entry did not mean St Peter's was prepared to rewrite all the rules. Then, of course, she would have found it nigh impossible to seek the information she coveted, because if the men were reneging on their vows, Faren supposed that by day they would epitomise model priests; any carryings-on would be nocturnal. Then again, if the men were involved merely in masturbation in the privacy of their cells, there was little chance of proving that activity. Fervently she hoped for more. This assignment was her baby, her idea, and she had no intention of coming out disappointed.

She picked up her suitcase. 'Here goes.' She sighed as she traipsed across the street towards wrought-iron gates. One week ago she had been ushered to the parish priest's house where Father Murray had interviewed her, and that, though far from opulent, was the total opposite of this dreary place. A web-coated bell squatted in its alcove by the gate. Faren pushed it gingerly with a fingernail while wondering if anyone would hear the clang. She shifted from one leg to the other as she waited, and was about to execute a further rattle when an elderly priest came trotting up. He offered no acknowledgement when she gave him her name, nor did he present a smile of welcome as he released the latch and hauled open the gate.

They stumbled across the courtyard in silence, Faren hindered by her case, and the old priest because he seemed anxious to put distance between them. If Faren had judged the exterior grim, it was nothing compared to the atmosphere that prevailed as the old man impatiently beckoned her in. Wistful at surrendering the summer day, Faren decided there would be little hard-ship in remaining celibate in this chilly, mute building. It gave off a distinct odour of neglect as her footsteps scraped on timeworn stairs. No gentlemen, these priests, Faren noted, as the man bounced up the stairs without offering to lug her case. Then again, he had at least fifty years on her, so perhaps her expectations were harsh. Panting for breath, Faren arrived right on the tail of her elderly leader, and with relief she dropped her bag at her feet. When the priest frowned at the thump, it set Faren to wondering if she had broken a golden rule of silence.

'Your room is along here, Miss Lonsdale. Please follow me.' The first words the old man had uttered.

'When I get my breath, Father, if you don't mind.' He clucked his tongue and waited, though Faren noticed his feet tapped a small on-the-spot dance. Then he flapped his black robe and went on. Sighing, Faren retrieved her bag and followed. Her room was behind the very last of about twenty panelled, heavily studded doors. After the priest had depressed the clunky iron lever and shoved open the door, he vanished as swiftly as he had appeared, leaving Faren alone in the centre of the room. She gave a startled yelp as the door thudded and settled back into position. The sombreness of the monastery was getting to her; she hadn't been in the place fifteen minutes. How was she going to survive fifteen days, if indeed it took that long? Surveying the room with a critical eye and finding the assessment lacking in any homeliness, Faren hoped her stay here would be far less than that.

Pleased that she had carted along her patchwork quilt, Faren slid it from the side straps of her suitcase and flicked it across the narrow bed. The bright, sunshiny colours leapt out, creating an illusion of warmth. How long she would need to stay here was a question she could not honestly answer yet. In addition to the austere surroundings, her meeting with the far from gracious old priest was sufficient to put a damper on this assignment. Then again, Faren reminded herself, she was here for work, not pleasure. If it proved a great success she would be up for promotion. She grasped the thought, a soothing remedy to assuage the sudden jolt of homesickness she felt for her own cosy flat.

Faren heaved her case up on to the bed. She set out an array of toiletries and hummed to herself in the otherwise leaden silence, and though far from squeamish, she shivered, willing to admit she found the entire set up unnerving. How did priests live like this year after year? And why were so many young men endeavouring to gain entry into this particular order?

When a sharp knock sounded on her door, shattering the silence, Faren's hand flew to her throat. She marched across the room. 'God, you frightened me!' she said accusingly, yanking open the door while realising she had taken the Lord's name in vain. Considering she was in the Lord's house – or near enough to it – Faren apologised to the man she found standing on her threshold. Sweeping him with her cool green gaze, she noticed his stance was sublimely arrogant for a priest. Totally unlike the more gentlemanly Father Murray who had interviewed her a week ago. When the priest made no attempt to greet her she said, 'Yes, Father?' It was impossible to miss his appraising stare and, when finally his gaze joined hers, he executed a wicked half-smile that caused her heartbeat to quicken. And she was certain he knew it.

'Welcome to our exalted ranks. The entire compound is buzzing with your arrival. And I was elected to come along and welcome you.' He smiled. 'How entertaining it is to have a young lady here.'

Faren caught the subtle message and a wave of excitement shot through her. The priest was flirting! This assignment might prove far easier than she had expected. Despite such brief acquaintance with the priest in front of her, Faren suspected that sexual release would be a priority for him. And before long she hoped to be able to prove it.

How would a man like this appease his frustration? she wondered. By pleasuring himself in the age-old method? Or did he perhaps sneak out of the building to visit a woman? Maybe a variety of women? She would seek his friendship and before long she would uncover the facts. Then, with any luck she would have gathered sufficient information for her research in the shortest possible time. She gave the priest a disarming smile. 'Am I correct in surmising it is a long while since St Peter's has permitted a female to run loose within the cloister?' she asked, her eyes meeting his.

'Correct. Like a mother hen. We used to have day staff, and Mrs Cheaters always kept the young ladies under her watchful eye. And now, not only are you permitted upstairs, but also you have the Fathers' blessings. That makes you someone special.' He was smiling at her with his eyes, his mouth quirking in mischievous promise.

With unmitigated joy, Faren realised her initial assumption was accurate; this priest was a very sexual man and he was coming on to her – albeit cunningly camouflaged – so that he could successfully retreat if his instincts proved incorrect. Faren gave him a smile, enough to show him she was interested. She did not need to act. The tall, impressively built male leaning casually against the doorframe with his arms crossed was a fine specimen of virile manhood. And his dark eyes gleamed in appreciation of her.

'Thank you for the welcome, Father,' Faren said.

'Karl Sterling, at your service.'

Faren suppressed a smile, wondering just how far she was meant to take that statement.

He extended his hand and as it touched hers she was conscious of delicious warmth that went far beyond her palm. Aware that he was waiting for her to return the courtesy, she blurted, 'Faren Lonsdale.' She wondered when he would touch her again. Totally at ease, Father Sterling nodded, the gesture acknowledging that he had succeeded, that indeed the chemistry was mutual. Just then Faren felt very certain this man had never failed to disappoint a woman, and would take it as a major defeat if he did. Why then, had he taken his holy vows? Out in the ordinary turn of the world there was no doubting he would be one hell of a ladies' man. And in turn the ladies would devour him. Immediately another thought flashed through her mind: had he entered a seminary for the pleasure of surrounding himself with men? But it was quickly contradicted by a saner thought: he was coming on to her, which in itself firmly cancelled out her rash assumption. The priest looked over her shoulder, his mouth quirked in a flare of amusement. She continued to stare. Then Faren realised he expected to be invited in. 'Would you care to come in, Father?'

Barely had she uttered the invitation when Father Sterling took a step around her, eager to install himself in her room. 'Should I close the door?' Faren asked, and felt foolish the moment the words were out. Father Sterling smiled, and again Faren felt an intense yearning for this magnificent creature standing before her.

'My presence is not exactly the correct protocol? Is that it?'

Faren was not so much bent on protecting the priest as she was herself, because, if this were a breach of the rules, she had no wish to be herded back out to her world before she had time to gather the information she sought. 'I think, Father Sterling, that I am very fortunate in being here. And I have no wish to jeopardise my position.' She paused. 'I'm sorry if that sounded rather pompous, Father. But I can't allow this encounter to ruin my chances here.'

'Close the door, child.'

She did so, then turned to find the priest still watching her.

Father Sterling's smile now was wide, crinkling the corners of his dark eyes. His sexy, white smile touched somewhere deep inside of her, and she felt pity for the scores of women who would lust vainly after him. She began to pick at her nails, capturing the priest's attention so that he reached out to still them. With his palm, warm and reassuring, covering hers, he said, 'Don't be nervous, my child. My colleagues and I will help you through the difficult early days. Like us all, you have made a momentous decision and we hope you never find cause to regret it. God will give you strength.'

Then he turned away from her and without awaiting an invitation, strolled over to her bed and sat down. 'Working on your room, I see,' he said, fingering a floral patch on her quilt as though he was genuinely interested in her attempts at interior decoration.

'Aren't they called cells, Father?'

'Ah, yes,' the priest conceded, 'but most of us call them rooms these days. It suggests a touch of home for us.'

'Home,' Faren murmured, a lump in her throat. She recalled that most of the novices at St Peter's were very young men. Like Faren, they also needed to feel at home here in this harsh monastery. Knowing it was imperative to her cause that she become friendly with as many of the inmates as possible, Faren shook off the vestige of unease brought about by the bleakness of the place. But before she could make any overtures of her own, the priest broke the silence.

'I must leave you now, Miss Lonsdale. I wanted you to know that although you are the first young woman to enter this Order, you are truly welcome,' he said, springing to his feet. He moved towards the door before Faren had a moment to take charge of the situation.

'Thank you very much, Father,' she said. In her job she had adapted to difficult situations before, though none as strange as this. And it would be foolish to allow the best chance of a source to sail out of her room. She must get to know him. With her gut instincts, Faren knew that if she wanted to unearth the truth about this Order, then adhering herself to Father Karl Sterling would, without too much time and effort, pay off.

'You haven't finished unpacking yet. I'll leave you to get on with it.' Would you like to come along to my room later?' the priest asked. 'My collection of textbooks could be very helpful to you.' Father Sterling gazed down

31

at her from his six-foot plus stature and smiled. Slow and wicked. 'Welcome again, Faren Lonsdale.' He stretched out his hand and for the second time that evening his palm touched hers. The room seemed to sizzle.

Faren looked up at him. Flickers of moonlight crept in through the open slats of the one tiny window, spotlighting the handsome features of the priest. The desire she felt for him was not altogether to do with his presence, but the fact that he was a priest, and therefore taboo. A heady aphrodisiac indeed. Familiar warmth invaded her body, and settled low in her belly. She swallowed. If she were a man she would have a hard-on by now. She felt fortunate to be female, for there was no visible sign of her desire.

'Would you like that?'

The priest was smiling at her and Faren suspected her expression was blank. Or worse, was her excitement showing? 'I'm sorry, Father?' He must be so used to women falling under his spell, and now here she was, joining the band of fools. She steered her mind away from lustful thoughts to concentrate on what he was saying.

'I asked if you would like to visit me in my room. I would be greatly honoured, Miss Lonsdale.' When Faren hesitated – though she could have cuffed herself for that uncharacteristic reaction – the priest seemed to lean closer, although he did not move one step, so that she felt his warm breath fan her hair. At that moment she knew she wanted to stand naked before him, to feel his warm, sweet breath in a more intimate place.

'What do you think?' Father Sterling said, his tone persuasive. There was a degree of intimacy in his voice that made Faren want to throw herself into his arms. But the initial physical move – if there was to be one – had to come from him.

Without trying to appear rude, Faren moved gingerly away, and, as if he knew the very emotions charging through her body, Father Sterling laughed. The sound of a confident man, totally sure of himself and of his power over the female sex.

He ambled to the door where he stopped to glance back over his shoulder. 'Turn left, third door from the end.' He winged one eyebrow. 'Say, in one hour?'

This could be the break she needed. It was unbelievable how quickly a priest had homed in on her, that is, if she was reading him correctly. Even though she felt happy with the amount of reticence she had shown, Faren knew it was not totally an act; she was in awe of the man. The bonus in all this was that the man was openly sexy. As she tugged his image to the fore, her body began to tremble, all feeling centred between her thighs. She knew what she needed to do before visiting the priest in his room.

With her suitcase flapped open and a trail of garments spilling across the bed, Faren unzipped her tailored slacks, tugged them off and kicked them aside. After releasing her cuff buttons her hand moved shakily to her throat and fumbled with the row of small buttons. She shrugged off her blouse, and let it drift to the floor. Then she stepped out of her panties and, with her right foot, flicked them high. As they sailed through the air an ambrosial wisp of her own special perfume escaped. She reached out to nab them, to bring the scent closer. Her pussy grew hot, throbbing, as she teased herself. She took a deep breath. The smell permeated her nostrils. The taste pervaded her mouth. Inches away, Faren held the scrap of underwear, her fingers squeezing the soft fabric. Then releasing. Squeezing and releasing; teasing her senses. Until, unable to endure the sweet agony a moment longer, she drew in the frothy scrap to cover her face, and inhaled deeply. The most heavenly scent on earth. If only they could capture and bottle the unique essence of female, she thought. Since her brief encounter with the priest, and in the excitement of knowing that within the hour she would see him again, Faren's arousal had escalated. With no way to secure her room – she made a mental note to see about obtaining a key – and after lugging the chest of drawers to sit firm against the door, Faren felt sufficiently secure to drag out her secret supply of magazines. Aware they were dynamite, she would ensure they were stowed in her case at all times. If discovered, she would never survive the fallout.

Normally Faren removed her bra before her panties but the temptation to be free was too much, and now the only piece of clothing shielding her body was her lacy bra. Impatiently she fumbled with the clasp, snaring the straps almost in one movement as they slid down her arms and to the floor. Though she was naked, the air appeared warm. Creating this illusion was her own burning skin, and as Faren's palm caressed one soft breast, then the other, her fingers teasing each in turn, her nipples began to peak. Her head fell back and she groaned as her hair feathered across her naked spine, shooting signals of pleasure to every nerve ending. As Faren's skin became more sensitive, the wetness gathered between her thighs, and she sank to her knees beside the bed and snatched at one of the sleek magazines. Naked women in all manner of poses, all blatantly erotic, stared back at her. Then she grabbed at a second magazine and, her breath coming in short gasps, she placed it with its counterpart on the bed. It consisted entirely of naked men. And all paraded magnificent erections. She raised one knee to open herself more fully and her fingers trailed along the swollen lips, playing with the slippery flesh. Just as suddenly, she lowered her knee and clamped her thighs together, centring on the pleasure, the heat, as she squeezed. She licked her fingertip and lightly touched her clitoris; her body quivered. She looked down at her pouty, soft flesh. The trimmed, soft curls let the bud of her pleasure centre peep shyly out.

Faren could feel the heat building up sharply between her thighs. Her dark, curly hairs clung damply together, the erotica on view having created a fierce ache deep inside her. Faren touched herself again, this time brushing a finger gently through the curls and stroking the seam of her sex while she hauled the second magazine closer. She wished she could have any one of those bulging hard-ons plunging inside her right now. Just looking at the man's erection jutting eagerly out from the tuft of pubic hair was so erotically stimulating, stirring her dew, that she felt the dampness coat her inner thighs. She wanted the cock to pulsate inside her, to fill her with its hardness. As she dipped two fingers inside her cunt she could feel that thick rod thrusting inside her opening, stroking back and forth, teasing and withdrawing, until only the purple head remained in the soft, heated flesh. Then as her muscles tensed, and she could bear the emptiness no longer, it would plunge deep inside her, embedding itself to the hilt. She could feel her breasts heavy with desire, and she pulled her fingers from her pussy to slide her hands beneath them. She cupped each globe, squeezing as she pushed them up and together, her thumbs stimulating her nipples until they were hard and swollen.

Hearing her own breathing so loud in the lonely room, Faren took a shaky breath, then shuffled the single mat across to ease her cold, hard knees. Arranging it beside the bed, she parted her legs, the rush of cool air a ghostly caress in her warm place, inciting her further. She dipped her slender fingers into her love channel, enjoying the moist heat of her soft flesh, her fingers slipping along, making wet, sexy sounds as she caressed her most secret place. Her own touch made her tremble, more so as she visualised the priest and imagined how his long fingers would feel massaging her pink folds, pulling gently on her swollen lips before dipping into the dark interior. Eyes slumberous, she made a tremendous effort to hold them open, to devour those visions before her. Her fevered gaze slid between naked female and naked male until they fused, the man's mighty cock entering the woman's welcoming sheath.

Gentling her touch, Faren imagined her soft finger pad was her lover's searching tongue as it swirled along the slick length of her. She felt the strength as it prised open her pouting sex to dip quickly and forcefully inside her. She could almost feel the raspy tongue sweeping the intimate reaches of her sex, searching out that other pleasure spot. Her eyes were slowly closing again, the pleasure point between her thighs the only tangible part of her body, as her finger, mimicking a lover's tongue, slicked up and down along the aggressive little shaft. Even as it begged for fulfilment, it refused to surrender to the frantic, rhythmic actions that it loved. She spread her legs further apart, moaning softly, feeling her juice covering her, matting her soft pelt, her lubrication sticky on the soft skin of her inner thighs. Inhaling deeply, she savoured the sweet smell of her passion. All Faren's smouldering senses were torched as her quickening excitement translated itself to every nerve-ending housed within her sensitised flesh. Again she took a deep breath, wanting to drown in this most alluring of all female perfumes, wanting to taste it, lap every wet morsel, and as she lifted her lids, her glazed eyes stared at the pictures on the bed, and she smiled. She would taste herself. Just as she had inhaled her own special scent with her panties draped over her face.

Faren lifted her damp fingers to her face and anointed the small indentation beneath her already dilating nostrils before she lowered one finger to her mouth. Her tongue flicked out, at first letting only the very tip of it touch her finger. Then with more courage, Faren stole liberal licks, using the length of her tongue, tasting her wetness that was every bit as exciting as her perfume promised, sweet and intoxicating. Each trace an exotic tang. Faren adored being licked, drenched with a man's saliva, caressed with his tongue, and she wished Father Sterling were here now. He would know how to slide his tongue between her lips, to lick her womanly place and nibble at her bud. The magazines and her fantasies were providing Faren with a powerfully erotic stimulus, invading her very core. She could have climaxed very quickly, but she wanted to savour the pleasure, wanted desire to mount again so that the most fantastic orgasm would swamp her. Panting, her sex pulsating, Faren relaxed her hands by her sides, gazed again at the proud cock pointing at her from the pages, as though begging to be allowed to bury itself between her swollen lips, and be devoured by her warm, wet pussy. Nimble fingers strayed between her thighs once more, rotating in the soft pink flesh, deliberately skirting the sensitive bead, while tantalising with their promise of exquisite pleasure. One hand left that warm, moist centre, skated along her flat belly and cupped a breast. Her breathing quickened as she rubbed her palm in circles, loving the hard coin of her nipple on the softness of her palm. Now two hands were busy, flicking and rubbing, then pinching, until her breathing escalated and she knew she must end the torture.

Faren stumbled to her feet, crossed her legs tightly to imprison her hand as her fingers rubbed her clitoris in a crazy tempo. She whispered dirty words; words that served to propel her into a frenzy. 'Fuck me! Fuck me, hard!' she cried, keeping a constant rhythm while she stared at the handsome young man with his huge straining erection staring evocatively back at her. Paper. Not flesh and blood, but as real to Faren as if he were in this room, pumping away at her, their sweaty bodies joined, their breaths mingling as his mouth came crushing down on hers. Two fingers disappeared into her opening. Her thumb pressed firmly against her clitoris. Fierce contractions swept through her. Faren closed her eyes, unable to gaze at the young stud so remarkably like the priest, concerned only with her own pleasure at this magical moment, as her pussy tightened convulsively about her fingers, clamping them in a possessive grip. Faren glanced down to watch the muscles in her legs tense, her knees shaking uncontrollably as her orgasm began to wave through her. Then, as the raging spasms subsided, she slumped down on to the bed with a satisfied sigh, crumpling glossy pages as she did so. Drained, depleted and deliriously sated, Faren shifted the magazine to one side, mindful of creasing the image of that delectable specimen of virile male, knowing that she would want to feast her eyes on his penis another night.

Several minutes later, when her breathing had quieted and her heart rate maintained an even tempo, Faren rolled over on to her back, arms widespread, legs dangling over the side of the bed. She sighed. 'What I need now is a real man with a real cock.' She shifted and levered herself upright to glance at her watch. Thirty minutes of pleasure. And now she must dress and visit Father Sterling. She needed a friend in this camp, and who better than a sexy friend? She would even make a bet with herself that before the week was out, she would know for certain if priests lived by their vow of celibacy.

Chapter Four

Karl Sterling strolled along the hall and stopped several doors away from his own room. He rapped, then let himself in. A young man was lolling on a bed, a sheaf of papers in his hands.

'I've just been to see the new candidate.' Karl pulled up a chair. He smiled slyly and waited for the forthcoming questions. He did not have long to wait.

'What's she like, then?' Drew Edmonds asked.

'Like something from heaven,' Karl said, startled at his disclosure when he had had every intention of keeping that sort of opinion to himself. One did not go around the compound spouting off such thoughts. And he had been at St Peter's long enough to know how to deal with carnal images. Besides, was celibacy not a man-made law? Looking at the priest now, he wondered how the young man dealt with his impure thoughts.

'Do you think she is nervous? It's a big step for any of us, but the first woman in our seminary must have extra burdens to carry,' Father Drew said.

'She seemed anxious, but I expect that's more to do with the strangeness of the place than the fact that I dropped in on her unexpectedly. A woman who looks like a goddess would have too much confidence in her appearance and ability to be anything else.'

The young priest perked visibly, then, clutching his crucifix to his chest, he asked, 'She's a blonde then?'

'Did I say that?' Karl shook his head, 'Brunette. With fire in her soul.' As Karl tipped back his chair, fingers locked behind his head, he felt immensely optimistic. Faren Lonsdale's soft skin would light his fire. 'Perhaps she's been sent to try us. Think what a temptation it will be to see her every day. Yes, I rather think Father Murray had the sin of temptation in mind when he allowed Miss Lonsdale to join us.'

'When will we get to meet her?' the priest asked, still fingering his cross, as though he were afraid that such a question would see him in hell.

'At breakfast tomorrow.' Karl felt the growing hardness against his belly and fought the urge to stroke his erection. It was time to leave Father Drew.

A shaft of light from the shaded wall lamp pooled straight down, leaving the rest of the passage in darkness. With her heart thumping, Faren dashed along the length of the passageway, her hand grazing the uneven surface as she sought reassurance in the darkness of the night. When she reached the third door from the end of the corridor, she stalled, palm pressed to her chest, waiting for her heartbeats to subside.

The priest opened the door on her first tentative knock. 'Um, hello,' Faren said, swatting a stray wisp of her hair away from her eyes.

He reached out his hand and gently clasped her wrist, wordlessly inviting her into his sanctum. As she waited for him to speak, Faren wondered if priests were allowed this degree of intimacy with a woman, before realising this was precisely why she was at St Peter's. The phantoms she had battled with on her way here seemed to have dulled her senses.

40

Father Sterling's warm palm stretched across the back of her hand. The innocent touch made her shiver. 'There. That's better,' he said softly, almost as if he knew exactly what his caress had accomplished.

Faren was beginning to think the priest was very astute. Then, as she mulled it over, she reflected it would be part of every priest's training, his function in life: to instil a confidence in his flock, act as the sounding board and the sponge for the congregation's troubles and expunge them of their so-called sins.

'I'll get those books for you. But while you are here, what do you think of my room?' Father Sterling asked.

Suddenly Faren realised she was concentrating on the man, rather than his room, and if he wished to hang on to the pretence of why she was here, then she, too, must adopt the deception. She dragged her gaze away from him to survey the room. It was dominated by burgundy leather and highly polished oak. And no stubby narrow bed for Father Sterling, like the one skulking in her room, she reflected. Thrown across the bed was a grey and burgundy duvet, matching pillows at its head. But for the two religious pictures and the crucifix adorning the walls, the squat candles, and a miniature statue of the Virgin Mary, Faren considered that she could be in any number of efficiently decorated bachelor pads. She wondered how he got away with it. 'It's great.' Certainly unlike anything she had expected.

Father Sterling smiled. 'How about a drink?'

His dark gaze held hers. Faren's heart leapt. She sensed she could learn so much from this priest. Already he was granting her an intriguing glimpse beneath the veneer of St Peter's. While gathering facts she would enjoy each sensual hint he had to offer. On the job she was her own responsibility; she would explore whatever St Peter's and its inmates cared to tender. Faren swished her hair across her shoulders and observed the priest watching her. 'Let

41

me guess, Father. Priests drink because they surrender their other pleasures?'

Her words were met with a chuckle. 'Are you trawling for information, Miss Lonsdale?'

Father Sterling remained smiling down at her, and Faren's pulse quickened. Was he on to her? It seemed impossible at this early stage. She was certain she had done nothing to alert him. Could he perhaps smell her sex? She could still detect a faint note. To steer her mind from its chaotic course, she moved away from the priest and wandered about the room. With desire surging through her veins, she wanted to fling herself into his arms, beg him to tumble her to the floor, rip off her clothes and straddle her. But what if this were a test? She would be kicked out so fast she would scarcely feel the boot. She swallowed hard, as if that distraction would banish the almost painful ache in her loins. Immediately the futility of the exercise became apparent as her skin seemed to tighten across her belly and the familiar warmth spread throughout her body, before settling in a heated throb at the juncture of her thighs. She wanted so much for him to touch her.

She watched the priest lift a whisky decanter from the bedside table. He took a swig. Then he moved towards her, offering her the bottle. He was so near she could smell his pleasant, whisky-scented breath. 'Not for me, thank you, Father.'

'Welcome to our Order, Miss Lonsdale.' Then he stepped back, smiling as he replaced the decanter on the table.

Faren's pulse accelerated. Her heartbeat thudded in her ears. Barely an hour entombed with scores of young men, and already her body was yearning for one of them. With this degree of temptation she was likely to sabotage her chances of an exclusive scoop. And then Faren's head cleared. Sabotage? No. This was what it was all about! She was on the verge of proving her theory. As she nibbled away at her lower lip, Faren reined in her thoughts. He had held her hand briefly when he pulled her into his room. Other than that he had not touched her. So where did she get the thought that she had proof, that her job here was done? Where was the evidence? What had Father Sterling done, besides welcome her? Perhaps he gazed at her a little too long. The fact that he exuded sexuality was hardly conclusive that her theory was correct. But Faren felt strongly that it was a step towards it, and it was over to her to see it proceed all the way. After all, she reminded herself, it was for the good of her career. But she shivered beneath her flimsy blouse as her mind's eye projected the priest's powerful body crushing hers into submission. She fought to keep her expression neutral. 'Look, Father, I think I should go.'

In reply he turned and tugged her towards his bed. He sat down and patted the spot next to him. 'Not yet, Miss Lonsdale,' he said, his tone suggesting that he expected her obedience. 'What harm is there in staying? I am a priest, after all.'

Faren thought she detected a slice of irony in that simple statement and, to manoeuvre the priest to where she wanted, she felt it wise to play the reticent young woman. At least for tonight. She suspected that Father Sterling was a man before he was a priest, and one who enjoyed a challenge, and the worst thing she could do would be to show her eagerness. 'Are you sure it's okay for me to be in here, Father?' she asked, inching towards where the priest sprawled, his long black-sheathed legs stretched out in front of him.

'I'm sure. For you are one of us now. Sit. We will have comfort while we talk.'

Faren sank down on to the bed beside him. He tipped towards her. Or was he merely using the momentum and over-exaggerating? An excuse to touch shoulders? 'I find it hard to believe that I'm a novice,' Faren said, trying for a normal conversation while her mind and body fought to betray her.

'It takes a bit of getting used to, I agree.' The priest's thigh brushed against hers. Then just as abruptly he shifted away.

One thing was certain: Faren could have selected no better subject than Father Sterling, for it was obvious he was a sensual man. It was unbelievable that he would be content in self-pleasuring alone, to the exclusion of all other sexual activity. This man would desire the soft flesh of a woman to assuage his passion, she was sure of it.

Whatever lurked within these walls, Faren had a hunch that the path leading to it would prove to be of the utmost joy. She hoisted her left leg, tucked it snugly beneath her and turned to face him. 'Why are you a priest?'

He gazed at her, a hint of amusement in his eyes. 'Why does anyone do a job?'

'Is that all it is to you, then? You must have had some reason,' Faren pressed. 'Did a ladylove scorn you, Father? Is that it?'

In a gesture Faren found already very characteristic of her new comrade, the priest threw back his head and laughed. Then he said, 'Look at me, young lady. Do I really come across as the type to be thwarted in love?'

His very tone, as well as his words, showed the priest's complete arrogance and Faren delighted in his cavalier attitude. It could prove very interesting. 'You're right. A woman would have to be out of her tree.' And she meant it; Karl Sterling oozed sheer sexual magnetism.

'Tell me about yourself, Miss Lonsdale.' His breath was a whisper in her hair.

Was it possible he was unaware of their adhering hips, his own potent and hard, pressing into hers? She felt her flesh begin to heat beneath the pressure of his flesh. 'I will if you will.' She really did want to learn more about him. 'For instance, how old are you, Father?'

He laughed. 'You drive a hard bargain, young lady. I'm thirty-two. Sydney born and bred. My parents retired to Palm Beach.'

'Wow.' Faren had visited Palm Beach once, when she was sixteen. She had never forgotten the magnificent mansions and the ostentatious dwellings which glittered in the fierce yellow sun, or the Ferraris looking ready to pounce from cobbled driveways, and the yachts which could sail away to the ends of the earth.

'Aah, you understand. The type of girl I would be expected to marry if I were free is more interested in her own ego than mine. I couldn't take the competition.' Startled, Faren glanced up to find the priest laughing at her and she grinned right back at him. 'Your turn now,' he said.

Recalling the cover story she had related to Father Murray at her interview, Faren cleared her throat as she prepared to condense her life's history. She raced through it with ease and when she was finished, she felt the priest's gaze on her. Her heart thumped. He was staring at her mouth.

'Why would a lovely young woman want to give up on love?' he asked, dashing her hopes as he looked away. 'Hmm?'

As he spoke, Faren prayed she could keep her excitement from spiralling to the surface; it was much too soon to surrender to the demands of her body. Testing her resolve even further, the priest's knuckles fleetingly brushed her lower leg on their way down to attend an itch inside his sock. She had never before thought an ankle could be so sexy. She took a deep breath. 'Don't tell me you don't know why I'm here, Father. When Father Murray made his announcement he would have embellished it with an explanation, surely?'

He laughed. 'I can see we'll need to be awfully quick to put one over on you.' Karl, obviously impressed, assessed her with even greater interest than before.

'So, I'm right?'

'Of course. The story is you decided against marriage in favour of the Church,' Karl said, unaware that what he quoted was exactly that: a story. 'Care to fill me in on the details?'

'I'd rather not,' Faren said, sliding her gaze away from the inquisitive priest. Her skin began to prickle with increased warmth as the blood pumped frantically along, pushed by a surge of adrenalin, and her fear at having her cover blown. Would the priest settle for that, or would he probe deeper? Faren's job prepared her for such crises in her working life and now she took refuge in her fabrication. 'The reason is embarrassing, that's all.'

'Share it with me. Why did your fiancé call it off?' Karl persisted.

A command rather than an invitation to share a confidence, she noted. This could be a trap. She must stick to the exact tale as presented to Father Murray during her interview.

'We didn't get along.' She watched as the slow grin started and turned into a devastating smile, just as – she was sure – he meant it to.

'Tell me about it, Miss Lonsdale. I'm an avid listener.' When she remained silent and stared back at him, Father Sterling continued. 'I'm a priest. Imagine you are in the confessional. Talk to me.'

About to blunder in and reveal her disapproval of the archaic idea of confessing supposed sins, and worse, that she had never entered a confessional, Faren stopped short. Facts raced through her mind. 'One does not normally gaze into the eyes of one's absolver while confessing, but in this case –' she shrugged '– I will tell you.' She sensed his mood and felt curiosity and a leashed excitement at what she was about to reveal. 'We were incompatible, Father. Sexually incompatible.' She hung her head, but whether it was for the lie itself or the fact that he might catch her out, she did not know.

Suppressed excitement hovered in the atmosphere, much as it had lingered in Father Murray's study. She was deeply attracted to this priest, as she was attracted to Father Murray, and with a bit of luck she just might find herself in the arms of one of them.

He shifted to his feet and stood before her. 'We'll leave our discussion there, Miss Lonsdale. Perhaps later, you may feel the need to confide in me.'

'Yes, Father.' She wanted to fall into his arms. She wanted to feel the hard wall of him crushing her aching breasts. She gazed up into his face and her lips parted. How would it feel to have his lips brush hers?

'It's time for you to go now.'

Her shoulders slumped. What had she expected? To be thrown to the floor and ravished?

'Perhaps we can meet like this again. It's heavy going in the early stages. I could give you some private instruction.'

Private religious instruction? Or private sexual instruction? A bevy of tantalising images floated before Faren. 'I thought you would be forbidden to fraternise with me, Father.'

'You are a novice priest now. Male and female do not exist.' But the manner in which his gaze held hers presented Faren with far more insight into what the priest was thinking than the words he was saying.

The water dribbling from the hot tap was barely tepid as Faren sluiced it over her face, flinching when droplets hit her warm breasts. The briefest toilette of a lifetime but for now it would suffice. She pulled a comb through her sleep-tangled hair. As she pulled a sloppy sweater over her head she was tempted to team it with old jeans, then, unsure if they were permissible attire for a young lady in this unique situation, erred on the side of caution. She had no intention of offending anyone, especially anyone with the power to banish her from St Peter's. This might be her only crack at her story. Blessing her common sense in packing a couple of calf-length skirts, she chose bias-cut denim for her first morning. Shivering, she stepped quickly into her skirt and fastened it at the side with a shoestring bow, wondering all the while if sun even brushed the monastery walls, let alone penetrated it. A shower would certainly warm her but she had slept past her alarm, having never before needed to stir herself at the ungodly hour of 5 a.m. Only the bell toll from somewhere afar had roused her.

Last night before retiring she had checked out the bathroom, peering into showers that mirrored the ones back at her old school; communal; not a curtain nor cubicle separating one from the other. An interesting experiment would happen this evening when she presented herself in the showers in all her naked glory. With a couple of hundred men in this establishment, Faren could count on a handful of priests using the ablutions at the same time. She could hardly wait to see the effect her presence would have on them. With added vigour, Faren nudged her feet into blue canvas shoes that she retrieved from beneath her bed. She knotted her hair at her nape, leaving a tendril or two free to frame her face. She applied lipgloss and decided that would do; it was imperative to prevent the slightest antagonism from the governing board of senior priests who had, along with Father Murray, granted her this chance.

The soft soles of her shoes assured Faren moved as quietly as the priests. At the clanging of a second bell she joined the steadily growing cluster of men who trooped from their rooms along the halls and down the stairs. Several men were openly agog on encountering a woman in their cloister, others mildly amused. A handful were openly admiring. This latter group would be her target, Faren decided, as she followed the stream towards the chapel. From the breviary that Father Murray had given her she was able to recite communal prayers. The forty-minute meditation after that Faren saw as an opportunity to doze but when she opened her eyes and yawned, it earned her a quick frown from the priest who stood at the altar surveying the assembly. By the time the breakfast bell sounded Faren felt light-headed; she had to get something into her stomach. Being awake – or half-awake, she amended – for more than an hour with no food gave her low blood sugar. From tomorrow morning on she would eat a biscuit in her room.

It took Faren several minutes to urge some feeling back into muscles that had cramped with the continual kneeling in the chapel, so that by the time she strode on the polished boards of the hushed breakfast hall many of the tables were occupied. She threaded through several long trestle tables, searching for a vacant seat, conscious of curious faces, of the blushes and sly glances.

'Miss Lonsdale.'

Faren searched the immediate vicinity for the familiar voice. She spied Karl Sterling and glided towards the table.

'Good morning, Faren,' he whispered, a secret smile hovering on his lips as she halted before him.

'Good morning, Father Sterling,' Faren greeted, congratulating herself on the formality, when she thought of him as Karl. It would be easy to slip. She sat opposite Karl in the space indicated and nodded politely to the young men clustered round the table. About to pick up her spoon to dip into the steaming porridge, she was checked by her neighbour, who mouthed the word, 'Grace'. Mortified, she gazed down at her plate and mumbled an apology.

An elderly priest stood on the podium and lurched immediately into prayer. Faren deciphered few words. The moment it concluded, cymbals of cutlery resounded across the hall. Faren took up her spoon and stabbed the corona of sugar. Squeezed between two men, she basked in the shot of pleasant warmth that permeated to her very bones, a warmth she would have welcomed last night. Minutes later, fortified with food, her body recharged, Faren itched to tear at her sweater but refrained, knowing it would be less than prudent. She cringed at drawing attention to her gender in the breakfast hall, and her full breasts would certainly do that.

'You seem to be acquainted with Miss Lonsdale already, Father Karl,' the priest seated next to Faren probed, unaware of her discomfort. 'How did you manage that?' Faren fielded the eye contact that passed between the priests, suddenly suspecting collusion between them, then glanced down to spoon more of the sticky porridge into her mouth. The young man seemed not to expect a reply. Instead he twisted in his chair, stuck out his hand and announced, 'I'm Drew Edmonds. Welcome to St Peter's.'

Faren accepted his hand, liking the welcoming squeeze of his fingers. For the first time she studied him. He certainly had an open, almost sweet face, with keen blue eyes, and his sandy hair undoubtedly had a will of its own.

'As Father Karl found you first, I am sure he has already appointed himself your guide and protector, Miss Lonsdale,' said Drew Edmonds.

'Indeed, Father Drew,' Karl answered, before giving Faren a warm smile. 'You have a spot of porridge in the corner of your mouth, Miss Lonsdale. That's it,' he said as her tongue snaked out and retrieved it; she wondered why, at that moment, she thought of sex.

She continued eating in silence until a scraping of bowls signalled an end to the first course. The aroma of fresh coffee fingered the air as someone jolted Faren's shoulder and she glanced up to find the housekeeper at her table. The woman nodded, and placed a rack of buttered toast and a pot of coffee in the middle of the white cloth. 'Good morning, Mrs Cheaters,' Faren said. She noted the wariness in the woman's eyes was every bit as transparent now as on the day they first met. She

50

wanted to tell the housekeeper there was nothing to fear from her, but doubted any affirmation of the sort would be believed; the woman apparently saw her as a threat. Dismissing her from her mind, Faren deposited a slice of toast on her plate. She waved a hand through the rising steam. 'Father, could you pass me the marmalade, please?' she said, speaking to Karl. As their fingers met round the jar, she glanced up. His head was cocked slightly, amusement touching his lips, and Faren's heart-beat seemed to falter; he was a magnificent creature, totally wasted in a seminary.

She dipped her spoon into the golden mass of mar-malade and placed a dollop on the side of her plate. Then she lazily spread it on her toast, covering up the excite-ment she felt at being seated so near to this man. Her teeth were clamped into the first bite when something brushed her ankle. An accidental touch? Or was it inten-tional? Her gaze shifted to Karl.

'I beg your pardon, Miss Lonsdale. My foot slipped.' His expression remained inscrutable.

Did she believe him? Faren had no time to mull it over, for the priests sharing her table began speaking quietly, anxious to introduce themselves. She smiled and chatted in turn, her mind barely on the conversation as she risked a glance at Karl every chance she got. Once, their eyes locked, and the priest was the first to look away.

A bell tinkled somewhere behind them, cutting into the hum of voices. Glad of the intrusion that took her attention away from carnal thoughts, Faren watched as the men seated opposite shifted restlessly, while Karl wore a look of mild annoyance. Faren sensed he was unlike his fellow priests. The intrusion did not appear to bother anyone but Karl. And Karl was the only one here giving her the odd furtive glance. She scraped her chair round, turning to face the stage.

The same elderly priest who had mounted the podium at the beginning of the meal took up position again. After a short prayer the priest looked up. 'I won't keep you long, my brothers. I know how eager you are to get to your lectures. We have a new colleague amongst us.' His eyes searched his audience. 'Ah, there you are, Miss Lonsdale.'

As if she could hide in this sea of men, she thought, as the priest smiled at her. Apparently he harboured no animosity towards a female interloper, and she returned the old priest's smile, aware that all attention was focused on her. Faren's major fear was that the men, more particularly the older priests, would resent her, and she felt the tension leave her as she realised she had their acceptance.

The priest began to speak again. 'To be chosen for St Peter's when young men are virtually pounding on our gates is some feat indeed. I trust, my child, that you realise the honour we have bestowed upon you?' Whether it was expected of her or not, Faren nodded openly, acknowledging the priest's accolade. With a satisfied nod he carried on. 'Gentlemen, I want you to show your generosity by welcoming Miss Lonsdale into our fold. But,' the speaker warned, 'if you are thinking to afford this young lady special concession, then I suggest you forget it. She has chosen to join us, therefore she must be treated as one of us. Thank you.'

A light clapping began at Faren's table, then echoed throughout the cavernous room as novices and priests acknowledged her, their true emotions etched clearly on their features for her to see. Faren, feeling very much as though she had sinned, dipped her head. When at last the applause faded she looked up into Karl Sterling's smouldering gaze. Suddenly scrambling to her feet, Faren knew she needed to escape him to get her thoughts in order, impossible though flight seemed in the crush of bodies surging in a human tsunami towards the doors. Then he touched her lightly on her elbow and her only course was to be buffeted along with him.

'We missed you in the showers this morning,' he said, once they were free of the crowd.

Faren's skin started to tingle. 'Am I really expected to share with the men?'

'No.' He laughed. 'You will have to use the same showers but you won't have to use them at the same time.'

'Isn't that a "special concession", Father?' she asked, a hint of laughter in her voice.

'One that had to be made, nevertheless.'

'Of course.' Faren pushed back her disappointment. A priceless opportunity would elude her if she showered alone. But she could hardly press the issue.

With the priest's hand now at the small of her back, Faren was guided out into the foyer and ushered towards a closed door. 'Are you permitted to touch me?' she asked, reluctant to complain when she was lapping up his attention. If anyone should see, she might be booted out before she met another priest quite like the enigmatic Father Karl; she realised she was counting on him being the maverick in this Order. He raised his eyebrows in what she thought was deliberate misunderstanding. Why was she making so much of this? she asked herself. While low in her belly she felt the heaviness, the tentacle of heat in response to the slight pressure on her spine. 'I mean, your hand.' And that seemed to make matters worse, for she could hardly wait for the time when his hands would fondle and explore her body. And it was going to happen. She would make it happen.

'Am I not guiding you? How else would you know to head for this door?' Father Karl said, reaching out to grasp the sturdy brass knob. It sounded very logical put that way, and Faren felt a fool. An embarrassed fool. However, the next hour passed pleasantly as she peeked into all manners of rooms, with the priest as an informative companion. As he pointed out utility nooks, recreation rooms, libraries, and study halls, Father Karl was content to answer her questions, though she curbed herself from any personal probing. The tour nearly at an end, he surprised her by announcing, without any prompting on her part: 'The priesthood wasn't my life-long ambition, though I'm content here.'

Curious, Faren stopped in her tracks. 'Was it a sudden decision, Father?'

He shrugged. 'A sudden decision like yours, you mean?'

Faren blanched at his sharp calculation. Had he seen through her deception? Impossible. If her cover were blown she would not be standing here, conversing with him. 'You know the reason I am here. And now I am asking you, Father. Why are you here?'

He repeated his earlier shrug, the casualness echoed in his words. 'A bit of a rebellion on my part. My father decided only sops entered the priesthood. I set out to prove him wrong.'

'A weird reason,' Faren commented, wrinkling her nose. Her gaze scanned the man beside her. He was no sop. Definitely very masculine. And yes, he would be the typical headstrong guy. But what a price! 'Drastic. And do you regret it?'

'Tell me your calculation, Faren.'

'That you are happy. I barely know you, but yes, I think you are happy.'

He smiled that heart-stopping smile again, a smile that no priest should give, and she felt the beginnings of familiar heat between her thighs.

The silence left by the novices since they had rushed off to lectures settled around them. They were alone in the vast hall. Faren shivered. 'Why is it "Father Drew"? And I noticed he called you "Father Karl".'

'Not until we are ordained can we reclaim our surnames.'

'Oh.' That explained Father 'Murray' and Father

'O'Malley'. She was suddenly thoughtful. 'I wonder how they are going to get round me?'

'That will have them stumped.' Karl laughed as he pushed open yet another door. This time he guided her up a steep flight of stairs.

'Where are we going?'

'You'll see,' he said, allowing her to go first.

The splayed hand that gently nudged her suddenly slipped to the swell of her buttocks. Faren sucked in her breath, and wondered whether she had imagined the brush of his fingers because she wanted it to happen. But the warmth lingered. And this time there was no apology. Was he merely watching out for her, ensuring that she did not tumble back if she should lose her balance on the sharp climb? Each time her legs flexed to take a step, she was conscious of the thrust of her bottom. It felt like some wickedly intimate secret, knowing that his eyes watched every movement of her body. In the beginning, Faren had expected to be a voyeur at St Peter's; now, she thought, there just might be more. And she would partake of whatever delights were offered, for what better proof was there than being the recipient of some good-hearted, frustrated lust by a member of the cloth? Her heart thumping, she said, 'How much further?'

'Only a few more steps,' Father Karl said encouragingly. 'Keep going.'

'Fine for you to say,' she grumbled, plodding on, her calf muscles so tight she felt they would give out at any moment. And then, blessedly, she was there. Her breathing laboured, her legs shaky, she halted on the landing.

Faren could smell the faint scent of soap that lingered on the priest's skin as he reached over her shoulder to give the battered door a push. It squeaked open. Sunlight struck her face. She smiled as she stepped out on to the roof, enjoying the sun on her skin, as it warmed her through her light knitted sweater.

'Everyone likes it up here,' Father Karl said, following her.

She walked over to the battlement to survey the city that seemed almost to spew into its harbour. From this distance the Sydney Opera House looked like a discarded biretta. Her city, she thought, a lump in her throat; she would never leave it. 'It's spectacular, Father Karl. The best view in all of Sydney is from the roof of St Peter's seminary!' She laughed, whirling round to share her joy, and, for one small moment, she wished this man could share her life.

Chapter Five

'So, what do you think of our new recruit?' Karl watched his study mate's face, homing in on the play of emotions that Drew Edmonds fought to conceal. Interesting. He chewed over Edmonds' reaction, snapped the top back on his pen, and pushed his lecture pad aside. Again he eyed the young man.

'She's all right, I expect.'

'Yes, she is that.' Karl paused. He knew Edmonds was waiting for him to go on, despite the fact that silence was meant to be observed. 'How would you like a little fun with our Miss Lonsdale?' Just as Karl knew he would, the priest paled, his narrow lips working soundlessly. Karl chose to rag the man a degree or two more. 'Come now, Edmonds, whatever can you be thinking?' Karl pressed him, delighted with the flush that was creeping from the thin neck into the chap's face.

'Fun? You mean, a sort of initiation ceremony?' Drew asked, while Karl gloated over his colleague's obvious discomfort.

Karl laughed, a confident man, too sure of himself to take offence at the dark looks which industrious fellow students flicked his way. Let the minions frown.

Edmonds continued to stare dazedly at him, and Karl knew he had the young man hooked. He shuffled his forearms until they were flat on the desk, his face so close to the young priest's that he could smell the oatmeal soap on his skin. He lowered his voice, less in consideration for the studying going on around them than his desire to keep his suggestion between the two of them. 'No, Edmonds, I do not mean initiation. Though by all means label it that if you wish.' With overt interest he observed the convulsive bob of the man's Adam's apple. A dead give-away. Edmonds would follow where he chose to lead. The young priest stared back at him with glazed eyes. What was running through his mind right now? For the first time Karl studied the delicate features – almost a feminine look – of the man seated opposite, and he felt a forbidden stir in his groin. Startled, he jerked back in his chair, cursing himself for allowing such a repellent thought – however fleeting – to form. He turned to scan the lecture room, gathering his wits so he could approach Edmonds with a plan.

When Karl twisted back to face his colleague, he was calm. 'Would you like to know our sweet new novice? As in –'

'I know exactly what you mean.' Drew flushed.

'Of course you do.' Karl smirked, remembering how he had tempted the young priest into breaking his celibacy vows with Cherry, one of the seminary's kitchen maids. At least the girl had awoken the man's sexuality. Karl guessed the younger man was still mortified at his carryings-on when above all else he wanted to become a good priest. The girl had been sensible and when she had bid goodbye, she promised never to breathe a word of the pleasures they had shared. Both men believed her. Now Lady Hampton, Cherry had risen to great heights and had far too much to lose to spout off about what went on at St Peter's, especially as she had managed – ludicrous though it seemed – to convince her new hus-

58

band that she was the virgin he coveted. Cherry had been the last of the girls employed to help Mrs Cheaters, the housekeeper. Now novices assisted her in the kitchen. Karl had figured that either the Church was too miserly to employ outside help, or that it wanted to purge St Peter's of all temptation. Probably a bit of both.

Ah, but now we have a new lure, Karl reflected. He pictured her soft hands stroking him, her wicked tongue exploring him. And her hair. Like rich toffee. He could feel it slipping through his fingers, brushing his chest as she slid down his body. His blood surged, coursing along to that one sensitive place, making his flesh stir against his thigh. His vocation, his vows, common sense and propriety, all faded into oblivion once the blood engorged his penis. He slid his hand beneath the table and squeezed his throbbing erection. After the bell, he would slip into the confessional.

Karl looked across at Edmonds and was surprised to see all trace of nervousness and embarrassment had fled. Instead, his eyes glowed. Are we like animals, Karl wondered, that we emit a smell, with sexual intent? An attractant? There seemed to be no other sane explanation for the rapid change in Edmonds' demeanour.

'What's this about the confessional?' The voice, though hushed, was firm now, composed.

Christ! Had he spoken out loud? A careless tongue was dangerous. 'It will keep for another time. Now, what were we talking about?' Karl smirked.

'What you propose is risky, to say the least. And what about my career?' Drew whined.

'And wasn't what you did with Cherry also risky? And what you do with your friends?' Karl said, unsure as to why he harped at Edmonds. What did he care if he sought out the willing seminarians? And why was he eager for Edmonds to bed Faren? Sensible answers eluded Karl. Then one came to mind. An inexplicable excitement to watch two beautiful people together. 'What do you think the rest of us here do? Do you honestly believe we abstain?' he scoffed. He leaned across his desk again, having accepted his clinical attraction to the young priest and slotted it away in his mind where it would stay. He shrugged at Edmonds' questioning look. 'A small handful here probably do. But most of us –' he paused, his dark gaze unwavering '– find a way.' A current of excitement seemed to charge the air. He's hooked, Karl thought, smiling, knowing that while he wanted Faren, he also wanted to watch a seduction between the novice and the young priest whom he had befriended from the very first day. And for whom he had been the instigator in the Cherry affair. And most of all, he wanted to indulge in a *ménage à trois*. But first, he had to make Edmonds comfortable with the novice. And though deep in his soul Karl convinced himself he held no desire for a man, somehow he wanted to see Drew Edmonds naked. To watch the lean limbs sink on to the young woman's curvy flesh, to see the rise and fall of tight, perfect buttocks as the priest took his pleasure in Faren, as he thrust deeply inside her soft, young body. With a shot of distaste Karl had a sudden and inexplicable urge to touch a man's flesh. Shifting away, widening his personal space, he set out to soothe Edmonds' fears. 'Faren will want you. I've seen her eyeing you.'

'She's only interested in you,' Drew protested, almost pouting. 'And she is to become a priest herself.'

The half-hearted argument brought a faint smile to Karl's lips. 'So? Has it stopped any of us?' With his palm he smoothed his hair, wondering why he was bothering to convince the tiresome man when he could get on with enjoying the girl and forget all about Edmonds. If the fellow was too stupid to take what was on offer then it was his worry, not Karl's. But he gave it one more try. 'Look at the Borgias! They flouted convention. Hypocritical old bastards, that lot.' He waved a dismissive hand. 'This celibacy thing is man-made.' If that failed to influence him, let Edmonds satisfy his lust in a man's body instead. But he knew the priest was weak. That weakness was rearing in him now. Edmonds wanted Faren, Karl knew it; the vibes sailed over that expanse of wooden desk and hit him square in the intuition. So when was Edmonds going to stop acting the sop and show some guts?

'Life is short, and did Adam stay clear of Eve? No. We wouldn't have these tools of the trade if we weren't meant to use them,' Karl continued, feeling the deep throb of his cock, imagining how it would feel in Faren's soft mouth. Soon, he promised. Soon.

'All right. I did it before, with Cherry, and I can only be strung up once for the same offence. When?' Drew asked, the height of his eagerness clearly obvious now he had made his decision.

Karl laughed out loud, ignoring the grumbles and frowns from fellow students. He figured they would be responding differently if they were in on this conversation. Maybe later, before Miss Lonsdale was chucked out on her cute little butt – because he was convinced she was insincere about a calling – he would gather a small group, an élite selection of priests, to sample the novice.

'When is all this going to come about, then?' Edmonds asked.

Karl grinned, and watched Edmonds fiddle with his pen, the ink staining his shaky fingers. 'Very soon, I think. In the showers.'

'But we have been forbidden to enter the bathroom between eight and nine every night,' Edmonds protested.

'I know.' Karl smirked. 'And I wonder just how many priests are going to honour it?'

'They are not all like you, Karl. They will not sin.'

'You plan to. But of course, you will then pay penance.'

A bell rang in the bowels of the building. Amidst the clatter of assembling books and pens, Karl scraped back his chair. 'Next week. If we are lucky,' he said. By then he should have had a right royal time with Faren. She wanted him. But then, he wanted her. He would hand her a surprise when he showed up with Edmonds in his wake. She was a sparky little thing, and Karl guessed she would love having two of them pleasuring her. He felt a stirring in his loins. He could hardly wait.

Faren was on the roof. After lunch it was compulsory to be outside. Over on the soccer field, boys were getting ready for a game. They were the first-year novices, and were very young, some as young as seventeen. Others, like Father Drew and Father Karl, strolled through the grounds, or used the walking track. For Faren, there was nothing. But she preferred it this way; nothing could surpass her hour spent here, smelling the ocean, the breeze lifting her hair. And Karl. Sometimes Karl would come. He would touch her arm. Casually touch her shoulder. Sweet anticipation, but how long was he going to make her wait? When the door squeaked behind her, she tensed. Would he touch her today?

She turned to greet him and watched him walk to-wards her. He stopped about a foot away. The air seemed to crackle between them. Something would happen today. Then he went and sat on the edge of the battle-ment. Faren sighed, wondering if she would ever move ahead with Father Karl. He wanted her. She knew he did. He needed a little nudge.

She strolled over to view the city from the eastern side, flicking her hair over her shoulders, walking into the wind so that it streamed behind her. Her legs weak with longing, she was about to turn round, to go to him, when she felt a feathery touch on her nape. A feeling of such joy swept through her that she thought she might burst. Her head fell back to imprison his hand; she wanted the touch to linger.

Faren's skin tingled with desire as Karl's free hand

trailed down one bare arm, circled her wrist, then spread her fingers to twine with his. Wordlessly he tugged her towards the door and she stiffened; surely they would not leave now? But he was clever, her priest, because Faren saw that they were safe from inquisitive eyes. She forgot everything except Karl's hands. Karl's lips. He lifted her hair to nuzzle the softness of her neck, and traced the pattern of her ear, and she shivered at his touch. When he turned her to face him, and brushed his lips over hers, sweet sensations coursed through every sensitive inch of her body, and Faren groaned, her fingers clutching his shoulders, wanting to bring him closer. She could smell candle wax and incense on his cassock, and at that moment she thought it the most seductive bouquet in the world. A hint of jasmine drifted from her hair as Karl wound his fingers in the silky strands framing her face. He gazed at her with dark eyes, and she thought him the most beautiful creature she had ever seen. And then, at last, his mouth crushed hers. She cried out in pleasure when Karl's tongue darted between her parted lips and slid sensuously against her tongue. She pressed her body into his and felt his arousal, and she prayed this day would never end.

When he came to her three days later, she knew there was no turning back. She had survived the rigorous rules, the punishing regime, awful food, for this.

She sensed the precise moment that Karl came up behind her; she leant back against him, and sighed when he kissed the top of her head. 'You left your hair for me,' he said, his voice husky with desire as he released her hair from the clips and let it tumble free. She swished it provocatively over the back of his hand and felt a shudder course through his body. 'Come over here,' he said, already leading her back to the shelter of the doorway. A shiver of pure delight swept through Faren as he tugged her to the ground, and then knelt behind her.

Karl kissed her below her ear, and nibbled on the sensitive lobe, his fingertips trailing across her shoulder and down her arm, and on to the hem of her sweater. Faren's skin tingled with desire when he reached the underswell of her breast and gently stroked. His hands followed the fine cotton bra round and back again to the front. She sucked in her breath as the wandering fingers dipped beneath the fabric to touch her skin.

'Karl,' she murmured.

'Sshh. It's all right. Just close your eyes. There now, isn't that perfect?'

Mesmerised by his husky voice, waiting for his touch, she arched her back. When his thumb and finger took her nipple and squeezed, her body quivered along with the sensations. He murmured in her ear, calming her. 'Beautiful, Faren. Beautiful, hard buds,' he said, squeezing again. She felt herself being lifted, and when she was facing him, he pushed his knee between her legs hard against her mound, and gratefully she writhed against him. With one busy hand teasing her nipple, the other expertly slipped the metal catch at her back, then the cotton loosened its restraint, her breasts falling free. 'There, that's better,' Karl said. He was so right, she thought. So much better. Now his fingers had more mobility and slowly they circled her swollen flesh, moving in to play with her nipple. She whimpered, then opened her eyes to look up at him, and he obviously sensed her momentary unease, because he said, 'We won't be disturbed.'

Faren hesitated, then realised this priest had even more to lose than she had if they were caught in this compromising position. 'If you say so,' she whispered, thankful for his reassurance and, most of all, wanting the seduction to continue.

Now he was dragging her sweater over her head, his voice murmuring praise, the air provocative, teasing her exposed skin. She shivered. He tossed the sweater aside then slipped her bra straps down along her arms, urging her to shrug out of the tiny scrap of underwear. 'So beautiful,' Karl said, as he lowered his head.

Faren caught her breath just as his mouth surrounded her aching nipple. His tongue poked and prodded as she trembled in his arms. Heat radiated from her breasts, all the way down to the moist mound between her thighs. She groaned, surrendering to the powerful sensations coursing through her. As Karl's mouth lifted, the summer air swirled and dried his saliva round her peak, tightening the skin. Immediately, he suctioned her other nipple, sucking so fiercely that Faren arched, crying out, pushing herself further into his mouth. His tongue took up the play as it flicked round the nipple, searing her, while his other hand kneaded her right breast. Her breasts felt heavy, engorged, so very sensitive to Karl's practised assault. She lifted her arms and her muscles stretched, firing ripples of pleasure through her upper body. When all pleasure was squeezed from her stretch, she dropped her hands and splayed her fingers aggressively through the priest's hair, inhaling its masculine scent. Loving the healthy tufts, letting them tickle her fingers, she used her palms to push his head closer, feeling his nose flatten on her breast, feeling the minuscule shift to the side so he could take a breath before turning back to suckle her once more. She could hear his breath, loud and raspy, as he tasted her, his tongue, never still, soft and wet and lapping at her skin. Delicious shivers arrowed through her as he left her breasts and tongued down to her navel, where he dipped and prodded, so intensely and rhythmically that it was almost as if his tongue were plunging inside her. She wanted his tongue to blaze further down, to seek out her soft, secret folds, but instead it teased her, content to bathe her belly with long, slow licks. Her writhing body conveyed its yearning; Karl responded, his mouth trailing over her flat belly once more, down to the fringe of her curls. The crotch of her panties was damp and sticking to her. She wanted to be naked for him, to have him taste her. And she wanted him to peer into her sex, to know every fold intimately before he finally entered her.

'Oh, please!' she cried, desire racing through her, the beat of her heart hammering in her ears.

His hand went beneath her skirt and dipped two fingers under the elastic of her panties. 'You're so wet.' His breath was hot on her belly. He played with her pussy, his thumb stroking the crease of her thigh while she pushed herself at him, wanting his fingers to enter her. Shivering with desire, Faren doubted she could bear it a second longer as each languid stroke heightened her arousal, bringing her towards the peak of pleasure. Her cunt felt heavy, on fire, the crack leaching its honey, scorched by Karl's tantalising tongue licking and prodding, and his damp roving mouth. She could feel the swollen lips part, and still his fingers toyed there, not entering her. Then he was tugging at her panties, edging them down her legs. And now, as he panted his way down, there was the ultimate treasure left for him to discover. She kicked one foot out of her panties so she could open her legs for him, and rucked her skirt up to her waist. She could smell the intimate scent in the air, and knew that Karl was aware of it too, as he took a deep breath and nuzzled between her thighs. She thrashed on the warm stone, aware she was crying out for more. 'Don't move,' Karl said.

The intensity of his tone stilled Faren, but it was difficult to resist the sensations that lapped at her, inciting her to squirm in her selfish quest for more. How could she remain passive when she needed to be stroked, needed his hardness inside her? Did he not realise what he was asking? 'Karl. Karl. Please.' She groaned, her agony raw and palpable, as she felt the moist heat and heaviness in her pussy.

'It's fine, my lovely. Be patient. I'm going to get to it,' he said.

When Karl finally lifted her trembling legs and positioned himself so that he buried his head between her thighs, Faren thought she would melt with pleasure. It was so long since a man had performed this most intimate of acts, and though she wanted it, desperately, willed it, Faren felt embarrassed. The emotion did not loiter; the silky pleasure of being licked overshadowed her mortification, and she relaxed into the blissful sensation. His probing tongue forced her lips to part, dipping as if to sup of her, before the cunning tool moved in slow, torturous curves, pausing now and then to tantalise her clitoris with a quick, fiery flick. When Karl changed pace, his head moving faster, rhythmically, she thought she would collapse with the sheer pleasure of the gentle strokes to her clitoris. As he shifted, she wondered fleetingly how it was possible he could kneel for so long on the abrasive surface. But had her body not long forgotten the slight discomfort she first noticed when he lowered her on to the ground? She shivered, her body yielding to the intense sensations his magic tongue inflamed. She parted her legs slightly, only to tighten her thighs as that roving tongue delved deep into her cunt. She moaned, her head lolling from side to side, slipping on her own silky pillow of hair. She was wet with a mixture of the priest's saliva and her own dew, but the swirl of air stealing beneath her flesh dried the moistness almost as quickly as it formed.

'Keep still,' Karl said before homing in on her again, but hesitating at her clitoris so that she felt warm puffs of air as he breathed on delicate tissue.

With his thumbs pressed on swollen flesh, he prised the outer lips wide apart, grunting with apparent approval before drawing the hard bead into his mouth. Faren reacted to the delicious sensations, thrashing about as he suckled her. She arched into his mouth, impossible though it was to get any closer. Then she felt tiny nips on her tender flesh, and even as she felt the sting of his teeth, the tongue soothed, teasing the sensitive underside of the erect nub. When Karl shifted her legs from his shoulders, she wanted to cry out in frustration, but as she started to protest she realised he was not going to abandon her. She looked up at him as he lowered her bottom to the ground, her body tensed to cushion the anticipated roughness on her flesh. Then Karl quickly pushed her heels hard against her buttocks and leaned over to kiss her full on the mouth, the kiss sweet and gentle, tasting of her. His tongue pushed into her eager mouth, exploring, tickling the tender roof, sweeping across her teeth. She inhaled her own sweet fragrance that lingered on his mouth. Just as her pussy was beginning to ache for the tongue that toyed with her own, Karl reached down with his hand to slip two fingers inside that velvety place. His long thumb flicked her clitoris, gently at first, then hard and fast. She bucked in his arms. She knew she was going to come and she welcomed it, grateful for his mouth still covering hers, fearful that she would scream for the explosive release. Even as she wanted the release, she wanted it to drift on forever, wanted to feel tingly and hot and sensual. She grunted beneath the mouth that still clamped hers, tightened her leg muscles, curled her toes and urged her climax on. As spasms rocked her, the priest's fingers fed the rhythm, drawing out the pleasure, and he kissed her hard, then opened his mouth to swallow her cry.

Draped over his arm, Faren gasped. 'Oh, my God. That was out of this world.' He grinned cheekily at her and she knew he had no need of praise for his skill. She closed her eyes. When she opened them again, she reached up to touch his face. A light sheen of sweat coated his golden skin; she pulled his face down to hers. She licked him. Fresh, clean, salty sweat; he tasted like some rare nectar. 'I want to curl up in a little ball and drift off to sleep in your arms,' she murmured, wondering how she had got so lucky.

But Karl was pulling on her panties, urging her to her feet. He slotted the metal clasp of her bra as deftly as Faren herself would. He slipped the sweater over her head. 'What's the rush?' she grumbled, reluctant to relinquish her euphoric state just yet. 'And what about you?' Her gaze dropped to his groin.

The bulge still in evidence, he smiled a little ruefully. 'Forget about me.'

'But it must be uncomfortable,' Faren said, amazed. Here, at last, was a gem of a man, one concerned only with his partner's pleasure, undemanding of his own release.

Karl laughed. 'It's not the first time I've had to live with a sore cock.'

The crude picture was a real turn-on and, despite feeling sated moments before, Faren shucked off her drowsy state, feeling the heat in her beginning to rekindle as the vision shot through her mind. She shoved Karl back, and as he sat on his heels she was fumbling for him. 'We have the time, surely?'

'Greedy little thing, aren't we?' he mocked.

But Faren knew he wanted this. He was so totally generous with his giving, and she wanted to repay him. She had branded him arrogant, and yes, he was arrogant, but he was also considerate, for he was prepared to walk away with an aching erection. She smiled as she reached for him. In her haste to discover him, her nails scraped over the tender head of his penis; he sharply sucked in air. She dipped her head and the tip of her tongue delicately touched the small bead of moisture on his slit. She licked her lips, drawing the salty taste of him into her mouth. Karl moaned, thrusting his cock at her as she opened her mouth to receive him. She sucked him gently, her right hand tickling his pubic hair while the left grasped the base of his shaft. Her hand roved up over his belly, fingers splayed, pressing the hard muscles, before moving off to trail over the smooth line of his hip, as she murmured her appreciation of his beautiful body.

'Swirl your tongue,' he ordered, gasping, and she obeyed, pulling her mouth away so that her tongue could lever and tease the ridge. Moisture leaked; she could taste him, and the power excited her.

Faren's thumb and forefinger moved round the base of Karl's shaft, ringing him, as she took his cock into her mouth again. Her head moved rhythmically as Karl thrust himself at her. She sucked hard on the ripe head, pausing now and then to flick and tease with her tongue. Her hand gripped the lower half of his thick penis, trying for a steady rhythm, a rhythm that was difficult to maintain with the priest's frantic thrusting. Then she felt his hands clasp her shoulders, steadying her, leaving her fingers free to caress him. She slid her hands down to his balls, cupping them, sensing his imminent climax as they bunched tightly against his stem. Her hand strayed to his small, tight butt. Her fingers roamed each perfect moon, exploring, squeezing. In response, Karl moaned, then more loudly as her finger trailed inside the crease, pushing hard against resisting flesh. Even as she burrowed, she felt him release the muscles, then tighten again to urge his climax on, trapping her finger inside the cleft. As the first hot spurt of his seed sprayed her throat, her finger pressed firmly on the small, tight ring. He writhed, his come hitting the roof of her mouth, dripping down on to her tongue. She swallowed, while Karl tried to push further into her. She eased back from him, knowing he was lost and incapable of realising how roughly he endeavoured to embed himself. When Karl shuddered, his thighs shaking against her shoulders, he expelled a long, satisfied groan. Faren held him in her mouth, feeling the rigidity drain away until his penis felt wrinkly and soft. She gave him one final lick, and then, with her palm flat on his belly, she pushed away from him.

'You are some surprise, little Miss Lonsdale,' Karl said, his breathing returning to normal as he tucked his little monster back into his pants.

About to say he was the surprise, she heard it; the faint ringing of a bell. Somehow, afternoon lectures were not going to be so bad.

With a brisk knock on the study door, Faren prepared her speech, believing it to be word perfect. She heard the priest's call to enter.

'Good afternoon, Father.' Smoothing her denim skirt over her hips, a pure reflex action, Faren waited until the priest gave her permission to sit. As he smiled at her, she envisaged little bother in wheedling a town pass out of him. But it was so soon to ask. However, she was far too excited to keep the stunning revelations to herself. She needed to see Martine. Even her editor could hardly expect such fantastic results so soon. And she wanted to surprise her.

'How did you find these early weeks, my child?' Father Murray asked, waving his hand towards a chair, indicating that she take a seat.

'Interesting, Father. Very different from what I originally expected, but exciting nonetheless.' If only I could tell you of my experience! she thought. And more to the point, how one of your flock has strayed. Karl Sterling was an accomplished lover and his lovemaking left Faren feeling utterly sated, but now she yearned for more. More of the same exquisite torture. And she wanted to feel his wonderful hard penis deep inside her. He wanted her and he would be back. If it weren't for the end of recreation hour, he would have taken her there on the rooftop. She wondered where it would finally happen.

'That is pleasing to hear,' Father Murray said. 'Your lecturers speak highly of your diligence. Now, is there something that can I do for you, child?'

Faren held his gaze. She found Father Murray attractive; perhaps if she worked at it, she could become his lover. The very thought caused a telling warmth in her loins. She wanted to use her fingers to stimulate her love centre, to give herself relief. The only way to do so was to state her request and get out of here. But, oh, what she would give to pleasure herself right here in front of the priest!

Father Murray cleared his throat. 'Miss Lonsdale?'

'Oh, I am sorry! I'm taking up your time, Father.' She expected him to dismiss her protest but he remained silent, waiting. All he did was gaze at her, his expression slightly questioning. Could she entice this priest to stray? Would he ravish her if the opportunity arose? She cleared her throat. 'Father, I need to go into the city. Tomorrow, if possible. I need to buy some things.' Faren's gaze held his. Could a priest tell when a person lied?

'Miss Lonsdale, this is most irregular. We do, of course, give passes from time to time, over and above the regular monthly pass. You have been with us for so short a time.' He repeated the time frame as if she had gone completely insane. 'Child, what can you possibly need in town that you failed to bring along with you?'

'Er, personal things, Father.'

She must have conveyed something in her expression, embarrassment perhaps, because the priest suddenly flushed, holding her gaze for a mere second, before he bowed his head on the pretext of studying the leather-bound diary in front of him. 'I'll write out a pass immediately. But please, my child, do purchase everything you might need.'

Faren released a quiet sigh. Her request had been granted with a minimum of fuss and without an elaborate excuse. 'Who gets to see my pass, Father?'

'Father O'Malley. He greeted you on the day of your arrival.' And catching her smile, Father Murray's lips curved in response. 'I know what you are thinking, Miss

Lonsdale. Father O'Malley's fine age makes him an unlikely custodian of young men.' He smiled. 'And now, of a young woman. However, he is quick of mind and whips round the monastery like a young terrier.'

Faren laughed. 'I had noticed.' And once again Father Murray bestowed on her a genuine – and, to Faren, very sexy – smile. As the priest rose from his chair, she followed suit. 'Thank you, Father. I really appreciate your sympathetic dispensation.'

Reminded of why he had granted the extra privilege, Father Murray hurried her to the door. 'Quite all right,' he said, ushering her out.

On the way back to her room, Faren made herself a promise. Somehow, before she left the seminary, she would spend time with Father Murray. Some intimate time.

Chapter Six

*H*ad the sudden power cut not blacked out the corridor, Faren never would have stumbled into the wrong room. Nor would she have ventured from the safety of hers, especially without the aid of candle or torch. By her estimation, she was more than halfway along the passage when it plunged into darkness. She decided to flounder on to her destination – surely she could find it? – Karl's room being nearer than turning back to hers. She shuffled along, fumbled for the door handle, and pushed. She breathed a sigh of relief. Karl's room. The glow from several candles suffused the room in an eerie light as she closed the door quietly behind her. About to call Karl's name, Faren started. A man stood looking at her with passion-glazed eyes. She held her breath, then realised it was as though she were invisible; the naked man, his zealous attention on his partner, was unaware of her presence. Two coppery bodies, slick with sweat in the cool room, were bathed in a series of shadowy flickers and candlelight. Frowning, Faren endeavoured to decipher the puzzling actions that played in the mysterious night-light in blissful ignorance of her. Then, unmistakably, the timeless tune of sex intensified in the room.

One of the men stood at full height, his beautiful body arched, his penis thrust into the mouth of his lover kneeling before him. Faren dared not make a sound, dared not move, least any shift interrupt their flow of desire. But what was she to do? Once sated, the lovers would unfurl from their passion and discover her. They would recognise her of course, for unlike the majority of St Peter's masses, her sex made it impossible for her to blend in. Would they be angry? Ashamed? How could she have been so stupid as to enter the wrong room? Suddenly, the sexual sounds of passion grabbed Faren's attention. The urgent thrusting was riveting to watch; their moans ignited a desire of her own. Licking her suddenly dry lips, she felt as though it were her throat holding the thick cock that rocked rhythmically, as though it slid easily in her saliva. In fiery response, her pussy began to ache. She tensed her thighs, feeling the damp crotch of her panties. She bit off the moan that threatened to escape her throat. She watched as the man placed his palms each side of his lover's face, almost feeling the intense grip, the pressure, as the priest rammed his cock into his partner's mouth until he gagged. Highly aroused, she yearned to join in. She wondered if she could creep over, touch the smooth, silky buttocks without startling him or interrupting his sexual flow. But she might earn his wrath.

Faren deemed it wise to back away before she did something foolish to betray her presence, when a voice, thick with desire, rasped, 'Get out of those clothes.'

For a few moments she froze, her gaze still on the tight buttocks of the priest on the floor. When finally she looked up at the man who had spoken, he withdrew his penis from his partner's mouth. Stepping aside from his startled lover, he advanced on Faren, his erection pointing threateningly at her, laminated with saliva glistening like a woman's dew. Faren breathed in the heavy smell of his desire. 'I'm sorry. I'll go,' she mumbled, backing away, but her flight was checked by the priest's grip on her arm.

'Come and join us.' He drew Faren over to the bed; she became aware of the other man getting to his feet, anxious to be a part of whatever was going to happen to her. They appeared calm, not at all vexed by their interloper's unscheduled appearance. The priests then sat side by side on the single bed, bodies touching, their rods jutting solidly away from their bellies. Candlelight radiated from the bedside table and Faren saw them more clearly. 'Are you going to get out of your clothes? Or will I do it for you?' the priest said. It was non-threatening. More seductive.

All thoughts of the wonderful material she was gathering for her magazine piece were tucked away to the back of her mind, as, with unhurried movements, Faren wordlessly answered the young priest, her clothes pooling around her. When she was naked, they bid she kneel in front of them. She extended her palms and stroked their hardened thighs, playing with the soft tangle of hairs before creeping towards the soft skin of their balls. Faren poked her finger gently into each man's scrotum and rotated the hard marble-like rounds she found there. In unison, the priests groaned, and as each man sagged sideways, the tip of their cocks met in a fleeting kiss, the erotic sight causing warmth and moisture to increase in her sex.

'Take Philip in your mouth,' the young man ordered.

As Faren opened her mouth, Philip's cock strained towards her, the heavy tool quivering with an almost uncontrollable desire. Just before she closed her eyes and took him into her mouth, she caught sight of the other man clutching his rod and beginning to masturbate. Philip groaned as her tongue danced round his flesh. For a moment she drew away from him so she could prod her tongue-tip into his slit. She tasted the salt of his excitement. He then surprised her by reaching for her naked breasts. He settled himself between her soft globes and squeezed so that his prick was wrapped in her warm flesh. She heard him sigh, and wondered if he had been caressed by female flesh before. As she steadied herself with her hands either side of him, he jerked, trying for a rhythm that would bring him to climax. His cock was hot and hard, and her breasts firmly clamped him as he moved in the shelter of her cleavage. Faren sucked in her breath, her crack so warm and wet that juice coated her inner thighs.

The man sitting beside Philip suddenly grabbed her hand and guided it to his erection. He held her palm flat against his flesh, letting her feel the exciting throb of him. Her fingers wriggled beneath his hand, seeking to grip his cock, seeking to caress him. As he sensed her purpose, he lifted his hand from hers, giving her the room to manipulate him. She trembled with the thrill of having one prick between her breasts and, in her hands, another which jerked as its owner bounced, lifting his behind off the bed in a silent signal for Faren to move faster. With thumb and forefinger she squeezed the base of his shaft, and at his impassioned howl she determinedly followed through, along to the glans. Wrapping him in her palm, Faren created a tunnel, and he jabbed along its length, as her thumb pushed at the velvety tip every time it was cheeky enough to poke through. Beyond control, he emitted raw, guttural sounds, and Faren sensed he was about to come. She wanted to glance and see how Philip was faring but at that moment a stream of semen shot from the other man. She pointed the spurting weapon at Philip and watched, fascinated, as it hit his sweaty skin in potent bursts. Warm come landing on Philip's skin triggered his climax, Faren sensed, because suddenly his hot liquid sprayed her and dripped down in thick rivulets to coat her breasts. After a final valiant burst of seed, his penis fell sideways and Faren released it. It lay dejected on the priest's heaving belly. Philip shuddered in the final throes of his ejaculation, his fingers digging into the soft sides of her breasts. When spent, he released her and flopped back on the bed, his penis a limp facsimile of its former glory.

After several minutes, Philip's friend stirred, and he came to Faren. 'You will maintain silence on what you have seen here tonight. It is God's will,' he said. 'You must devise your own penance for your lapse.'

Philip's eyes remained downcast. Then Faren watched open-mouthed as both men hastily threw on their cassocks over their nakedness and, down on their knees, began in earnest to repent the wickedness of their mortal souls.

Faren got to her feet, wincing at the stiffness in her muscles. She hobbled towards the heap of clothes. She must get to Karl's room; he would be wondering what had happened to her. He might even think that she had wimped out.

'Here, use this.' Philip chucked her a towel, still gripping his crucifix as though the devil himself might appear at any moment. Grateful for his kind gesture, she smiled her thanks; she could hardly trot along to see Karl with semen encrusted to her skin.

Faren fired her panties across the room. They hit the white tiled wall and fell into a red mound. She shivered as a thrill shot through her when clothes were shucked off, the air lovingly caressing her; her legs were free to fly in whatever direction without restraint. Her tired feet relished the cool, ceramic squares as she admired her lithe body in the mirror which ran the length of the entire back wall of the bathroom. We are all little voyeurs of ourselves, she confirmed, and then, with a final self-appraisal, she whipped round and headed for the showers. With a choice of at least thirty showerheads, she could use a different one every day for a month, she thought, grinning. All this space seemed ludicrous, and she smiled at the image of pandemonium were she to share this communal facility with all the novices and priests abounding in this seminary. Today her mind had been far too occupied with Father Karl – she liked to think of him that way sometimes, it was so decadent, so sexy – to bother talking with anyone else. Father Drew had shown remarkable interest, as if he were on some adrenalin charge, and kept intruding on her daydreams, trying to drag her into conversation. Well, she was not going to think about him now, and she reached out to twist the mixer dial. Was Father Karl waiting, perhaps thinking she would not come?

As always, the soothing jets of water spraying on to her abdomen ignited a familiar tingle between her legs. The entire back wall was lustrous stainless steel, rivalling a mirror which was without the dense fogging that a mirror inevitably acquired in a steamy atmosphere. The biggest turn-on of all was when she could watch herself, and here the golden opportunity presented itself. She thought that the men here must get quite a charge out of gazing at their own reflections. And the reflections of others. This way they could surreptitiously look, without being caught and accused of lustful desires. Surely it was a great turn-on for each man? But now, watching herself proved arousing for Faren, and she began to pose, hand on jutting hip, while her eyes took in every inch of the pert, coral-tipped breasts, and the triangle of hair which was such an exotic shade of reddish-gold beneath the yellow fluorescent light. Combing her fingers through her thatch, she thought of the times when she was away at school, and had unwittingly intruded upon classmates performing contortions beneath the sprays of water. Once the meaning of their actions became clear, Faren had tried it herself, been left unsatisfied, and wondered what the attraction was. Orgasm in this manner was impossible for her, but perhaps with her body fully awakened, the 'water treatment', as she had heard the girls call it, might be within her reach.

With this in mind she sat down, opened her thighs, and positioned herself beneath the fall of water. She propped herself up on her elbows, aiming her sex so that it could receive the rapid pelting from the shower. Though it was highly pleasurable, and she relaxed under the steady beat, clitoral stimulation was inadequate; she soon gave up, realising orgasmic release was improbable for her.

Disappointed, Faren jumped to her feet. She ripped open her new packet of French Vanilla soap and proceeded with languorous care to lather her body, the slippery surface of the soap sailing over each shoulder and down along her arms. She rested the soap in the inbuilt dish and, hands sudsy, swirled them round each breast. Already her nipples felt hard with the promise of expert fondling as her fingers craftily crept towards the centre of each breast. With the flat of her palm she rubbed, such an erotic charge now her skin was slippery. The sexual current hot-wired to her private parts and she sucked in her breath sharply, but still she dallied, lingering on the silky skin, caressing herself. She dropped one hand to play dreamy circles along the tightness of her belly, bringing every inch of her sensitised body to life, as she watched her reflected movements. When Faren found the ache that radiated from the soft place between her thighs unbearable, she pressed the heel of her right hand on her mons. Until she got to visit her sexy priest, her aching bud would have to be satisfied with her fingers. Still pressing down on her mound, Faren stroked her middle finger between the plump folds of distended flesh, slowly, teasingly, until her finger rose over the erect bud. She pushed her finger firmly on the tender tip, an action that caused her to suck in air between her teeth. Now she concentrated on stroking the tiny shaft. She knew it would be peeping from its hood, although only for a moment; very soon her clitoris would be aggressively prominent, demanding a definite rhythm, overtaken by its greed for more. As Faren pondered on this, her hand kneaded her pouting flesh, applying indirect pressure to the clitoris. So small, so deviously hidden, and the centre of her pleasure.

Under the pelting of water, Faren stretched while she watched her reflection in the shiny wall, feeling her legs tighten, feeling the glorious extension of each muscle, the rigidity of her body sending pleasurable waves flowing through her. As her finger flew along her moist channel, she heard the heavy pant of her breathing quicken in time to the frantic rhythm of her hand. She groaned, and forced her lids open again so that she could watch the speed of her hand between her legs. She needed to be filled with a probing, pulsating cock. Father Karl's cock. And if their afternoon tryst had afforded more time, Faren knew the priest would have pleasured her as she had wanted; she would have welcomed his penis, holding him in her velvet sheath, because, if she knew anything, it was that Father Karl wanted her every bit as much as she wanted him. Now, as she daydreamed of her maverick priest – tall and dark and smouldering, and definitely naked – Faren's left hand dropped from where it caressed her breast to the fringe of curls, distractedly playing and tugging. In her mind's eye, Karl approached, his cock thick, magnificent, and glistening beneath the strobes of bathroom lights. She slowed the rhythmic stimulation of her clitoris, instead teasing it with the tip of her finger, as that cheeky bud reared, poked through her bush, and attempted to connect with that elusive finger.

Above the noise of the splattering shower she heard footsteps. Faren whirled round, and gasped at the sight of two men dressed in identical black trousers and short black tunics. A strip of pristine white collared their necks.

Instinctively she covered her privates, slinging one arm across her breasts – which even then slid a little in the silkiness of her soapy skin – while the other hid her bush. It was Karl. He had grown tired of waiting for her. She swallowed, and wondered how long they had been watching her. No one had watched her masturbate before.

'Where have you been, Faren? Surely you have a torch? And now I find you in here. What's going on?' Karl said, glaring at her.

'Sorry,' she mumbled, her gaze sliding between the two priests, the second of whom looked decidedly shamefaced. What was Father Drew doing here? She had marked him as being dedicated to his calling; had she been so wrong about him? Was he another priest who would take his pleasure and follow it with a night of self-reproach? Her hands remained covering her bush. Recovered from her initial fright, Faren did not hide her body for the sake of modesty. Despite Father Drew's obvious unease, she suspected she provided an arousing sight, one more erotic than if she were to make a blatant display of her nakedness.

'What have we here?' Karl hooked her panties, which lay in a small scarlet heap, with the toe of his shoe. He flipped them carelessly, a mere frippery as they sailed through the air towards his companion. Father Drew expertly caught the feminine item. 'Go on, Edmonds,' said Karl. 'You know you want to.'

Father Drew needed no further urging. He lifted the gossamer panties to his face. While Karl laughed, Faren gasped but her eyes remained locked on the younger man. From this distance she failed to see Father Drew's dilating nostrils savouring her most feminine of scents, but she knew he was sniffing, watched it in the contractions of his neck, heard his long, drawn out sigh, and listened while he inhaled deeply once again. 'What are you doing? You shouldn't be in here!' she said. Against

her better judgement, Faren's skin prickled as she anticipated what the appearance of these two priests meant.
Were they offering her a package deal? Sex like this had
never been a part of Faren's repertoire. But, why not?
Her skin began to tingle. Another added factor in the
young priest's unexpected appearance with Karl was that
a priest's flouting of his vows was contagious. But Faren
already knew this, having recently had a fascinating
insight into Philip and his lover. And she was not going
to count that as a threesome because, to Faren, that
would have meant ministering to her needs, her desires,
not merely being used. If she so wished, tomorrow Faren
could pack her bags and leave. She frowned. She had her
proof. Why wasn't she elated?

She looked up to see her scrap of underwear being
bandied about between the two men. 'Stop it!' Faren took
a step towards them but her foot slid from beneath her.
She squealed and Karl rushed forward, grabbing her. Her
slick body slid right out of his arms. She landed on her
bottom, legs splayed unladylike, giving Father Drew an
unimpeded view of the innermost folds of her sex. Mortified, she quickly clamped her legs together.

Karl unzipped his pants and freed his penis. As it
popped out Faren could not take her eyes from the play
before her. She watched as it grew and darkened into a
magnificent erection. She reached for it, feeling Karl's
shudder convulse through his body the moment she
circled her fingers round his hardness. With the touch of
her hand, a drop of moisture beaded from the eye.
Delicately, Faren stuck out her tongue and lapped the
tiny pearl. His cock, so terribly sensitive, seemed to
flinch, but Faren positioned her lips in a firm ring round
the plum and sucked, confident in the knowledge that it
quivered with desire. She sucked hard, greedily, taking
more of him into her mouth, while one hand drifted
down to his balls. Working briskly, she shot a sideways
glance at the young spectator, gratified to see his tongue

toiling to moisten dry lips, and his face flushed, shiny with sweat.

'I love it, little one.' Karl spoke through gritted teeth, withdrawing his prick from her eager ministrations. 'But now I've got to fuck you.' He flipped over on to his back, dragging Faren with him so that she straddled his hips.

The engorged cock twitched against her thigh and Faren shuffled up to align her sex with his. She raised herself above him, smiled down into his eyes and lowered herself with infinite care upon him. Karl clutched the base of his cock, guiding it so that she might swallow him whole, but the mischief in Faren made her tease him. She jerked up, anticipating the sweetness of total penetration, but denying them both. Just then Karl gripped her hips and guided her down on to him, impaling her with such sweet pleasure that Faren cried out. They remained still for several moments, Faren delighting in this, her sheath stretching for the priest's thick cock. As she rotated her hips, he groaned, then she began to ride him. She heard herself panting, harsh breaths merging with the pattering shower, as she increased the tempo, moving rapidly up and down on his erect penis. She leant further into him so that she could rub her stiff clitoris on his hardness. She thought of the priest, watching behind her as she bounced on Karl's body. He would see her releasing Karl's cock and the wet cock plunging back in again. The thought of being watched, together with the sensations and the pounding, spurred Faren to even greater arousal, and she felt near to coming, more so when Karl's hand feathered down her spine and into the crease of her behind. She sighed as he touched each soft moon in turn before bringing his hand round to press a finger to her clitoris. Now, with each thrust, there was also direct friction on her bud, and she shivered, knowing she could not hold on for Karl, needing to have her release. As she let herself go, the force of her orgasm gripped him, and he came inside her. Karl's groan was loud as he thrashed about. After several spasmodic jerks his hard body relaxed beneath hers. Faren collapsed on top of him, the soft moons of her behind in full view of the second priest. She smiled against Karl's chest. It was the first time she had welcomed his penis into her treasured place, and, if she had any say in the matter, it would not be the last.

'What is it?'

'Just wondering –' she whispered, the shower muffling the sound of her voice from Father Drew '– if we turned him on.'

Karl chuckled, his breath brushing her cheek. 'If we didn't, then he's made of stone.' His fingers played along her spine. 'Did you like him watching us?'

'Hmm. And you?'

'What do you think?' Karl said.

'If I knew, I wouldn't ask.'

Karl refrained from answering. Instead, he sat up, toppling Faren, and looked towards Drew. The young man hesitated. Karl said, 'A few Hail Marys should expunge your sins. And if it still bothers you, tomorrow I will hear your confession.'

The tip of her tongue poked between Faren's lips as she glanced up at Father Drew. She heard him draw a deep breath, then with trembling hands he fumbled with his leather belt. Like the young priest's hands, Faren's legs were shaky, every nerve-ending alive in sweet anticipation. It was not quite what she had envisaged, this threesome. Greedy little Faren wanted both priests working on her simultaneously. Sliding her gaze to Karl, she encountered his broad, sexy smile. Did this excite him? Or was he looking to humiliate his colleague? She shrugged. Whatever was going on between these two was best left to them.

When Faren glanced back at Father Drew he had already divested himself of black, and his thumbs were hooked into white briefs. Already wanting more, her pussy contracted sharply at the sight, eager for that first glance of the young male's complete nakedness. Her gaze darted from man to man. Her mind's eye ran through each priest's physical attributes. Attracted to both, Faren freely and dispassionately admitted that Father Karl was by far the most aggressively attractive of the two. The sheer masculinity and total arrogance of her dashing priest as the dominant partner in their sexual encounters only added to the excitement. About to muse on the inevitable loss of Karl as a partner once her deed here was done, Faren heard her thoughts intruded upon.

'Turn around.'

Father Drew's terse command appeared at odds with the gentle character of the man she had viewed during earlier meetings. Such an order Faren expected from Karl, but when she had spoken with Drew at mealtimes he was quiet, introverted almost. And above all, very polite. 'Isn't it always the quiet ones,' Faren muttered, as she raised her eyes, admiring the thick penis that stuck out fiercely and proudly from its forest of hair and throbbed with impatience to find its promised mark. She shivered, feeling cold without the needles of hot water which had been spraying her nakedness. As she started to turn for him, wondering if he was going to take her in her sex or – a frightening thought – anally, Drew stopped her.

She saw how Drew's body shook, undoubtedly aroused by her coupling with Karl, but still battling demons, she suspected. She could smell him already, that unique animal scent that emanated from his body, the musky fragrance arising from his genitals. He stuck his head right between her thighs and inhaled, and Faren was conscious that Karl's scent would be mingling with hers.

'Have you washed? There!' Father Drew's voice quavered.

Green eyes flashed at such impertinence. 'Of course!'

'Then wash again. I want to see you,' he said quietly, his gaze unwavering from her damp bush.

Faren's hackles subsided a notch. She had taken his words as an insult, when all he wanted was to witness her probe and finger herself, create a turn-on for him. Her gaze flicked to Karl. He was grinning, enjoying every moment of this game.

'Yes, little one. Show us how a woman cleanses. Then if you are lucky, Edmonds might be persuaded to show you how he wants it done.'

'Perverts,' she muttered, low enough that only she could hear. It was humiliating to have to bathe in front of these priests, though Faren could not deny that she felt the sweet building of arousal, a desire to primp and preen, to touch her swollen folds in front of her appreciative audience.

After he handed her the soap, Father Drew sat back on his heels, his prick standing rigid, a bead of moisture poised on the purple tip. Sensuously, Faren glided the cake of soap round her breasts, across her stomach, releasing its vanilla fragrance, teasing down to the fringe of curls, then away again, until Father Drew pleaded for her to wash her furry mound. Now the priest's eyes were alight with desire, not a shadow of guilt marring his face. He licked his lips and his breath came fast. Karl lounged on the periphery, an interested outside party, content to watch. Beneath her fingertips, Faren's hair curled and lathered.

'Squat!' Father Drew demanded. 'How can you wash yourself properly like that?'

Faren obeyed. A new game. Cleansing so intimately for spectators, watching while a thick penis quivered and leaked, waiting to penetrate her, while her cunt throbbed with need.

'Open your lips.' Another command from Father Drew. Lust had triumphed, had changed him into an arrogant beast.

Karl laughed, enjoying the display. Faren glared at him. If Drew did not fill her soon she would scream with frustration. But there was something almost forbidden in touching herself in front of witnesses. With the first two fingers of her right hand Faren spread the puffy flesh, and heard both men gasp as she opened to them. That traitorous piece of flesh, the nub which was her most sensitive part, flaunted its need. Faren tried to shield the obvious. But then her nipples were hard; a sure sign that she was as aroused by the rough orders as the men were themselves.

Just then Drew grabbed the soap from her shaky fingers and lathered her. Moments later he slung the soap aside. Now his fingers rubbed the satiny folds, burrowing between the puffy lips to feel the wet slit. Faren's back ached with squatting, her thighs ached, and she felt her legs might give out. As if Drew had only now become aware of her discomfort, he gently pushed her backwards and her bare bottom hit the cool floor. She began to shiver. 'Here, you're cold,' he said. With that comment he twisted the temperature dial to full force. Faren gasped as warm water hit her face and pelted her body, warming her flesh until she was pleasantly soothed. Drew grabbed her by the ankles to move her face from the spray, then spread her legs once more. Faren's attention never left the priest's hard penis and he knew it, because he grinned at her and for one second touched it to an aching nipple. She moaned. She sensed movement in Karl's direction and flicked her glance that way, reluctant to take her eyes away from Father Drew's engorged cock for more than a moment. It appeared that Karl could no longer rein in his desire, that the little scene being acted out before him proved too arousing to remain merely an onlooker. His pulsating dick was testimony to that.

Karl padded closer, the pooling water dammed by Faren's prone body sloshing about his feet. Then he too knelt alongside her, bending his head to kiss a rosy peak before sucking it into his mouth. He held the weight of her breast in his palm as he suckled, and she closed her eyes. He let go of her nipple to whisper, 'You're doing fine, my dear.'

Father Drew commenced a gentle kissing of her ankles, then her calves, his hands inching along ahead of his mouth, blazing a trail. A quiver rode over her, touching every inch of her body; two priests may have been a fantasy, a harmless fantasy, but right now it was real, and it felt fantastic. She surrendered to the pleasure that both men accorded her with their wet hands, moist mouths and light kisses.

'I think she's ready,' Karl grunted as he released her throbbing nipple. 'You first.'

Drew, with a mouthful of scented pussy, was unable to reply, but the grunting, moaning sounds could only be pleasure as his streamlined hips moved in unison with his busy head. Faren wanted to scream; the sensations were so erotically powerful and beautifully exquisite, with Karl alternating between her breasts and Father Drew licking hungrily in the dampness of her pussy.

'Turn her round.' This time Karl's voice was thick with desire.

A startled Father Drew lifted his head and then together they flipped her over. With his arm beneath her stomach Karl hauled her to her knees; Faren expected them to crumple under her at any moment, weighed down by the relentless waves of desire that continued to lap through her. Her hot core threatened to explode in orgasm but she held off, wanting to hover near the brink before surrendering to the ultimate release. So she waited for the priest to enter her, and when he at last touched her sex with his, she buckled.

With strong arms, Karl hauled her up again. 'That's it, Edmonds,' he encouraged. 'You're doing just fine.' He began chanting sexy words and rude suggestions that spurred the humping man to move faster.

When Faren first heard the yelp she thought the young

man had come, and although he stopped his thrusting, his cock suddenly pounded into her, his balls slapping against her as he disappeared to the hilt. Shocked, and then with a new excitement, Faren realised the extent of what was happening. Karl had positioned himself behind his colleague and had entered him. Why the thought should excite her so much, Faren was at a loss to explain. She only knew it did, and now that the priest's initial shock seemed to have dwindled and his narrow passage accepted the thrusting cock, he took up his earlier rhythm. Her mind's eye on the scene behind her, coupled with the pleasure Father Drew's hard member was giving her, was enough to trigger Faren's climax. Giving way to the scream that came from deep in her throat, she marvelled at how vocal she had suddenly become. She hoped no one would investigate, but with the shower gushing, the noise would mask her cries and the grunts of the men.

Following close behind Faren's earth-shattering climax came muffled groans, the priests surrendering to their own blessed release. The movement within her body slowed. Drew's cock slid out of her, and suddenly aware of the rawness of her knees, Faren collapsed gratefully.

She had scant time to regain her breath when Karl, the first one to compose himself, smacked her bare bottom. 'Your hour is up, little one. Get dressed.'

Chapter Seven

When Faren breezed into the office of *Splash!* magazine the following morning, Julie Perkins, the teen-
age receptionist, glanced up. 'Hi, Faren,' she said. A
smattering of guilt clouding her pixie face, she whipped
a fat paperback into her desk drawer.

'Good book, Julie? You've discovered erotica, have
you?' Faren teased the blonde, who immediately blushed.
'Is she free?'

'Yes. Go right in.'

'Thanks, Julie. Catch you later.'

When Faren burst through the door Martine was
perched on her desk flipping through a manuscript, her
slender legs crossed at the ankle and the telephone
hugged beneath her chin. 'Check that story on university
students prostituting to pay their fees, will you, Bas?'
Martine said, as she glanced up, and waved Faren
towards a seat. 'I'll see you here within the hour.' Martine
broke the connection and slipped off the desk, smoothing
down her pencil-slim, caramel skirt. 'I didn't expect to
see you so soon. You must have some news.'

Faren's news, her sole reason for risking Father
Murray's wrath by approaching him for permission to

come into the city, was to tell her editor she had cracked the case. Now, suddenly, she stalled. Why should Martine know what her reporter did? It was personal. And there was another reason for wanting to keep the hours of passion to herself. 'I had to come into town for some personal items,' Faren lied. 'And of course, I wanted to pop in and see you.'

Martine appeared deep in thought as she ambled about the room. Then suddenly she strode over to the handsome leather chair and sat down. Faren met her gaze. 'You've cracked it? Already?' Martine asked.

Faren's hesitation lasted only a moment and, she hoped, went undetected. 'Not exactly.'

'Oh?' Martine frowned. 'What does that mean?'

'It means –' Faren explained '– there is one priest who is absolutely stunning. Tall and dark and definitely very handsome. Every woman's dream stud.'

'And?'

'He's flirted with me.' Something made Faren hold back the truth. If she got pulled out of the seminary now, when all she had experienced was a small taste of the wild passion that was Karl Sterling, she would surely wither. He breathed life into her. Who would take his place? She knew of no other who had the powerful sexual expertise of her priest. Hastily she fought to push the provocative visions of Karl from her mind; if she were to dwell on those, she would soon be sitting here squeezing her thighs together, drifting off into a secret mist of pleasure and remembered passion.

'Well, that's a good sign.'

'Pardon?' Faren's gaze connected with Martine's dark brown eyes, and found them watching her shrewdly. Had she blown it? 'I think so, too,' she added hurriedly, realising she had heard her editor's comment after all, and, as the older woman reclined in the depths of expensive leather, Faren felt the tenseness leave her shoulders.

'But it's not enough to pull you out. Not yet. Can you stand to be in there a while longer?'

'I'll have to, won't I?' she said, ever-hopeful that her show of reluctance would seem genuine. If only Martine knew! Bruised and sore, feeling remnants of the previous night's lovemaking that did nothing to diminish her zest and sexual appetite, Faren had rolled out of bed this morning more alive than she had done in years.

But she was not at all surprised when top editor Martine Danson, far too shrewd to be conned by any reporter, warned, 'Faren –'

'OK. OK! This priest. Father Karl. Well, we sort of – No. I'll have to gather more substantial evidence than a quick bit of petting below the battlements.' For some obscure reason she refused to confess to the bathroom scene with not one, but two priests. Was it a fear that Martine would pull her off the case? Her editor might well be satisfied with that lot, but Faren wanted more. More proof. More pleasure.

'And you don't wish to give me details?' Martine's astute gaze seemed to bore right through Faren.

'It was only a bit of a fumble,' she said casually, fighting the urge to relive every moment of Karl pleasuring her, and reluctant to air such personal details to her editor.

'Why, Faren, you're embarrassed!' Martine crowed. 'How on earth can you be embarrassed? You told me about your last little scene with that bastard, Jack, and that was pretty juicy.'

Of course, she realised now how foolish she had been to confide her personal affairs to her boss, but they had both met Jack at a press party, and Martine had always asked. In Faren's view, at the time, Martine had had the hots for Jack herself. 'Well, I didn't care for that prick, did I?' Though not the love of her life, she had been comfortable with the relationship. Then she had caught him devouring her flatmate on the kitchen table when her untimely appearance made no difference, and the bastard had kept on slurping away.

'And you care for your priest?'

'I guess I do.'

'Faren,' Martine spoke firmly. 'Tell me. We've discussed sex before. Apart from Jack, all in relation to your work. And that is all it is now. Where is my bright and breezy reporter who danced into my office and told me she would be taking up residence at St Peter's? Also, young lady, don't believe I am so easily duped. You know me better than that.'

Looking up at her boss, Faren caught the wry smile and wondered how she had supposed for a moment that Martine would be satisfied with the fringes of her news. The woman had not got where she was today – where Faren planned on being one day – by taking people at face value. No, it was not in Martine Danson's nature to believe that people told her all. 'So, what do you want?' Faren asked.

'Start at the beginning, my girl.'

Faren realised her editor's curiosity was justified. This woman paid her wages. She was on a job. She gave a resigned sigh. 'It was freezing, that place, but it could have been nerves on my part. At least, adding to it. And it was warmer in Father Karl's room.'

'You went to a priest's room?'

'Yes. I went to his room.'

When Faren had finished her tale, Martine's dark eyes still glittered with the excitement that had first appeared with her opening statement. 'My God! You really have dropped yourself into a hornet's nest!'

'I know. But something else is going on. Remember I told you about the lengthy waiting list to get into St Peter's? There's got to be a connection.'

Martine nodded thoughtfully. Then she smiled. 'You're asking me to let you stay, aren't you? Even though

94

you've got enough to make an enlightening little article for *Splash!* You're enjoying it, Faren! Come on. Admit it.'

Faren squirmed. 'All I'm trying to say is there's more to that place than meets the eye. Besides, this celibacy bit I'm doing; well, all these things happened with me but what about when I wasn't on the scene? Where are all the women?' As Martine sent her a sly smile, Faren tensed. She had omitted mention of walking in on two men pleasuring each other, and of her participation. 'Do you think it's what we figured in the first place?'

'Precisely.' Martine appeared thoughtful again. 'But this Father Karl sounds very much the lady-killer. So, there's got to be more. You're certain about the housekeeper?'

Faren flapped her hand in the air. 'Forget her. Karl would never be attracted to her. I told you. All I've managed to fathom is that Rosemary Cheaters has the hots for Father Murray. Whether he returns her feelings or not, I have no idea.' She paused, her finger on her lips while her mind returned to her first morning. 'There must be girls in the kitchen. Unless, of course, they enlist the help of the novices. It would be impossible for Mrs Cheaters alone to cook and serve all those priests, yet she was the one to bring coffee and toast round.'

'Right, here's what we will do. I'm in full agreement that you stay there. This could be bigger than we both expected. Keep your eyes and ears open and, whatever you do, maintain your cover.' The ivory telephone on Martine's desk trilled. 'Look, Faren, I have a meeting, but keep up the good work. Can you phone me?'

Faren chewed her lip. 'Bit risky from there, I reckon. Someone might overhear. Perhaps if we could talk in code, I'd manage it. You ask the questions and I'll keep to "yes" and "no".'

Martine picked up the telephone, putting a decisive stop to the annoying interruption. 'Won't be a moment,' she said briskly into the mouthpiece before jabbing the mute button. 'We'll see what happens, Faren. If I don't hear from you, I'll see you in – what? – two weeks? Three?'

'Right. I doubt I can get any more special leave.'

As Faren was about to disappear out the door, she was called back. 'It is safe in there, isn't it?' Martine asked, frowning.

Faren, her good spirits restored, grinned. 'There's not a thing to worry about.'

Faren had hit peak-hour traffic so that it was forty-five minutes later when she arrived at the seminary gates. 'Good evening, Father,' she said, dismissing the elderly priest from her thoughts as she gazed up at a restless pink and charcoal sky. A sense of contentment enveloped her as she strolled through the courtyard, breathing in fresh salty air instead of city pollution, while an ocean breeze ruffled her hair. Immersed in thought, Faren failed to concentrate on where her legs were taking her. She collided with Father Murray, her soft breasts against his hard chest, and, as they bounced off each other, they both laughed.

'Forgive me, child. I confess I failed to see you.' Father Murray smiled down at her. 'The only excuse I can offer is that I was deep in thought.'

'And I had my head in the clouds.' As Faren admitted this she glanced skywards again, and her periphery vision caught a slight movement at a second floor window.

'Did you have a good day in town?'

Faren swung her gaze back to the priest. 'Oh, yes. Yes, thank you, Father.' But her tone was wary now. Could someone have seen her enter the magazine's premises?

'Good. Good,' he muttered as he stepped round a relieved Faren and prepared to head off to wherever it was he was heading. But he turned back. 'Were you told this morning that the council requires a report from you at the end of the week? You are to hand it in to me.'

'No.' She frowned. 'What kind of report?'

'Oh, nothing to be alarmed about, child. Your opinion on the lectures. How you feel about St Peter's. That sort of thing. All our new entrants are required to write up a simple report. We like to know our people are settling in. Check with Mrs Cheaters before you start, if you wish. She is always very willing to help.'

He sounds almost anxious, Faren thought, wondering why the priest wanted to get the two of them together. Did he perhaps hope they might become friends? 'Mrs Cheaters? But isn't she your housekeeper, Father?'

'She is. But Rosemary also helps the new students, and was an invaluable asset to me on my arrival. She's been here fifteen years and is well clued-up on the running of our little clique. She would be happy to help. With anything, I'm sure,' Father Murray added lamely.

Aha, but regardless of what you may like to believe, you are uncertain, aren't you, Simon? thought Faren. 'Thank you, Father. I'll remember that,' she said.

'If anyone gives you any – shall we say – trouble, you will come to me?'

Faren experienced an almighty tummy turn. Her legs felt shaky. Did he know something? Had someone seen her on the roof with Father Karl? They had met innocently for days, but novices were forbidden to form friendships, and pairing off with Karl would undoubtedly be misconstrued. Perhaps Father Murray had heard something of what went on in the bathroom last night? At his next words Faren relaxed.

'Not that I am expecting anything of that nature, Miss Lonsdale, don't get me wrong. St Peter's is a very disciplined community and we all get along, even if at times it requires a bit of an effort.' Father Murray shook his head. 'I really don't know what possessed me. My students are fine young men. They embrace celibacy vows.

Of course they – Forgive me, my child.' Shaking his head, Simon bid her goodnight, mumbling as he marched away, apparently still chastising his wayward tongue for its foolish rambling.

Faren smiled to herself. Then remembering the silhouette at the second-floor window, she stared up to where she knew the housekeeper still surveyed the courtyard. Rosemary Cheaters saw herself as Father Murray's protector, that much was obvious, and was most certainly his lover. Therefore the woman was watchdog to her possession. Faren mused, her gaze sweeping the forbidding architecture that loomed ahead of her; she would relish solving the conundrum that was Simon Murray before she relinquished the mixed-up, tight-knit universe of men who took solemn vows and turned quisling. Before she defected from St Peter's to a far saner world.

From his fourth-floor window Karl observed the intrepid Faren Lonsdale. She really was a delightful little thing. He watched as she gazed up at one of the east-wing windows, her neck so slender, shoulders braced, wind-fashioned curls whipping across her face. Suddenly she moved, striding out with her proud chin tilted, her glorious mane plucked up in the summer breeze and Karl felt a stirring in his loins. He vowed he would make slow, tender love to her. There had been so little time. And he had derived a voyeuristic pleasure from watching Faren and Drew Edmonds together. But Karl was a very sensual man and it mattered to him that his lovers also derived their pleasure from being with him. Egotistical though it was, he counted himself a rare breed, a man who delighted in bringing a woman to the ultimate orgasmic peak by his considerable skills. Tonight it would be different. Tonight he would take all he wanted, while ensuring his young lover enjoyed herself in the process, of course.

Hands thrust into his pockets so he could stroke his

burgeoning erection – brought on by both Faren in the flesh and seductive images of her – Karl turned away from the window to focus on the young man fidgeting in one of the chairs. 'So, Edmonds, what is it you have come to say?' His confidence in the priest was misplaced. He had thought to make a man out of his colleague, but now, observing the body language, the restless gaze, he sensed Edmonds wanted to wimp out. Edmonds' next words proved it.

'We were very rash last night. We could have been caught.'

'But we weren't. So, what about it? You didn't do enough penance, is that it?' Karl sneered.

The young man licked his lips several times. Oh, yes, thought Karl, he wants it all right. But which of us is he unable to resist the most? Faren's yielding body, soft and warm and moist? Or mine? My thick hardness sinking into his tight rear end?

Karl's cruel streak surfaced. 'You liked me in that tight orifice of yours, Edmonds.' And as he predicted, the young priest flushed. Karl sauntered menacingly towards the seated man, knowing with unguarded relief that he would never touch a man again. But it had been an experience, albeit one he had only ever harboured as a fantasy.

'You are embarrassing me, Sterling!' But Drew was once again quenching parched lips.

Karl smiled before he turned away. 'You haven't been to the confessional, you said?'

'You know I have another year of study before I can hear confessions.'

Karl threw back his head and laughed, producing a strangely robust sound laced with harshness that was sure to make the other man shudder. 'I'm not talking about confessions. Would you like to go into the box?' He eyed Drew speculatively, noting the puzzlement in the inconstant blue eyes and knowing, without waiting for it to be confirmed, what the priest's answer would be.

'I don't know what all this is about, Sterling. But I've seen the confessional, if that's what you mean. I've even confessed my sins in there. I grew up in Sydney.'

Karl nodded, looking thoughtful. 'What about last night?'

Drew blanched. 'Obviously I couldn't – until I can –' Drew's eyes remained downcast. 'You are the only one I can confess to, Karl. I stayed up all night. It was the proper penance for my sins. But heart and soul remains heavy. Karl, will you give me absolution?' the priest pleaded, his fingers twisting his frock.

'If I must. But later.' Perhaps another time he would reveal the secret of the confessional, Karl decided, conscious that Edmonds was not ready to be plunged into the thick of things. 'And now, old man, I must kick you out. Miss Lonsdale will be awaiting my talented ministrations. Unless –'

'What?' Drew asked, wariness apparent in his tone.

'Do you want to join in?' Karl watched while a burst of excitement vied with guilt in the young man's expressions. Edmonds wanted to be a good priest, but now he had tasted forbidden fruit. So much for his bleating about repentance.

'With Faren?'

'Who else?' As the priest's eyes trained on Karl, an eloquent spark lit the sometime-cold depths, and Karl's insight blessed him with the knowledge of just how ardently the younger man wanted the spunky new recruit. Apparently the boy would sin and wallow in remorse later. 'Come by later. If I'm not back in a couple of hours, wait,' he said, sending Drew to the door alone. It did not bode well to appear overly friendly with any one compatriot, close friendships being actively discouraged by the older priests, who remained staid in thought and outlook. 'Don't linger, man!' Karl hissed, as Drew poked his head round the corner to check if the hallway was clear. Exiting by stealth only encouraged inhabitants to look askance, whereby openly visiting, usually on the pretext of seeking advice or study help – with doors left open – failed to invite closer inspection. He watched as the young man stepped from his room, only to stop and turn back with obvious confidence restored.

'Will she come?'

Karl's mouth curved in a knowing smile. 'In more ways than one.' As the priest flushed like a virginal female, Karl laughed. 'I sure know how to push your buttons.'

Chapter Eight

*K*arl headed for Faren's room, and as he walked across the deserted hall, he wondered if it was wise to trust Edmonds. He liked the fellow well enough; he was pleasant and bright, and respected by his peers, despite being quite the teacher's pet. So why did he trust Drew Edmonds? With Faren. With his drink. And soon with the secret of the confessional. It was much too early for such a revelation. Edmonds needed to be fully corrupt before that secret could be shared. He smiled. Unexpectedly he found the corruption of the young priest an exciting pastime and was eager to observe just how far he could push the man. Last night had been a mad aberration on his part. That was all there was to it; a receptacle for his lust presented itself and he, like any passionate man, had taken it. But Karl knew he was lying to himself, an intolerable weakness that he refused to condone in others. True, the pink cunt with its provocative lips which were so tantalisingly displayed as Faren lay sprawled on the shower floor had been an irresistible temptation. But it was the young man's white buttocks tightening before him that had made it impossible for

102

Karl to contain his lust. His prick beginning to stir, Karl hastened his strides.

Faren opened her door almost immediately following his knock, and he entered quickly, aware in an instance of her natural perfume, the healthy scent that emanated from her. Laid out on her bed were a black cassock, white collar and black trousers. A clone of every costume worn at St Peter's. 'You've been kitted up, I see,' he said. She nodded, her hair swishing about her shoulders, inviting him to reach out and touch it. Though she wore it in a top knot during the day – loose, it would be counted as an enticement – he had had to keep himself from touching its softness. Now they were alone in her room, away from prying eyes.

Karl stepped towards her and fingered the gently swaying tendrils, closing his eyes as he inhaled the ambrosial essence of her; clean and sweet, and delightfully fresh. She leant into him, the length of her slender body pressed suggestively against his. He drew her into his arms, lowered his mouth to her parted lips. With his mouth crushing hers, Karl trailed his finger on her throat, where the skin was soft and warm, but warmer still where he dipped beneath the scooped neckline of her dress. As he traced the swell of her breast, Faren whimpered, firing his desire further, so that the ache for her began and ended in his cock. 'That's nothing, little one,' Karl said huskily, feeling her soft flesh ooze beneath his splayed fingers, her nipple a hard coin on his palm. Almost savagely he yanked at her dress to free her ripe breasts. She arched into him, and he held her buttocks, lifting her so that she settled provocatively over his hard bulge. 'You little devil,' he whispered, her silky hair tickling him as he placed his lips near the plump earlobe. 'You're every bit as naughty as your cat's eyes suggest.' And his thumb landed sharply on the exposed nipple, tilted so his nail dug in for a moment, and she cried out, before he lowered his mouth to the injured flesh to soothe

103

what he had harmed. As he captured her nipple, drew on it long and hard, she moaned, clutching his hair, ramming his head ever closer. When he shifted slightly aside to nibble, he watched her hand come up and clap over one breast, and he immediately covered it with his own. After two gentle squeezes he thrust her hand aside and hungrily snuffled for the nipple. With her lower body frantically gyrating against his, Karl knew she was conveying her readiness, her restless mime telling him how desperately she wanted him.

She was more than ready; the heady love perfume rose from her sex. God, how he loved that smell! He would savour it. Karl, a connoisseur, would sniff the subtle notes, tease her tender skin until he knew she would do anything at all to have him embedded inside her. His body rejoiced in her whimpers, which incited him, his skin tingling, causing his cock to ache and his balls to tighten. As Faren's moans grew in intensity – louder and longer and more frantic as he teased – Karl dropped to his knees to tongue the sweet skin to her navel, and the scent of her was even more intoxicating now as she writhed against him.

'Please. Oh, please, Karl. Touch me.'

'Tell me. Tell me where you want to be touched.' But even as he spoke his hand was cupping her mound, kneading and pulling at the skin, and he smiled at the knowledge that each tug would be working its magical friction on the hard bud. He dipped a long finger between the fleshy pleats. She groaned then, and he began to caress the satin softness of her, to stroke with a regular rhythm, as Faren panted, her head thrashing from side to side. But when his skilful fingers stopped short of making her come, she grabbed at his hand, pushing it as hard as was possible in the confined space against her tiny shaft. 'No, my hungry little one. Not yet,' Karl said, watching the glazed eyes clear, open wide and plead mutely with him. In reply he lifted her effortlessly in his arms and strode across the room. He backed down on to the bed and secured her on his lap.

With Faren astride him, his penis sought the hot core of her. With little assistance from him, she lifted herself into position above his cock, a dreamy smile on her face. He knew she intended to squat, to impale herself on his throbbing flesh, but he did not wait; instead he surged upwards and they were joined, his penis immersed in the moist, intimate softness of her body. His hand came up to snag the damp tendrils of her hair, to brush from her face the lengths that clung to her skin. 'Wasn't it worth waiting for?' he whispered, and knowing Faren was beyond teasing, that she might at any moment scream for exquisite release, he fitted his palms beneath her buttocks, taking her weight, and lifted her, guiding her in an ever increasing rhythm so that she, too, could enjoy the act of feeling her body expand to accommodate his.

'Karl. Oh, Karl.' She was almost weeping now, moved to heady emotional heights as he, too, experienced the adrenalin which pumped through his veins and lifted him to a state of heightened awareness and exquisite pleasure.

He loved to have her bounce, sometimes teasing him until the head of his cock was the only part of him left inside her. He could feel himself quiver, waiting for her to move slowly down his length, widening her so that he could be swallowed up in her warm, wet darkness. With both hands firmly on Faren's hips, he held her to him, not allowing her to escape and tease him. His pubic hair joined with hers, damp and curly and entangled; it was impossible to know where his ended and hers began. She ground herself on him, releasing such sweet pleasure that he gasped, his fingers digging cruelly into her. He pushed her so that she leaned away from him, looking down at where they became one, then he pulled her close again and dipped his head to take her nipple in his mouth. As he sucked lustily, she clawed at his shoulders, frantic to lift her body again, wrenching herself from his busy mouth. His hand slipped from her hip and ventured behind her to play seductively along each prominent bone of her spine. She sighed as he lubricated his finger in her slit, then dipped into the crevice of her neatly rounded bottom, opening her wide and planting his fingertip just inside the puckered flesh. He watched her bite her lower lip, and held her gaze, pushing his finger slowly until she took him to the knuckle. She did not lift herself so high now – perhaps the pain was more than she could bear – so he thrust up to meet her and, conscious of the rigid length of his finger through the wall of her other opening, felt her shiver as his cock embedded itself.

As though sensing his climax was near, she whispered, 'Not yet.' When he withdrew his finger she gasped, and he placed his hands on her shoulders to still her. Perplexed, she stared at him. 'Why did you stop?'

'Faren, Faren. It's either yes right now, or I stop.' He laughed shakily.

'Oh.' Her slow grin, when it appeared, was, he noted, one of triumph.

'Yes. Oh.'

She squealed in protest as he lifted her from where she was spiked, and, if her opening felt bereft, then so did his prick at giving up its warm sheath. He tumbled her on to the bed, pushing her legs wide and nuzzling her pussy. Now her squeal of surprise turned to contentment as she gasped at his expert loving. He lifted his head from her so that he could probe her with a finger instead, feeling inside the dark tunnel, his other hand opening the swollen lips wide, examining and exploring her intimately. He slid his finger in and out while she bucked, knowing she was trying to match his rhythm so that he would stimulate her for maximum pleasure. But as she met the tempo and stayed with it, Karl abruptly withdrew his finger. Her howl of protest at his unfeeling action was replaced with a soft sigh as his tongue came into play, swirling along her slit, lapping at the honey that ran and spread over the satiny place. Purposefully he ignored her clitoris, knowing with instinctive cunning that that was where she wanted him most of all. His tongue dipped into her entrance. Squashing his nose against her clitoris, giving her the pressure she needed, he inhaled the rich, exotic scent of her. Then with a finger he delved ever deeper into the hidden depths, swirling round inside her until he reached up to press her G-spot. Faren's fingers pulled at his hair, tugging hard when she liked what he was doing to her. When he replaced his finger with his mouth, he felt her seeping dew on his top lip, inhaled the fragrance of her sweet desire, her own sexual note, and Karl became ever more aroused, his prick near to bursting point.

Finally, he withdrew, and, holding her thighs, he clapped her legs together. With his palms on her knees he pushed them back to her shoulders, exposing her, crudely showing another view of her luscious pussy. Then he bent to lick the length of her sex. He heard her whimper appreciatively, felt her tremble. With long laps along her wet channel, tasting her and inhaling her musk, his mind's eye smiled as she whispered his name and begged him not to stop. He did stop, to rest his tongue, to let her stretch her leg muscles, as he lowered her back on to the bed. But he did not stop the loving. He tickled her glistening nest, pushed his thumb on her clitoris so that she gasped, her eyes flying open at the sudden fierce touch of him. He used his thumb to stroke and press, to stimulate with ever-increasing speed that part of her that was so very sensitive. As she came close to her climax her head lolled more, and her whimpers became deep groans, as if willing her orgasm to claim her, willing him to retain the pressure, the invigorating rhythm. Karl watched the clenched hands unfurl as Faren gathered a handful of bedcovers, squeezing the fabric as if this would make her come. She was arching into his thumb, her bottom raised so that her clitoris maintained continuous contact. In one abrupt action, Karl slid two fingers into her slippery opening, his other hand not leaving her clitoris. It was then that he felt the spasms, the wet interior clutching at his fingers as she came. He glanced down at her thighs, watched the muscles tense and her legs tremble as her climax swept through her. He watched the small, satisfied smile spread across her face as he guided Faren back on to the bed.

'That was beautiful, Karl,' she whispered, her smoky, green eyes raised to his.

But he was far from finished. As Faren languished in the aftermath of her climax, Karl reached for her long hair. On his knees, straddling her, he moved up and along the bed, settling his cock at jaw level so that he could hook the glorious silk of her hair and wind it round his shaft. It felt so good! So soft! He used it to caress his flesh, backing out of the soft passage so that it rippled round his erection. The softness was almost more than he could bear. He slid easily back and forth, never withdrawing completely, should he lose the gentle caress. Sighing, he pushed his rear end back, feeling his balls jiggle against Faren's face. He felt her hand come up and cup him, squeeze him. As she fondled him, he set a tempo, his finger grip on her hair tightening as he sought a fiercer grip from her along his shaft. He continued to lunge into the makeshift sheath, wondering, as he was now placed further along her head, how Faren liked having his rear in her face. When he felt her finger snake its way behind his testicles and press, he felt an immediate urge to ejaculate, but smothered it, sitting sharply down on Faren, her chin digging into the base of his shaft so that that too, was almost a trigger.

'I want you in my mouth, Karl.'

Almost a demand, he considered, and Karl would allow no lover to demand. 'Too bad,' he said. 'I'm calling the shots here.' His cock wanted to be in the soft, wet mouth, nearly as much as in that other soft, wet aperture, but his arrogant mind rebelled. He slipped down Faren's body, feeling the perspiration-damp flesh, and with one hand guided his prick to caress the swollen lips that seemed almost to quiver as his plum touched. She opened her legs wide for him and he saw that her lips were parted in readiness for more pleasure. Her climax had not drained her; instead, it set her up for more. The heat of her pussy caressed his sensitive flesh for several minutes and he felt her relax in the slow, sensual love-play. When he felt imminent loss of control, he rested his cock against her wet and eager entrance, and with one fluid movement he was inside her. The heat of her, her moistness, was almost his undoing, but he resisted, wanting so very much to feel his cock slide into her soft tunnel before he surrendered completely and came inside her. With all feeling centred on his organ, Karl still remembered his lover's needs. He ground his pubic bone against hers, then, while he was thrusting, pumping himself into her, his skilful thumb pressed and prodded her clitoris so that she, too, could be taken up with the storm. He held on as long as he could, waiting for Faren's sex to grip his, for the sound effects to tell him she was over the edge, and then he blissfully let go and followed, feeling the power of his penis as he spurted his seed. Even as he began to relax in the exhilarating ebb of his climax, he knew this special time eclipsed everything he had so far shared with his sweet little novice.

His lover slumped against him. Her rapid heartbeats echoed his. The smell of fresh sweat and sex was intoxicating and already he yearned for their next tryst. Their breathing settled into regular, comfortable rhythms, and Karl stood up, lifting Faren with him. Although reluctant to relinquish contact with her soft body, he relaxed as he recalled the night was only beginning, and that he had further pleasures planned. 'Get dressed, Faren, then come along to my room.'

'Why, Karl?'

'You'll see.' In the afterglow of sex, she was more desirable than ever. 'Don't be long,' he ordered.

Chapter Nine

Who the hell does he think he is, ordering me about like that? Faren thought, feeling strangely irritated as she recalled her lover standing before her and looking down his aristocratic nose with infuriating calmness. But a tingle raced along her spine, effectively eclipsing her annoyance, as she recalled the scent of his skin, and his animal sex appeal.

Issued only this afternoon, her cassock beckoned from the chair where Karl had flung it before he ravished her, and though she glanced with longing at the garment, she knew how foolish it would be to don it tonight. It would end up in a crumpled heap in Karl's room and she needed it pristine for its first appearance in the morning. Besides, there would be no one about, and if she should chance to pass a fellow student in the corridor, then it would hardly be anyone of seniority. This spurred Faren to leap back into her hardy denim skirt and cotton sweater. What could Karl possibly want? Surely he had slaked his desire for her; he had certainly pleasured her more thoroughly and skilfully than any lover before him. Would he really want to make love to her again tonight? The weakness after his loving was still with her, so that her fingers trembled as she used them like a shoehorn to pull on her canvas shoes. About to start for the door, she remembered that her passion-tangled hair must look a sorry sight, and she brutally brushed through the rope-like lengths. She had wanted him to come in her hair, to have his semen drip down the wavy strands, so that his unique scent formed a halo round her. But it was impractical, and she was now glad of his restraint. She could hardly have strolled the hall with hair like Medusa!

Karl answered her first knock, and, as he pulled her into the room, Faren experienced the same turbulent emotions his touch always roused in her, knowing the fire was licking along every one of her nerve endings – despite the recent loveplay – yet helpless to control it.

Then, spying Father Drew, Faren started. She wondered why he was here. Heat surged through her body as she recalled the two priests sharing an act of passion, an act she assumed was a first time for both; Drew had been every bit as startled as Faren. Her assumption was that Karl was essentially a lover of the female sex, yet last night he had been happy to sample forbidden fruit. She shrugged. Who was she to judge? Already bubbling inside, waiting to erupt, was the rush, the evocative charge that she herself had got from it. Was there to be a repeat performance tonight? Unlikely, she thought, as Karl's finger tipped her chin until she was looking into his eyes. He smiled and Faren's heart did a crazy little leap. With thumb and forefinger he stroked her throat, resting on her pulse there, his pupils dilated and seeming to see right through her. Could he see through her charade? Was that what he was looking for? Her growing feelings for Karl were not part of her act; what she felt for him was honest admiration, despite his breaking of sacred vows. Her belief was that celibacy was a cruel canon, man-made and insidious, and Jesus Christ would not have asked for it, for it denied a closeness that mankind had every right to claim. Her lips parted, and she gave silent thanks to her god for Karl's rebellion as her priest bent his head, taking her lower lip between his teeth, biting gently, his breath sweet and warm on her skin. When she moaned, Karl sucked, then ran his tongue along the inside of her bottom lip, across her teeth. She quivered in his embrace, her arms going about his neck, pulling him closer, wanting to absorb his body into hers. At first his kiss was gentle, then hard and hungry, until he pulled back, his mouth soft and tender on hers. He let her go.

Faren remained in a daze until Father Drew loomed over her, catching her about the waist. His touch failed to ignite the extent of the aphrodisiac, power and energy that Karl's touch always summoned, but nevertheless Drew's gentle hold caused excitement to surge along her veins in warm anticipation. She glanced over at Karl to see that all tenderness was gone. In its place was his smirk – his trademark smirk, she thought, stiffening – as he watched the tousle of emotions that surely played out in her expression.

'Remove your clothes,' Karl ordered, and Faren lamented the loss of the sensitive man.

It gave him a charge to dictate to her like this, she knew. It also aroused her. She had never before met a man like Karl Sterling, so controlled, so demanding, and yet so attuned to a woman's needs. But it appeared that now it was to be Father Drew's turn. Briefly it slipped through her mind that she now had extensive proof of St Peter's priests flouting their celibacy vows. How many priests did she need to witness indulging in various methods of sexual pleasure to have her own journalistic question answered to her complete satisfaction? Was she merely procrastinating so that she could remain here longer to sample the priestly delights? Almost immediately Faren denied that thoughtful assumption; any researcher knew that a handful out of several hundred proved an inaccurate assessment. So, for now, she must stay. In the meantime, she would continue to enjoy the sensual performances of these two priests. And she wondered how many sexual encounters with different seminarians she would consider a reliable number to prove her theory, and ultimately serve her assignment.

But now rational thought was being squashed, even as Drew squashed her back against the wall, so that her head clipped the crucifix that dangled on the bedroom wall. A thrill rushed through her at the thought of being on display for her lover, of being watched by him as the younger priest made love to her. Drew was dipping his shaky fingers beneath the elastic of her panties, tugging them down so that the cool night air caressed her bare skin. He lifted her leg so she could step out of them. As he bore her back on to Karl's bed and knelt astride her, his cassock rucked up to his waist, it was as if he was fired by uncontrollable lust. She waited for him to release his erection, and Faren realised she was again about to experience every woman's fantasy, for there was something so wildly sexual and taboo about being ravished by a priest. From the day that Karl had first pleasured her, she found that she was reliving that fantasy. Father Drew still wore his briefs, a wet spot visible through the fabric, and she watched as he roughly pulled the material aside, releasing his erection. She lifted her hand to help him free his balls. At her light touch, Father Drew flinched, and, as he regained his composure, he edged himself towards her face. Once in position he rotated his hips, his smooth, satiny penis rubbing along her face. Faren could smell desire mixed with sweat as his cock travelled along to her hairline to plough through the silky swathe. And he groaned, collapsing on top of her so that the sprinkling of fine hair beneath his balls tickled her nose and she inhaled the full scent of his desire. While Drew stabbed his penis through her hair, Faren opened her mouth, her tongue sweeping in leisurely wet strokes across his scrotum until he moaned louder. Faren took the sac into her mouth and Drew shuddered, his thrusting becoming more frantic as the erotic softness of her hair caressed his cock.

Faren forgot her spectator priest until she felt a wandering hand on her breast, and the rub of nipple between finger and thumb. Her legs bucked, opening wide, only to close again as they searched for something on which to clamp her sex, but there was only the air, until Karl penetrated her with two fingers, circling inside her, caressing her. Her moans echoed Drew's deep sounds as he continued to use her hair like a sheath, and Karl manipulated his fingers to open the fragrant, pliable entrance to explore her more fully. As Faren felt the opening of her lips, her thighs pushed wide, the softness of Karl's mouth was in her damp triangle of hair. It toyed maddeningly there before moving to nip at her stiff bud. Unable to see him, with the thrusting figure blocking her view, she could feel Karl's masterful hands opening her again to explore her, and while one hand played there, his other came back to her clitoris. She felt him retract the hood so that the clitoris would be fully exposed to his dark, prying eyes. Then his tongue probed, flicking madly on her vulnerable bead in a decisive rhythm that matched the rhythm of the man finding such wanton delight in her silky hair, and as Father Drew ejaculated, shouting his blissful release, Karl's thumb replaced his tongue and pushed hard on her button. She spiralled downwards on exploding sensations that shuddered through her, her muscles contracting around Karl's fingers which were firm and still invading her.

The younger man climbed off the bed. She reached up and patted the stickiness in her mussed up hair, then turned her attention to Karl. He was stripping, and firing his cassock into a corner, divested himself of all encumbrances. Thoroughly sated as Faren thought she was, her gaze never left Karl's rigid cock, marvelling at his sexual appetite, licking her lips in anticipation as the velvety penis homed nearer. She knew what he wanted. It was in his eyes, in the muscle that twitched at the corner of his smiling mouth, as she reached for his pulsating cock. Before he dipped it into her warm, moist mouth, she teased him, her hand fluttering between his thighs, stroking his heated skin, feeling the taut muscles as his penis strained towards its goal. And then she cupped his scrotum, and weighed the tightness, smoothing her thumb across the wrinkly skin, back and forth through the sparse hair, until she elicited a harsh groan from her lover and drew him into her mouth, extending her jaw so she could take all of him. First she caressed his cock with her tongue, playing tunes of skill round the ridge before she began to suck him. Hard. As he began thrusting, Faren placed her hand around the base of his penis to guide him to a mutually comfortable rhythm. She heard his satisfied grunt, then slowly, as she coaxed him to withdraw, she flicked her tongue across the satin tip, and dipped into the tiny eye, driving him into a frenzy. She backed away, depriving him of her moist mouth. Karl opened his dark, glazed eyes, but with no warm mouth encompassing his throbbing flesh he began to growl, and Faren whipped away from the hands she knew he would use to bring her head down on him once more.

'Wait.' And she was behind him, pushing him face down on the bed. She trailed her fingers down his back, her mouth following, until she reached the base of his spine. She parted his smooth buttocks, her tongue dipping into the cleft, licking the length of him, until he was writhing madly beneath her. Hearing a sharp intake of breath, Faren was reminded of their voyeur. She had forgotten Father Drew, and on the periphery of her vision she saw that, once again, he sported a proud erection, and she watched as his hand came up to caress it, eyes closed, moaning with each stroke. Faren directed her attention back to Karl. It was his turn now. As she continued to lick across the tight skin of his buttocks, her right hand reached down and underneath to pinch his balls lightly. He jerked, the involuntary movement giving her searching fingers room to fully encompass the ridged sac.

'Stop, or I'll come.' Karl's voice, though muffled, was harsh, as if he did not really want what her fingers were doing to him.

Smiling to herself, Faren complied, moving away from his genitals to smooth her palms across the small of his back and then along his shoulder blades, feeling his tension ebb. Although he relaxed back on the bed, within seconds Karl was thrusting against the mattress, grunting, his tight mounds rising and falling, clenching and unclenching, and the sight so aroused Faren that she experienced an arrow of sweet pain that shot through her aching sex. Again she forgot Father Drew's presence, so taken up was she with touching Karl's tight butt and the resulting pleasure that seemed to transfer from its firmness to travel down her belly and warm her between her thighs.

It was then that Drew's release sang loud in the confines of the room. Faren whipped her head round to watch the jet of thick semen spraying from the eye of his cock. There was something seductively arousing in the sight as she keenly observed the culmination of the priest's pleasure spurting towards the bed. It plopped lightly to the floor as he sagged to his knees, his rod rapidly becoming forlorn and limp. Swinging her gaze back to Karl she saw his buttocks quiver, and realised that Drew's noisy release had triggered her lover's climax. Suddenly he jerked round to face her, as though wanting her to see the consequence of her simple massage, gripping his shaft so that his come fell back on to his naked belly.

Now Karl, too, lay lifeless, and his penis withered to a soft, sleepy snake-like creature. Fascinated, Faren gently squeezed. 'I like it soft, like this,' she told Karl, almost shyly, pumping and flexing her fingers, relishing the feel of malleable flesh, until Karl stilled her hand.

'Don't,' he said huskily.

Disappointed, she complied with Karl's wishes, halting the playful touches, and instead glanced over at Father Drew, who was now on his haunches, leaning back against the wall, apparently replete. Like his comrade, his breath was slowing, the loud rasps now mere whispers of air, but Faren found her breathing escalating. Two soft pricks somehow managed to make her feel like popping them together into her mouth, and the power she possessed to make them grow hard, should she so desire, was exhilarating. Gifted with dual orgasms tonight, first in her room, and again here with Karl, still she yearned for more, greedy as she had become since sampling the pleasures of St Peter's. She must have drifted into a daydream, because suddenly she became aware of fingers caressing her, of the aching, throbbing insistence of her sex.

'More, my greedy one?' Karl asked, and as she wet her lips in reply, he laughed and signalled to the second man to join him.

Was there some unspoken orchestration between the priests? Faren wondered, when Drew lifted her from the bed and sat her on Karl's lap. Facing away from Karl, it was titillating to look at Drew while unseen hands went beneath her bottom, and lifted her until she fitted above the soft head of his new erection, then lowered her until her vagina expanded and he was embedded fully inside the satin sheath. She closed her eyes, her head lolling back against his chest.

'That's right, little one. Tickle me with your hair,' Karl said. And she obeyed, happy to do as he asked, swaying softly so that her silky tresses caressed him, swishing until the need to straighten became too strong to ignore.

Suddenly, Drew was kneeling before her, kissing the

fringe of swollen breast, playing a finger across its hardened nipple. He bowed his head to take the peak into his mouth. Looking down on the priest's sandy hair, Faren wanted to kiss it, and as she bent to follow through with the urge, he suckled her, a sharp, firm motion that made her gasp and arch towards him. At her sudden movement, Karl bucked beneath her, and she visualised those tight buttocks as he thrust ever deeper into her. The stimulation of her G-spot was intense and frequent, and instinctively she bore down to meet his next thrust, anxious to sustain the friction. He held her tightly by her waist and pulled her down, and as her lower body was hammered against his, his cock deep and hard, Faren whimpered, knowing she was going to come. Though she tried to hold off for Karl, it became an impossible feat; the plundering of her, the rapid and strong suction on her nipple by the young priest at her feet, ensured her arousal remained near the summit. As she came, she sent Karl over the edge and he cried out as his own excitement peaked and overflowed into orgasmic relief. He fell back on the bed, towing Faren along with him who was glued to Karl by entwined limbs and sweat. The nipple that Drew had been so lovingly caressing now popped from his mouth. The air that chilled the wet, swollen peak sent shafts of pleasure darting along Faren's body to her throbbing pussy, and she whimpered in the glorious aftermath of sensations that continued to wash over her.

No sooner had her limbs ceased trembling than Drew's fingers caressed the soles of her feet before circling her ankles and slowly moving upwards to play along her calves and behind her knees. By the time the languorous journey reached the crease of her thighs, all that Faren wanted was to stretch her legs and point her toes, regardless of how drained she felt. 'No,' she groaned, loving the way her sensitised skin responded to the priest's touch, but too exhausted to reclaim the energy she needed to climb to the delicious heights of orgasm again tonight. 'Please, Drew!' she cried, thrashing her head from side to side across Karl's prone body.

'You want it, Faren, you know you do.' And though Faren felt she should argue, she knew she would let it be, for he was right. Since joining St Peter's, the sexual feasts were too numerous, too vibrant to refuse, and as Drew's slender fingers found the swollen petals of her sex, brushing first the outer lips, then cunningly, the soft inner flesh, Faren knew she was lost. 'Would you like my tongue there?' he asked. And she groaned her answer, but the priest played cruel. 'If you want my tongue, you must tell me.' And she flinched as she felt the flick of his finger on her rearing clitoris.

Writhing on top of Karl she felt him begin to stir in the cleft of her bottom, firing her desire to an even greater degree, and she yelled to the man tormenting her. 'Please, Father! Your tongue. I want your tongue!'

It was a triumphant Drew who lowered his head, first nuzzling her, before the wicked, wet tongue lapped and supped her nectar. Faren jerked as his tongue followed her every unspoken desire, and, in her muzzy passion mist, she wondered at the enormity of her appetite. Would it never be appeased? Was she condemned to this new, greedy sexual world where her ferocious appetite hungered for more? And more?

Covering her breasts now were Karl's strong hands. He pushed his palms hard and flat so that her aroused nipples were like pebbles in a soft blanket of sand. Against her behind, Karl moved, grinding himself, while Drew's hands fastened against her hips, holding her immobile as his tongue probed and saliva seeped down and under her, coating Karl's stiff cock so that he could move more easily against Faren's skin. She was indulging in sensations from both quarters when suddenly the tongue stilled, and Faren felt instead the soft mouth closing about the nugget of her desire. And then, as Drew sucked and flicked his tongue, and Karl's able

120

hands lightly pinched and teased her nipples, she heard a loud gasp and knew Karl was going to come in the cleft that was adroitly lubricated by both Drew and herself. As he trembled beneath her, Faren's excitement reached its pinnacle and, with Drew sucking forcefully on her clitoris, remained on its glorious path. Her fingers dug cruelly into Karl's undulating hips as a spine-tingling orgasm rocked her, her body trembling on the one cushioning hers.

Once again Faren relaxed back on top of Karl, feeling utterly sapped as the rapid rise and fall of his breathing lulled her into blissful relaxation. But Drew refused to leave her alone. 'My turn now,' he said.

He was beginning to mirror Karl at every turn, and Faren surmised that it was Karl's influence that gave the younger man unbridled confidence to play with her in this callous, sexual manner, to be macho in his demands. 'I'm too tired, Drew,' she groaned as he took her by the upper arms and hauled her to a sitting position. Helping her, Karl eased her off of him, and she felt her damp buttocks touch the coverlet.

'On the floor. Kneel,' Drew demanded, a smirk on his face and a burning light in his eyes, as if Faren's protests were merely token expressions.

Dreamlike and sated she moved to sit on the floor. He was enjoying himself, Faren supposed, being in charge of the sexual play, unlike last night when Karl had surprised him by entering the forbidden orifice. Last night? Was it only last night? Since then it seemed she was destined to ride the seductive Ferris wheel. Where was the shame that had earlier marred Drew's features? she wondered. Did he take his pleasure and worry about the consequences later?

Impatiently Drew flipped her round until she knelt on all fours on one of the coarse mats, and, with his foot, he pushed her legs wide apart before sinking down behind her. She felt his hairy chest relax along her spine and as she supported his weight, he pulled her back towards him so that her bottom fitted snugly against his erection.

In rocking momentum they continued, the priest seemingly happy to have his cock just there. She heard Karl move off the bed, heard the rustling of his clothes as he dressed. Was he watching her? It excited Faren to think that his eyes were upon her, and though only moments ago she had complained that all desire was spent, as Drew reached round with his right hand and fingered her clitoris she knew she was wrong. He butted up against her further to explore lower down her slit, and dipped two fingers into her entrance, before snaking his hand back up over her belly, leaving a trail of lovejuice.

As Drew moved back so that his skin lost contact with hers, Karl hunkered in front of her. He wore his black cassock, and Faren had no idea what he had planned until he swept up the voluminous garment and covered her head so that she was in total darkness. The smell of sex was confined in the tent-like structure, and although she could not see, she could sense Karl's nakedness beneath the robe.

She struggled but Karl held her head still. 'No. It's okay. Leave it. It will intensify your pleasure, I promise.'

With his assurance Faren relaxed, trusting him as she had never trusted a man before, knowing that even with his arrogance and macho commands, Karl always ensured his lover's pleasure came first. When rough fingers touched the underside of her sex, Faren wriggled, insinuating that she was ready for further manipulation. When the fingers disappeared, they were replaced by something wider, softer. A cock pushed slowly into her; she knew it was Drew's cock because she could smell Karl's right in front of her. But in her own personal blackout beneath the priest's gown it could be any fantasy male; the thought incited her, and her pussy relaxed, ready for whatever cock wished to make the journey into her. Faren felt herself widening as the head of the invading cock cushioned itself inside her, the midnight darkness consuming her as her arousal rocketed. Hands were playing with her engorged breasts, squeezing and stroking, and as the priest behind her revved his thrusts in time to his excitement, she pushed back, encouraging him to plunge deeper. Hard thighs slapped the back of hers and she felt them quiver with need and knew his climax was imminent. She began to whimper, her sex splayed wider every time he plunged, his bush grazing the cheeks of her bottom as they joined. With her head drooped, her body penetrated by the man behind her, and in the sensory deprivation triggered by the black robe, Faren's head swam, and just as she thought she would pass out from the seductive setting and the intensely pleasurable feelings, the priest cried out and shuddered inside her. He jerked for several moments, then sagged across her back, toppling her with his weight, until she was stretched out on the floor. Faren's breath rasped raw and painful in her throat. Drew's panting breath blew warmth across her shoulders, gradually slowing, and then he kissed her spine before rolling away from her.

The dark cloak was removed and she turned her head to see Karl smiling down at her. He stretched down to help her to her feet and again she marvelled at how gentlemanly he could be. When it suited him. He handed Faren her clothes and she slipped first into her briefs, her breasts jiggling as she balanced on one leg. Both men watched as she slid her arms through her bra straps and reached to hook the metal clasp at her back. She smiled wryly, realising her dressing was nearly as big a turn-on for them as her stripping.

Karl pulled her into his arms and then brushed back her matted hair. 'You need another shampoo. Go and shower,' he said, giving her a small shove towards the door. 'You won't be disturbed tonight.'

'Pity. I'm rather partial to that thing in your pants,' she

said, wickedly, on her way out. At the door she turned to look at the two priests who had given her so much, admitting to herself that she would miss the nightly entertainment when the time came to leave. But her inquisitive mind had found further reason to prolong her stay at St Peter's. Somehow she thought Father Drew was a raw recruit, and had been sexually inactive until Karl had coerced him into the bathroom and encouraged him to make love to her. So, until she had further proof, she would assume that each man housed at St Peter's masturbated. It was the only sensible solution.

Chapter Ten

'You don't think she will report us, do you?'

'My God, after all this you are still a bloody wimp, Edmonds! Why the hell do I bother with you?' Karl scowled at the young priest. 'We need some variation next time. Are you with me?' He noted the residue of sweat from his colleague's recent exertions. Whether Edmonds was willing to admit it or not, Karl knew he was attaining an inordinate amount of pleasure and stimulation from his high jinks with Faren. He also knew that Edmonds was now as hooked on sex as it was possible to be, even if the chap could not look Faren in the eye unless engaged in pleasure. He guessed that there would be another sleepless night for Edmonds. He should be more like me, Karl thought, I have already forgiven myself. 'Before you leave, come and sit down a minute,' he said to Edmonds. He sensed the man's nervousness; perhaps Edmonds thought he was going to touch him. That one incident in the showers had been an aberration, and despite the fact that he had enjoyed entering Edmonds' tight little butt, he had no plans to succumb to the same madness in the future. But he smiled wickedly; the priest was too much of a victim.

'I'm not going to eat you,' he said to him. On the heels of that thought Karl wondered briefly what it would feel like to have another man's cock in his mouth. Doubtless he would never know. When his colleague began to relax, Karl asked, 'What do you think of our novice?'

'I thought that was obvious, Sterling.'

Karl threw back his head and laughed. 'I've made a man out of you since introducing you to Faren.'

'I don't like what you are implying.'

Karl deemed it prudent to back off, or at least to make a show of doing so. He enjoyed baiting Edmonds, but perhaps it was time to quit his bit of fun. For now. So he said, 'I don't want to make an enemy of you, Edmonds.'

'Then what is it you want?'

Cocky little bastard all of a sudden, Karl mused, as he gazed thoughtfully at this new man. Heaving a sigh, he moved across to the single window set high in the wall above his desk. 'I'm bored with what we've been doing.' He turned from the night to face his companion, thinking of the idea he had mulled over but avoided mentioning for so long. 'Are you game to try something different?' It was a hunch, eloquently backed by the other's body language and perhaps even a touch of telepathy; otherwise he would never have voiced it. At least, not yet. 'Any ideas, Edmonds?' Karl strained to hear the mumble. 'Repeat that?'

'I said mirrors. I've always wanted to do it in front of mirrors.'

Karl failed to cover his surprise. 'You weren't a virgin, then? Before Cherry the kitchen maid?'

The priest scoffed, his cheeks reddening. 'Of course not! Were you?' He flung back the insult.

And it was Karl's turn to snort derisively. 'Christ Almighty!'

'And what about boots? And a G-string?'

'My, my. You are a surprise.' Carried along by a *mélange* of colourful fantasies, Karl added, '"A surprise,"

126

I said. Not a shock. And it so happens that jackboots alone are enough to stir me. And –' chin resting in his hand, visualising the scene, he decided '– no. Forget the common G-string. A leather thong that cuts into her crack and emphasises her lips while covering only the vital bud. Now, that would be something!' Feverish blue eyes stared back at him and he sniggered. Edmonds was almost drooling.

'Do you think she'll go along with it?'

'Leave it with me, old man. Like you, our lovely Miss Lonsdale is every bit as eager for a variety of sexual experiences.' Not to mention yours truly, Karl reflected, conscious of the restless stirring in his pants as the idea planted itself even more firmly in both brain and cock. 'She'll go along with it.'

Ten minutes later he was alone on his bed and gazing up at cracks in the plaster ceiling. He shivered, experiencing again the thrill of having Faren. Ah, but she was so malleable beneath his expert hands, so willing. But he was right to pursue a change; he might even crave a change in woman before long. Right now, Faren pushed his senses to the limit and beyond, satisfying his every need, although Karl confessed he was hungry for a little more. It was too early to introduce either Edmonds or Faren to the secrets of the confessional, though if the steadily growing waiting-list was anything to go by, then half of Australia knew about it. At this stage he doubted his two playmates could cope with it. More than likely Faren would be shocked; it was unsuitable for female relief. Before their little playtime in the shower, he had assumed that Faren would be shocked by a *ménage à trois*, and her expression when she had spied them both that night confirmed this. That little scene, along with tonight's, in Karl's mind still failed to introduce the conventional concept of a third party, but he was acquainting his new partners in the ways of forbidden fruit. When the time came for more sexual adventure, they would both be ready. In fact, Karl mused, breaking into a wide smile, they would both be begging for it. With Drew Edmonds' willing participation, plus the eagerness that reminded Karl of himself at the beginning of his sexual initiation, the game was already touched with spice. And that priest panted for more, even if he did spend all of his free time in the chapel riddled with guilt.

Faren Lonsdale, though obviously greatly enthusiastic, was a mite more complex. He was not convinced Faren was here to take her vows. A sixth sense – that acute signal that rarely failed Karl – made him suspect there was more to that young lady than she chose to show, and he would heed that instinct now, keep watch for any inconsistencies. And that was why he refused to reveal to her the secret of the confessional. Somehow, he knew it would not do for her to have this insight into exactly what went on at St Peter's, only to toss the chapel life aside because she missed her creature comforts. He smiled. In his opinion, the pleasures he found here in the seminary compensated for the loss of a layman's pleasures. Karl had had no intention of becoming celibate the day that he made the momentous decision that had shattered his mother's heart. Rather than detracting from his sexual magnetism, donning priestly robes had in fact enhanced it. He planned to sustain all of those pleasures. 'Yes, Faren, my little love, you will do just fine.' And he took hold of his cock and began to masturbate himself, slowly at first, then, as his excitement mounted, quickening his strokes, until he ejaculated.

Life for Faren at St Peter's was far less restrictive than she had originally imagined, and was far less disciplined for her than for her male colleagues, and, though happy to take advantage of it, she recognised the hypocrisy of it all. Faren supposed this meant she was not fully accepted; perhaps her presence here was seen even as trivial. Mulling this over, she knew it to be beyond her control, and while she did everything in her power to display her dedication to the Order – pseudo-dedication though it was – she was wise enough to take advantage of the extra freedom granted her. With this in mind, and two free periods looming ahead of her, Faren donned her white bikini, marvelling at the whim that had seen her toss the tiny scraps of Lycra into her suitcase. Not for a moment had she expected to have the opportunity to actually wear it, and now here she was, preparing to visit the beach while her colleagues attended lectures in Greek and Latin and whatever other languages the senior priests could cram into the afternoon. In a moment of hesitation, as she debated what she should wear to conceal her half-naked state – being neither brave enough nor foolish enough to walk through the seminary clad only in a bikini – she wondered whether she should whip quickly into the city to report to her editor. Just as quickly she decided against the trip. The lure of sand and surf loomed irresistible, the warm promise of sun toasting her skin. There would be another time for Martine, she assured the tiny voice that argued against a trip to the beach.

After deciding that a beach robe was little more appropriate than the scanty attire it was meant to hide, Faren struggled into a peach sundress, pulling at the crotch of her bikini pants as she did so. Firmer than everyday briefs, it cupped her mound nicely. She straightened her dress, then put a motley straw hat on her head and, with towel and sun lotion slung in her bag, let herself out of her room. Feeling fortunate to be vacating the building for a few hours, Faren's gait was lively, with an alluring swing to her hips. She craved fresh air on her skin and, as she hit sunlight, it seemed impossible that one could feel so cold in the edifice behind her, while the sun shone elsewhere. Now it teased her bare arms, burrowing beneath her skin, it seemed, to her very bones.

With a squeal of laughter she shot forward at a run, anxious to feel sand beneath her feet. The ocean was a mere nine minutes' stroll from St Peter's, and sprinting, Faren made it in less than five. She gasped as she stumbled, sand oozing between her toes. When her breathing returned to normal she sat up and wriggled her bottom, shaping an intimate bowl to her body. Then flat on her back with her eyes closed she listened to the pounding surf and the reel of gulls as they piloted out to sea. A spectrum of brilliance spiked beneath her closed lids, enrapturing Faren with seductive memories of her time on the rooftop with her priest. She sank further into the sand as she settled back to reminisce.

A dangerous practice, dozing beneath the fierce glare of an Australian sun, and Faren knew she had succumbed when she was roused with a trickle of hot sand playing upon her bare midriff. She opened her eyes and gazed up at the man above, his torso shading her face, a wry smile on his lips. She reared, the sand spilling to her bikini line, and she brushed at her hips, removing the grains that dug into her tender flesh.

'Sorry if I startled you, Miss Lonsdale,' Father Murray said, looking anything but apologetic as his eyes gleamed down at her.

Before Faren's throat could form words she licked her lips, wishing she had thought to bring a drink with her down to the beach. But there had been little time to plan and, with characteristic impulsiveness, she had grabbed the moment, with visions only of sun and sea and no thought of refreshment. Apparently Father Murray read her mind because he indicated a cooler pack that sat like an oasis in the desert. 'You look as though you could use one of these,' he said. He hunkered to snap open the vinyl lid, squatting over her at knee level.

Faren did her best to keep her gaze from wandering to the dormant protuberance in his shorts. Moisture beads dotted about the neck of the green bottle he offered her made her think of a phallus glistening with a woman's dew. She shook her head, banishing the image, thinking now only of how that refreshing liquid would ease her parched throat. Gratefully, she accepted the proffered beer, the chill of the glass very welcome on her sweaty palm. 'You are a lifesaver, Father.'

'Glad to be of assistance. And call me Simon, please. In private, at least.' His eyes squinted as protection against the sun.

'You should have a hat, Father. Sorry. Simon.' In her mind she had often thought of him by his given name, so it should not be too difficult to use it now. She also wondered if there would be private moments.

'You, sensible lady, have a hat and I forgot mine. I have the refreshments and, I gather, you forgot. But I'm willing to share.' He laughed, and Faren thought about what else he might be willing to share. 'What do you say we move over to that tree?' He reached out to haul her to her feet. Finding it difficult to assimilate this relaxed, light-hearted man with the serious priest she normally encountered, Faren obediently followed Simon as he trudged across the beach, his pace hampered by the cooler, his rug and her bag, she hampered by her bare feet sinking into burning sand. 'Come on, slow coach,' Simon called, glancing back over his shoulder.

Faren smiled, a surge of happiness flooding her, wanting so very much to catch him up, feeling the strain of her calf muscles as she tried to conquer the dunes so that she could walk alongside this new Father Murray. Despite her best efforts she failed to match the priest's strides, and so she contented herself with viewing his legs and the backward thrust of his neat buttocks as they strained against the almost old-fashioned beach shorts. She felt a strong urge to run her hands over his delectable rear. Smiling to herself, Faren supposed she should be unshockable at any lustful thoughts these days. Though far from a saint, she knew the importance of a façade while on a job. But as a young woman enjoying her sexuality, she guessed the impetus to caress Simon Murray's cute butt was due to his being a different animal, his formality finally erased.

By the time Faren reached the grassy embankment, Simon was already settling himself beneath a phoenix palm. The man motioning her to sit proved an exciting contrast to the restless priest she remembered from her interview. She allowed him to take her hand, to drag her down beside him on the tartan rug. 'Now, isn't this much better?'

'I love the sun,' Faren argued with a slight shiver. Then some imp inside her said, 'And unless you baked yourself on a sun bed, so do you.'

Throwing back his head, he laughed. She felt a potent impulse to touch her lips to his throat and suck his very lifeblood, and when Simon's laugh trickled away and he looked at her, his eyes were puzzled. She shook her head. She needed to be on her guard. If he should suspect her amorous yearning for him, or for any of his colleagues, she would be herded out through those iron-jawed gates faster than the surf pounded into shore. Acutely aware of her precarious hold at St Peter's, she had wanted time for her blockbuster scoop. But now she wanted time for a different reason. To cover the sudden stillness, she ventured, 'I'm surprised to see a priest with a tan. I really didn't think you would be allowed to sunbathe.'

He smiled lazily at her. 'We have free time. Not too much, I will admit,' he added as she shot him a disbelieving glance. 'But we do partake of some pleasures. Sun worshipping is one.'

'I meant the immodesty of dress.'

'Ah.' Simon shrugged as if that was all there was to say.

They fell into a companionable silence and Faren distractedly plucked at the grass that tangled with the rug's fringe. A gentle breeze rustled fronds above them, fanning their two scantily attired bodies. She lazed back on her elbows, her gaze drinking in Simon's golden skin. She wanted to splay her hands and learn its texture, to touch the pale pink nipples with her tongue. With a furtive glance below his waist she was disappointed to see his penis, not swelling as she had somehow expected with the tension sizzling between them, but soft and squishy beneath the thin fabric of his beach shorts. Normally she relished the softness of a man's penis, and after squeezing and pumping it to life, watching it grow long and thick within seconds. Now she felt her power diminished as his cock neglected to respond to her intimate presence. Why had it failed to respond? In her bikini she was more than half-naked, with the swell of her breasts revealed, and the very obvious feminine pout between her legs. What voluptuous young lady wanted to know that she failed to excite a man? No matter that he was a priest. Did he find her so unattractive? Though she felt like pouting at the very idea of a desirable man ignoring her considerable charms, she dare not venture to disprove it. It could well have deep repercussions which would land soundly upon her and upset the stability of her presence here at St Peter's. But if Father Murray were to make the initial sexual approach, Faren could respond to the overture. Otherwise, she would live with the fact, and accept that he was indeed indifferent to her feminine charms.

With a sigh she turned from him, pulled her legs up and hugged them. Resting her chin on her knees, she narrowed her eyes and gazed at the water, waiting for Simon to pierce her reflection. When he finally intruded, his posture echoed her own with scarcely a hand space between her smoothly tanned thighs and his hair-roughened ones. Faren's good spirits bounced back. She turned her head. 'Sorry, Father. I was out there, across the sea.'

'Dispense with the "Father", remember? At least, when

we're alone. I asked how you were coping with the enforced constraints on your life. The loss of friends?'

'I'm enjoying it, Simon.' She chuckled. 'I mean, I don't find my life narrow at all.' And when he returned her steady gaze, a teasing light in his, she said, 'It's true. Oh, I know so much liberty has been taken from me. But in return I have gained so much.'

'In what way?'

His gaze was questioning now, Faren noted, and if she was reading him correctly, a hint of something that was almost suspicion crossed his features. How much did he know of what went on in that fortress? More than she had given him credit for?

'I love the language classes. And ancient history,' she said. Was it merely her imagination, or did Simon seem relieved?

'But you could do that anywhere outside. In any of Australia's universities.'

'Yes, I could,' she agreed lightly, but how could she reveal that it had never crossed her mind to involve herself in such riveting studies until they had been forced upon her in her guise of novice priest? She came up with the truth. 'I have a thirst for knowledge, Simon, which I am only just discovering now. Rediscovering, if you like. I had been caught up with boyfriends and everything I did revolved around them.'

'Your fiancé?'

Faren nodded, silently chastising herself for her slip. How could she have forgotten the bogus fiancé? 'Women get caught up in relationships and before they know it they are absorbed, at one with their partners, no longer their own person with their own identity.' She rested her head on her knees and watched a cheeky sparrow as it darted closer, hoping for a crumb.

'You feel so strongly about this, Faren. Have you realised in the seminary you have no real identity? Here you are also absorbed, swallowed up as one.' When she made no comment – though she could have slapped herself for her *faux pas* – Simon continued. 'This is why I want you to be sure. Why I am giving you this trial period.'

'And I must do my utmost to prevent lousing it up, Father?' she asked, launching her toes forward so that the grass tickled the soles of her feet.

He nodded. 'And you must not louse it up, Faren.' After minutes of contemplation, Simon lurched to his feet. 'Come on. Race you to the water.'

She scrambled to her feet in a mad dash to catch up and laughed as she tore after him, feeling the coolness of the turf change to a baking heat as she landed on the sand. Simon was already in the water, stroking powerfully out and over the breakers, as Faren's toes touched the frothy fringe. Then she was taking playful leaps over the waves before tumbling into the sea, the taste of salt on her mouth, the first sting of seawater in her eyes. Gasping, she reached Simon, who was treading water in the deceptive calm beyond the breakers. He grinned, then dived beneath the waves. He grabbed her ankle and pulled her down under the water while she tried vainly to twitch away. She came up spluttering, her hair like long tentacles plastering her face and gripping her breasts in sopping strands. She laughed as she scrubbed her eyes with the back of her hand.

They swam about in wide circles for several minutes, each risking a peek at the other, enjoying this new and playful side that until now had been successfully hidden and bound by sanctuary laws. Simon struck out for shore. With a small leap Faren was on top of the water, swimming a relaxed crawl after him, letting the boiling waves push her on until her feet touched the shelf of smooth sand. Beyond the water line Simon stretched out his hand and dragged her from the surf, his laughter cutting out as she emerged, dripping. She followed his stare. Two cold pink nipples peeped insouciantly over her bikini top

– a plump bead of water on each hardened tip contrasting beautifully with the white fabric – and pointed straight at Simon Murray's bare chest. With a small cry she wrenched her hand free of his. He turned away as she hooked her thumbs into the white scrap to haul it over her heaving breasts.

'Simon. Simon! I'm sorry,' Faren choked as she stumbled from the sea, all sense of fun squashed by what he must surely have seen as blatant seduction.

Her cry stopped him. He refused to look back at her and his voice sounded strange. 'It's not your fault. It was unintentional, I know. The force of nature. And I can hardly blame you for that.'

'Simon!' Unheedful of her cry, Simon sailed on, and by the time Faren reached the spot where they had luxuriated so companionably, he was hauling on loose cotton slacks over his saturated shorts. Quickly Faren set about shielding her drenched bikini, mindful of the revealing nature of the tight fabric as it clung to the cleft of her sex, and upset about embarrassing him further. She reached out to touch his arm, to recapture the new and precious friendship, when a voice had her spinning round.

'There you are, Father Murray.' The housekeeper nodded to Faren. 'Bishop Latterly phoned. He asked that you return his call as soon as possible.'

Simon's lips thinned, and he frowned. He was not all that mad at her after all, Faren thought. And he seemed reluctant to leave her. 'All right, Mrs Cheaters. I'm coming.' As the woman marched across the grass, Simon's sigh was heavy. 'I must go.' He had already turned away when he stopped and looked back over his shoulder. 'We need to talk some more, Faren. About your reasons for being here. Please present yourself in my office after vespers.'

Faren took her time getting back. She took several refreshing dips and luxuriated in the sun until she felt her skin begin to burn. She was oddly concerned about

Father Murray's directive. One worry after another sifted through her mind until she settled on the one thing that she feared the most; somehow he had discovered that the priests were pleasuring her and he was going to ask her to leave. Though it was a possibility, she did not seriously consider that he had unearthed her profession. Or so Faren convinced herself. More than likely, someone had seen her enter Karl's room. Worst of all, had they heard what was played out behind the closed door?

Chapter Eleven

'What do you mean by seeking me out?' Simon stalked across the frayed carpet, stopping only to kick at discarded clothes that littered the room. The problem was when his foot connected with the feather-light garments, they offered no real substance for his anger.

'The bishop wanted you, Simon.'

She could plead her case all she liked but he was far too wily to be fobbed off by a weak excuse from his housekeeper. 'And every time he needs me, you come running to the beach? You know I expect to be left alone during my free time, unless I say I'm coming to your room. No, Rosemary. You came scuttling down because somehow you knew that Miss Lonsdale was there.'

'And what if I did?'

When Rosemary was in the wrong she always adopted the defensive. And, Simon thought, she knows damn well that she is in the wrong this time. 'My free time is exactly that. Free! And if I choose to spend it on the beach by myself or with one of the novices that is my business. Understood?'

'You've wanted her from the moment you set eyes on her. Can you say otherwise?'

'Who elected you my keeper?' Simon asked, deliberately ignoring her question, unwilling to be dragged further into defending himself. 'You forget I can be rid of you very easily.' He watched her blanch. 'I suggest you keep your suspicions to yourself.'

'But, Simon.'

God, how he hated it when she whinged like this. How he wished he had never taken her to his bed. On his arrival at St Peter's she had been the exemplary housekeeper, anticipating his every wish, and when she covertly offered her body to him, Simon was flattered, seeing it as an easy way out for sexual favours. He had seen an element of goodness in her, and he thought them friends. The pleasuring was mutual, and only recently had he begun to suspect this possessive streak in her. Now it was apparent her emotions travelled a notch deeper, and she was making it clear she intended to hold on to him.

Even as he was analysing the relationship, Rosemary was down on her knees, lifting his cassock, her greedy fingers working on the zip of his fly. God knows he would rather jerk off than be beholden to her ever again; only his prick refused to acknowledge what his mind commanded. The perfidious flesh was burgeoning beneath the pressure of her palm.

'Let's not argue, Simon. I love you. We have so much.'

Simon nearly tore himself away from her then. Love? His fingers knifed through his hair. Was he that deep into the mire? How had he allowed this to happen? Though he had suspected it would be difficult to rid himself of Rosemary's attentions, he had not counted on just how difficult. He wanted to protest, to end it now. Tell the woman how wrong she was. Be rid of her, for God's sake! But his cock decided otherwise. She was poking his aching flesh into her mouth, and Jesus, it felt so good! He closed his eyes and started to rock back and forth, revelling in the wet, soft place, so soothing on his cock.

'You want me to come in your mouth, do you?' he grunted, taking his frustration out on her as he plunged into her mouth. 'I've got a better idea.' His words came on every thrust he made into her waiting mouth, her tongue plundering the eye as if dredging his seed. Sensing his climax was near – an angry climax at the injustice of having lost his chance with Faren – he pulled his cock out of the warm tunnel. He felt his seed begin to spurt and he held Rosemary's head steady before him, lining up his cock, and watched his semen spray across the startled woman's face, jet after jet hitting her mouth, her cheeks. Then Simon gripped his weapon and shot the last of his seed into her eyes and her hair. His knees buckled and he dropped to the floor. The crude sexual action would show Rosemary that he controlled this sexual partnership, but as he forced himself to look at her bewildered gaze, he immediately regretted taking his frustration out on his lover. What was happening to him? He wanted to cry out. To lash out. He wanted salvation. He buried his face in his lover's semen-soaked hair. Priests were not supposed to desire the pleasures of the flesh, but how could a man vanquish natural, God-given urges?

Several minutes later he gently moved her away from him. 'Pull your panties down, Rose,' he whispered.

The soft nylon swished to her knees. She opened her thighs to him and Simon's finger slipped into the damp furrow beneath the tight curls. He heard her whimper as his finger touched the soft flesh, heard the long sigh as he probed and stroked her lips. He began to lick the semen from her mouth. She clutched his shoulders, moaning wildly each time he sucked the stickiness from her face, each time his finger penetrated her. With his free hand, Simon gripped one fleshy hip to steady her, as his finger rocked her lower body in its rising rhythm. His finger delved deeper into her, his thumb rubbing her clitoris, feeling the bead rotate under his ministrations.

Rosemary's hand was on his, shoving his thumb hard against her tiny shaft. As the sweet, sexual smell pervaded the air, Simon realised she was near to orgasm. He pushed his finger harder and faster into her. She ground down on to his thumb and gasped, and he shifted his hand from her hip to clasp her bare backside. The tensing beneath his wrist told him when she peaked, even before he felt the spasms grip his finger. Quickly he withdrew to poke his half-erect member inside her, so that the most sensitive of his flesh might feel her contractions. As Rosemary cried out he felt her spasm, felt her sex expertly gripping his flesh. His cock hardened.

'May I use the telephone?' Faren asked Mrs Cheaters. On her walk back to St Peter's, Faren made the decision to contact her editor, and had sought out the housekeeper in the dining room.

'Miss Lonsdale, I feel I must tell you that as a novice you were out of order, parading around in that scrap of material no bigger than a couple of eye patches, giving the come-on to a good man like Father Murray.'

Faren's mouth dropped open. She had not lured Simon Murray to the beach with her. He had approached her, playfully filtering sand through his fingers on to her exposed belly. If anyone should be labelled provocative, let the label stick to the priest. But she could not say this to Mrs Cheaters, who obviously saw it as her duty to protect precious Father Murray from the likes of her, a wanton novice.

'I was on the beach first, Mrs Cheaters. And it is a free beach. Father Murray joined me.'

'He is a good man. A good priest. Unlike some I could name.'

Faren's gaze remained unwavering. Did the housekeeper know something? Or was she guessing? If she suspected Faren's nocturnal activities, had she reported them to Father Murray? Turning away, she sighed, her purpose in seeking out the housekeeper forgotten as she reflected on these questions. Tonight she would learn what Simon wanted, and now it seemed in all likelihood that he knew what his housekeeper knew.

'You can use the telephone in the living room,' Mrs Cheaters called after her.

'What? Oh, yes. Thank you.' Once in the living room, Faren closed the door behind her and leaned on the solid wood. No wonder she had forgotten her call, what with the daft woman jumping on her the moment she was spotted. She closed her eyes, busily narrating in her head what she would say to her editor, when the door shoved hard against her back.

'Doors must stay open when using the telephone. House rules,' Mrs Cheaters announced.

Faren stifled a groan. 'Fine,' she said. Though it was a nuisance to have to revoke the privacy on which she had planned, it was much wiser to keep to an innocent conversation with her boss. She dialled the number and glanced pointedly at the housekeeper until the woman moved out the door and away from the room.

Faren muttered under her breath. Then, 'Oh, Julie. It's Faren here.'

'Hi, Faren. How's things?'

'Fine.' A very innocent exchange, because the receptionist had no details of this particular assignment. It was far too much of a time bomb for it to spread any further than *Splash!*'s editor.

'Are you busy? The magazine is a madhouse with –'

'Julie, please. Just put Martine on.' The last thing she wanted was to have Julie spout out across an open line that she was speaking to a staff member of *Splash!* magazine. It would blow her cover into fragments. Not forgetting the potential loss of her new sensual self which was beginning to mean so much more to Faren than she had realised.

'Faren. What's up?' Her editor's smooth voice purred over the wire.

'Oh, very little. I have a meeting with Father Murray later this evening.' Faren chewed her lip. Why had she not realised how restricting this call would be?

'So, are you worried?'

'Look, I don't really know. I wanted to talk but –' Faren lowered her voice, though she could see the house-keeper was too far away to hear '– I still have an hour free. Can you meet me? I don't have time to get into the city and back, and besides, it's impossible for me without a pass.'

'Sure. Where?'

'Just drive down towards the beach. I'll wait fifteen minutes before I leave here.'

'You've got it.'

'Fine.' Faren sighed. Until now she had not realised how much she wanted to talk to someone about the case.

Twenty minutes later, settled in her editor's BMW, Faren suddenly felt very silly. 'Thank you for coming so quickly, Martine.'

'What's all this urgency? And couldn't you have told me on the phone?'

'You know I couldn't, Martine. Lord, I feel so stupid now,' Faren said. Stalling, she streaked her fingers through her hair. 'Maybe I'm going nuts, but I thought they were on to me.'

'What do you mean, "thought"? You think otherwise now?'

'Now I just feel damn stupid!' Faren laughed shakily, recalling the prickle of dread when Simon requested her presence tonight. That had burgeoned until she was galvanised into calling Martine. 'Father Murray wants to see me tonight. And it sounds ominous.'

'Isn't he the one you met initially? The priest who offered you one of the valued novice places?'

Faren nodded, before realising her gesture would be

143

missed. Martine would never take her eyes from the road and risk an accident merely to study her passenger's expression; she was too proud of her crimson status symbol. 'That's the one. But why would he want to see me?' Faren asked.

Martine shrugged, eyes trained on the gathering traffic as they neared the promenade. 'You tell me. Surely there's nothing sinister in that? Seems to me you're overreacting, my girl.'

'Yeah, maybe you're right.' Faren sighed. 'Though I'm prone to play things down rather than overreact.'

'And you got me out of the office for this?' Martine ducked into a parking space and yanked on the hand-brake. Faren waited for the motor to be shut down, knowing she would not have the woman's full attention before then. 'Here I was, thinking you had some earth-shattering news to share, or, better still –' Martine flashed a bright smile '– you'd discovered a way to smuggle me in.'

'I'm working on it.' It was a jest, though her boss seemed to think otherwise.

'Really?' said Martine.

'Don't get your hopes up. Depending on what Father Murray sticks me with tonight, I might be reporting for duty in the office tomorrow morning.'

'But you'll try?'

'What?'

'To get me in.'

Faren laughed. 'Martine, I never knew you were a sex maniac!'

'You hid it pretty well from me, too,' the older woman delivered slyly. 'Are you attracted to this Father Murray, Faren?'

She mulled over the question, tossing over whether she should admit to it, while knowing full well that today she had wanted more from Simon than just the simple friendship he seemed to offer. 'I guess I am.' Why

144

not go the whole hog and confess to Martine? 'That first day, I embarrassed him, you know? And I considered him a challenge, knowing I wouldn't get to him with blatant seduction. After Karl, well, I was so caught up in his obvious sexuality that I relegated Simon to a non-event. Now, I wonder.'

'But that's not what worries you about tonight?'

'Good Lord, no! I'm more worried that he has cottoned on to me; either that I'm doing an investigative piece, or that someone has reported my nocturnal visits with Karl. I don't know which to worry about the most.' She glanced at Martine's chunky gold watch. 'Anyway, I must get back.'

'I'll drop you off. Can you ring me tomorrow? You've got me rather curious about this meeting now.'

'Yes, yes! But come on, start up.' Faren looked anxiously around while Martine started the motor, reversed carefully out, and with a wide sweep executed an illegal U-turn.

Sitting in Father Murray's office, she watched him, her unease growing as two more priests joined them. The addition of these priests signalled a sinister strain to the meeting, which Faren concluded could not possibly be social. She extracted a tissue from her sleeve and, with unobtrusive movements, rubbed first behind one ear, then behind the other. Before heading down to Simon's office she had slipped her finger into her panties and dipped into her moist slit before dabbing it behind both ears. Then, she decided, perhaps a touch at the jaw-line, and she had trailed her fingertip along its contour. All because she had read somewhere that men were not consciously aware of what attracted them to a special woman, but every woman exuded her own unique perfume, and tonight she wanted to lure Simon into her arms. How foolish was her plan! If these three men caught her scent, she would be in deep trouble.

'Faren, this is Father Patrick O'Connor and Father Tom Mullahy.'

Simon's smile failed to reassure her, failed to still the wave of panic that had begun to assail her the moment she spied the priests. It did not bode well. If it were Simon alone, then she may have had a chance to persuade him to keep her on at St Peter's, allowing her time to prove herself, but now, with the addition of the two older priests, Faren felt a sense of doom veil her. Courteous in her greeting, she assumed an air of nonchalance and forced back the memory of the day she had perched on the edge of the same cracked vinyl seat. That day she had prayed for Father Murray to give her a chance; it was all for her scoop she told herself, to push her further along the coveted ladder. But now there were other reasons.

'Miss Lonsdale?'

Oh, Lord! Was she forever destined to wander off into a daydream when in this office? 'I'm sorry, Father. You were saying?'

'We have some questions to put to you, my child. Would you be so kind as to answer them truthfully?'

'Of course, Father.'

The priest introduced as Tom Mullahy cleared his throat. He stubbed out his cigarette in the heavy glass ashtray beside him. 'This is in place of the written report Father Murray mentioned to you. Please do not think we are prying. That is not the purpose of our questions. It could be embarrassing to us all, but I assure you they are necessary if we are to make a fair judgement.'

Faren's skin prickled. What the hell was that supposed to mean? Was this to be every bit as bad as she had imagined? 'I'm ready, Father.'

'Right.' Father Mullahy shuffled the papers on his lap but his eyes refrained from seeking notes. And then Faren realised there was an absence of notes, of information written down; it was purely a ploy to appear business-like. 'Would you like to begin, Patrick?' As the second priest shook his head, Father Mullahy turned to Simon. 'Perhaps you could start then, Simon?'

Simon nodded, his eyes never leaving Faren's. Beads of perspiration hugged his hairline and her stomach did a little flip; this looked serious. And she was hot. Dressed in the heavy cassock, she squirmed, silently cursing the heat building up along her legs, the thick black fabric covering nearly every inch of her. Recalling the warmth of Simon's office, Faren had dispensed with all but the most basic of underwear, and now she wished she had shucked all but the voluminous garment. She parted her thighs and they peeled away. Immediately she experienced the benefit. Both arms she fitted on the armrests either side of her, giving her skin a waft of air that refreshed inside each sleeve. A state of relaxation – and this meant a comfortable temperature – would convey a modicum of ease and control, which would be in her best interests. She wished she could deal with only Simon. She could have controlled him. Being together like any young couple on the beach today proved that he was beginning to thaw. She wondered how many times he had elected to go through his rosary to clear his conscience for the sin of seeing her nipples.

'You remember the reason you gave for wishing to enter St Peter's?'

'Of course, Father.' And three pairs of eyes watched her as she spoke. 'I was jilted.'

'Quite so.' Simon sounded apologetic and now his eyes refused to meet hers.

Faren waited, her gaze sliding to Father Mullahy, then to Father O'Connor. Both, she guessed, were in their early forties and moderately attractive. And each had something simmering beneath the surface. Just what the hell was going on? She said, 'And it is my fiancé's defection that you wish to discuss?'

'What we wish to discuss with you tonight, my child, is sex and pleasure. Or the lack of, as the case may be.'

'Pardon?' This was unexpected. Unless Simon was now going to say that it certainly seemed as if she did enjoy sex, and that some vindictive person had reported her. Someone had seen her in the showers. Or on the roof with Karl.

'We feel –' and the priests alongside Simon nodded '– that the priesthood is an enormous commitment, especially for a young lady, and we feel it our duty to present you with every chance to revoke your decision.'

'Why should I want to do that? I have no intention of changing my mind.' Faren's shoulders relaxed, releasing the tension in her arms as she realised her fear of being tossed out of St Peter's was not about to materialise – at least not tonight – and tonight's subject was to be a discussion on her inadequate sex life. She hoped she could contain her smile.

'Maybe you will, my dear. Maybe not,' Simon continued. 'Nevertheless, you must have every opportunity to do so, and we would rather you decided early on in your training than later. It costs a great deal to train each novice, and when Father Mullahy and Father O'Connor approached me two days ago, we came to an unanimous decision.'

'What decision?' Faren asked, narrowing her eyes at each man in turn. Each priest bore beads of perspiration across his brow, but she felt little sympathy. Let them suffer in their full regalia.

'Do cease that infernal mumbling, Patrick.' He turned back to Faren. 'It pertains to your self-confessed inability to enjoy sex. As every young lady should, Miss Lonsdale.'

Father Mullahy spoke without a hint of embarrassment as he lay the topic of why she had been summoned out in the open. 'What we plan to do tonight, with your permission, of course, is to instruct you in the ways of sex.' Faren watched as he theatrically licked his lips, and it was then that she realised this was not a hoax. 'Stand up.' Father Mullahy's tongue flicked out, his greedy eyes devouring her.

As she did so, Faren felt the familiar yearning between her thighs, and realised her cunt was already lubricated. Her nipples were straining in her bra, seeming to drill through the lacy cover to the coarse fabric of her gown. Her body tingled all over; she could smell the heat of her sex and wondered if her scent was as apparent to the priests.

Father Mullahy and Father O'Connor had come round the desk and were standing beside Faren before she was aware of them having moved. 'Lock the door, Simon. The last thing we need is that clingy Cheaters woman tracking you down.' Mullahy guffawed.

'Don't be afraid,' Simon whispered as he brushed past, taking her trembling as fear, rather than the desire that was already building inside her. She heard the key gyrate in its lock. If anyone should seek Father Murray and find his office door secured, what would they think?

'Of course we are talking of more than the birds-and-the-bees stuff,' Father Mullahy said.

'Faren.' She turned to face Simon, who spoke so softly, with a gentle reassurance, as though afraid she would bolt from his room. 'You do understand how important this is? To you, Faren. If we let you throw aside the outside life, at least without trying to resurrect your sexual desires, we would have failed in our duties. We are the glue of foundering relationships, and just because you are a novice instead of a member of our flock, that is no reason for us to be remiss in our attention to you.' Unable to think of a reply, Faren nodded,

'Slip out of that thing, young lady,' Father Mullahy said huskily, and Faren slid the voluminous garment down along her arms and over her hips to the floor, the seductive trail of cloth holding each man's rapt attention. She stood in her pink bra and waited for Simon to slide each strap from her shoulders. He stood just looking at

149

her, and Father Mullahy, more eager than his colleagues, reached for her first.

As her breasts were exposed, two perfect mounds, each man seemed to catch his breath. She heard Father Mullahy's groan, an agonising rent of desire, and a deep response echoed in Faren. Her breasts were sensitive, and coupled with the tightness in her belly, sent a swift message to her sex. Her personal scent permeated the air as, with Father Mullahy's dry lips attached to her nipple, her arousal escalated. Her lids fluttered, blocking out Simon's sad eyes and Father O'Connor's obvious discomfort. Did Simon wish it were his mouth tugging at her breast? Is that why he looked so betrayed? But Faren swept the thought from her mind until pleasure was all she cared about. Swiftly the priest's saliva moistened his lips, and she flowered in his mouth, the nipple seeking the soft promise of lips and tongue. He came up for air. 'Now the knickers.' Hot breath, feathery and seductive, tinged with nicotine, floated over her skin. Her senses were alive to the air, to every light massage of his tongue. As Father Mullahy pulled away and dragged in his breath, he cursed. 'Je-sus! I haven't even got to the best bit yet, and I'm ready to explode.'

Faren kicked her briefs aside and opened her legs. She heard Father Mullahy's whistling breath as he dropped a hand to her tight curls. His finger twirled in the mass, the little finger dipping quickly between her intimate folds. She gasped and prepared to ride his hand; just as quickly the stroking was over and he rubbed her natural dampness in her bush. 'What a good, sensible girl you are, my dear. No shaven pussy for you, eh?' When she failed to answer he stuck his arrogant face close to hers. 'I can give you the kind of sex you never dreamt existed.' He jerked her tight curls, the sting sharp as the hair was strained from her mound, and the tingling shot into her swelling clitoris.

Weak in the knees, she let herself collapse in his arms

and he laughed, breathing noisily in her ear, his crucifix digging into her. She turned her face away from his smoky breath. When she turned back his black-covered arm was swiping across his brow, soaking up sweat.

'Tell us how you liked that, young lady. All is not lost.' Then he whispered in her ear, 'You have a responsive pussy there. Did you spend time with inexperienced young bucks? Did they think only of their own pleasure? You need mature men to teach you excitement. You, my dear, have come to the right place.' Faren objected to his smile; it held an edge of cruelty. 'Anyone else for a turn while I get myself together? This little lady here has me all aquiver with the wettest pussy I've fondled in a long while.'

'Please don't speak about me as if I had half a brain and no feelings.'

Without warning, Father Mullahy loomed over her, then he ducked his head and Faren felt his teeth sink into her neck. Shaken, she stumbled back and was checked by Simon's comforting hand.

'Tom,' Simon warned. 'We are here to show Faren she can enjoy what men like to do. Don't put her off.'

'It's a bit late for that.' She wanted to swear at the brute. Better still, she yearned to slam her knee into his balls. Instead, her nails dug into her palms, a reminder to hold her temper. This sojourn at St Peter's was proving more interesting by the minute. Tom Mullahy, I'll ruin you in the next issue of *Splash!*, she vowed.

Father O'Connor asked, 'Where's the ice?' He kept his gaze averted, reluctant to meet Faren's.

She saw Simon produce a red and silver ice bucket from behind his desk. Obviously this night of tuition was well planned. It was all fodder for her story, and she might enjoy it as well, though she would keep a wary eye on that prick, Mullahy. 'What are you going to do?' she asked. To these three priests she was an unenlightened lover. All her sexual encounters had been

151

straight, without props, and bordering on the boring, she realised, as she compared them with what she had so far shared with a few of St Peter's inmates. Now she shivered, as if already feeling the frozen cubes skim her skin, silently questioning what part ice could play in sexual games.

As she watched, Father O'Connor plunged his hand into the bucket and hauled out a handful of crushed ice. It dribbled down and circled his wrist before it was blotted against his cuff. Faren wondered if he, too, would promise her sensations she had never dreamt of. The priest pushed her back down on to the carpet then waved to his colleagues to assist him. Father Mullahy roughly grabbed her wrists. Her muscles pulled as her arms were yanked above her head. Simon fell to pinioning her ankles.

'Apart man. Apart! What's the use of having her legs clamped together like that?' Mullahy said disparagingly. 'How long is it since you fucked a woman?'

Shocked at Mullahy's scorn, Faren saw Simon flush. He gently parted Faren's legs, his grip on her ankles easing. She was just beginning to relax under Simon's tender treatment when her body bucked at the sudden glacial coldness between her thighs. She would have cried out, but a hand clamped her mouth. 'Shush,' he said. 'It's only cold for a moment.' Her muscles relaxed. 'There now, isn't that bliss? The ice melting inside your hot tunnel. Mixing with your love dew.' She felt her flesh withdrawing tightly into itself, savouring the pleasure of spiky ice which slowly melted into smooth, flat pebbles before her pussy had time to register the chilly sting. She squirmed; it was the most mind-blowing experience she had ever known.

As Father O'Connor worked on one breast, swirling his tongue round the swell and grasping the nipple at each final orbit, Father Mullahy was on his knees, snuffling at the neglected breast. He curled one hand into her fan of silky hair. As her excitement mounted, Faren's head thrashed, the prickly carpet abrasive on the soft skin of her cheeks. A widening puddle forged under her, leaving emptiness, as the ice thawed in her hot cavern and the residual cold left her vagina numb. Simon is right, she thought, for while the ice lasted she was in a perpetual state of arousal.

'Tell us what you want, girl,' Father Mullahy demanded. 'Don't be shy. This is a learning experience for you. How would you like a cock in that frozen place? We will leave it there until that nice little cunt of yours warms up. What do you say? What do you want Simon to do?'

'Nothing.' Gritting her teeth against each merciless sensation that, with each flick of a tongue, washed her nipples, she waited for Simon to intervene.

'You're lying. Really lying, girl,' Mullahy said in a singsong voice. 'Simon, as she isn't owning up to a preference, perhaps you might like to show her your repertoire?'

In response to the priest's question, Simon's fingers were creeping along her legs. He stopped to stroke a sensitive spot behind her knees before moving gradually to her thighs. As he caressed her, Faren took delight in the highly charged sexual assault that was storming her and drenching her with desire. It was not solely because three knowledgeable men laboured to inflame every unspoken desire, but that Simon, a man who starred in her fantasies, was finally touching her.

'Oh, my,' Father Mullahy remarked. 'Our girl is enjoying herself.' And as if her pleasure was an unwanted response, the priest sank his teeth into the soft underswell of her breast.

As she cried out in protest and tugged to free her wrists, he tongued the raw area, and the puff of breath that followed as he blew on her skin incited her, the pleasurable sensation leaving her wanting more. She could feel Simon's fingers probing her sex, exploring, gently pushing inside her. She felt him open her as though to peer inside, and then he let the lips close again. The priest's fingers trailed the crease of her thighs and she moaned softly, luxuriating in the tenderness of his loving. He must have sensed that she wanted more, because suddenly she felt his little finger snake to the underside of her sex, and then behind her, seeking and then pressing the spot of rose flesh. Rhythmically, Faren moved her hips so that she arched to meet him, and Simon wisely matched his finger thrusts so that she reached full enjoyment of his skills. Just as her orgasm nudged in greedy anticipation, Faren relaxed, and allowed the feeling to ebb, deciding to play this erotic game out to its end. If she came too early, they may figure their job was done, and right now she was going to milk all this marvellous pleasure for just as long as she could.

'Need more stimulation do you, my girl?' Tom Mullahy grunted as he turned to dip a paw into the ice bucket. He flicked his fingers, yowling as the crystals bit at his flesh. Splinters of ice flew to splatter on Faren's heated skin. Faren bucked as the shards melted and the priest's large hand covered one breast. She shivered and turned her attention away from Mullahy to Father O'Connor, who chose a larger cube with which to torment her. He held it lightly to her breast, and she steeled herself against the unrelenting glacial assault, until numbness eclipsed the chill and the usual soft mound felt firm and inflexible. But as the frosty sensation wore off, and a warm tongue replaced the ice, the contrast in sensation was so great that she felt herself peaking. 'She's coming. I can feel her!' Mullahy winked at O'Connor, who toyed with the last dregs of cube, swirling it round her hard nipple.

'Don't talk as if I'm not in the room!' she hissed, her teeth chattering as her body shook. In that moment Faren was unaware that she was speaking to her superiors and could ruin her chances of staying on at St Peter's. She could comprehend only that she drifted, alternating between excitement and exasperation, loving what was happening to her body, but mad as a bull that she was being thought of as merely some vehicle for the priests' lust. But pleasure came again, and she thought only of herself when Simon moved his finger inside her and pressed firmly, diligently searching for her G-spot. She groaned when he proceeded to caress her with tiny rotations of his finger pad. As his thumb reached along her moist cleft in its search for her clitoris, she sucked in her breath. The gentle explorations were as welcome as the hard thrusts. When contact with the bud was made, Simon pressed and released in time with her frenzied undulations. Within seconds, an orgasm waved over her so powerful, that it reached down to the very tips of her toes, encompassing her in an exquisite climax. Faren's throat filled with a scream. Then Simon's sweet lips were on hers, swallowing her cry.

They allowed her no time to rest and, as the glow of pleasurable exhaustion faded, soft flesh tapped her abdomen. She glanced down to see Father Mullahy's erection, the velvety head tapping her skin as he manipulated his cock with one hand. She was wondering what would happen next, when he shoved Simon away from her. The younger priest's fingers slid out as he fell back, and Mullahy straddled her, before rubbing his penis in the soft pink oyster of her sex. 'Oh, baby, you are wet! And I bet it isn't all ice! My cock wants you. What do you say to that? Do you want it inside you?'

Patrick, Tom Mullahy's cohort, dug Faren in the ribs. 'Answer the man!'

Brave man, she thought. Arrogance seemed to rub off every conceited priest in this place and instil the meeker fellows with a spirit that otherwise might stay hidden. 'Yes,' Faren whispered now, thinking only of how she

yearned for Simon, but some quisling emotion tran-
scended lucid thought, and all she knew was that her sex
was aching and on fire. Right now she was not going to
be picky.

'Faren, are you okay?' Simon asked. 'You are enjoying
this? Just say the word and if you want us to stop, we
will.' All Faren could manage was a slight nod. She did
not want anyone to stop.

'Your breasts are rather small for a bit of tit fucking,
but if I squeeze them together, like this.' Tom Mullahy
puffed, punctuating his words with his actions, until she
gasped.

If she could recount her little exploits with the two
young priests that night she had stumbled into the wrong
room, it would take the wind out of this guy's sails. But
she refused to rat on them. They deserved their fun. Let
this conceited buffoon discover his error himself. Besides,
she thought, as her chin stabbed at him, she had ample
breasts for any real man.

'That's it. Now, hold those glorious globes together.
There's a good girl. Tighter. Push them in hard.' Apparently satisfied with the degree of firmness that now
clutched his thick cock, Faren heard him grunt as he
rocked back on his heels and set up a fierce pace.

The tunnel made of yielding flesh was dry and
uncomfortable for Faren. In contrast, her sex throbbed,
aching for a stiff penis to penetrate her. Then her lower
body lurched, as something wet, soft, and oh, so sensuous, burrowed between her swollen lips. Because Father
O'Connor was busying himself by wrapping lengths of
her freshly shampooed hair round his swollen penis, she
knew – though Tom Mullahy, industriously working
himself between her breasts, blocked her view – that it
was Simon playing with her. As his skilfully swirling
tongue played in her slit, it seemed that he would ignore
the one place that she urged him to touch. She lifted her
bottom high as she dug her heels into the floor to steady

herself. She thrust her groin into his face. His lips captured her swollen clitoris as, with a sucking noise, he drew it into his mouth. She bucked with the intensity of the sensation that enervated her limbs which were now so heavy that it was only a moment before she flopped back down on to the floor. Unbelievably, as Simon's tongue lapped and caressed her, suckled and excited her, Tom Mullahy's urgent thrusts between her breasts grew more pleasurable, sending a fierce heat down between her legs. Then Simon's tongue was swirling again, stopping only while he nibbled gently on her sex lips, before dipping and stroking the smaller pleats. Suddenly his tongue invaded her opening, sending turbulent waves shivering through her. As Faren's climax racked her body, her spasms imprisoned the priest's serpentine tongue. Simon's nose stayed buried in her fragrant curls, snuffling in the dampness, stimulating her clitoris until she was spent.

Her jerking body excited the man that straddled her and, with a shout, he came between her breasts, squirting up along her neck, several drops splashing on to her lips and dribbling into her mouth so that she tasted hot, acrid semen. Her excitement, paired with Father Mullahy's climax, shot a message to Father O'Connor, who played lovingly with her hair. He increased the tempo of his thrusts and moments later echoed his colleague's shout, jetting his sperm. It dribbled, hot and sticky, and settled in the curve of her ear.

As both priests rolled away from her, Simon continued the sweet torture, delicately tonguing her belly now that her prone body was all his. She closed her eyes, wanting only Simon, glad the others had gorged on her, had slaked their thirst, so that she could now enjoy him alone. Her eyes flew open when she felt something gliding over her face. Father O'Connor was dabbing a tissue, blotting away spilt semen, mumbling incoherently to himself, although Faren suspected he was praying for his mortal soul. What a lovely way to live, she thought; commit sins then ask for absolution. But she reassessed her earlier view of the priests. Though they sought their own pleasure, scarcely troubling themselves with hers – despite their claim to this at the outset – she had been pleasured, and they were not all bad; one priest was cleaning up his spill while the other kissed her tenderly.

The two priests pulled away, their hooded eyes watching Simon at play. Faren's eyes closed, blocking them from view. In her darkness, Faren could hear the soft murmuring of the men. Their laughter. 'Simon, what the dickens are you doing down there? Haven't you mastered the art of cunnilingus?'

Mullahy, she thought, you do enjoy ridiculing Simon. So she tensed her muscles ready to claim her next climax, if only to prove Simon an expert lover. She blocked out all sensation but the swirling tongue, and lifted her legs to twine them round Simon. With firm pressure, she urged him harder against her. She rocked and squirmed as his mouth clamped on to her hardened bud, his tongue never ceasing its slippery work as he sucked her clitoris into his mouth. With every racking spasm that spread greedily through her, Faren thrashed. A scream rose from her throat and she swallowed it when a priest covered her mouth with his. She shivered. There was something terribly wanton in having a man's mouth on her lips, while another man's mouth was caressing her more intimate lips, she thought, as the exquisite spasms rippled through her sex, then slowly petered out. Legs dangled, limp and useless, as Simon moved her away from him, stretched himself along her naked body and kissed her full on the mouth.

Chapter Twelve

Simon was nibbling on her lower lip when Father Mullahy intervened and pushed him away. 'Oh, no. We haven't finished with you yet, my dear.' Faren shook her head.

'Uh uh. I'm dead serious,' Father Mullahy went on. He put out his large paw and yanked her to her feet.

Her legs would have folded under her, but Simon's arm shot out and gripped her by the waist. 'Tom, it's enough for one night. You can saturate a student with Greek or French or whatever, and he will only absorb to his brain's capacity.'

Father Mullahy yanked Faren behind him to the far side of the desk, swiping a hand across the clutter, clearing a space. 'Now, sit yourself down here. No, wait. The chair will be better,' he said.

'Tom!' Simon protested.

'He's right, Tom.' Father O'Connor's glance darted between the two men.

'Haven't you listened to a word I've said?' Simon asked, gripping the edge of the desk.

Father Mullahy rounded on his companions, brushing their objections aside. 'I'm not trying to teach her Greek, you idiots! Her brain is the last thing she needs to use. All she has to do is play dead if she's jaded. But this little lady doesn't want to play dead, do you, my dear?'

It was obvious he expected her complete acquiescence, for he pushed her into the chair. She hissed through clenched teeth as her bare backside touched cold leather. She could feel her damp thighs sticking to the leather, and wondered what would happen next. In this position her pussy was inaccessible to the priests, and they were not about to let her go yet.

'Right, here we go.' Mullahy rubbed his hands together. 'One leg over here. That's the girl.' With his running commentary he lifted her right leg and positioned it over the armrest. 'Now the other leg.'

Despite everything that had gone before, Faren was mortified, so vulnerably open before three pairs of alert male eyes that her posture seemed terribly crude. One heel slid off the armrest and even before she could dislodge her leg Father O'Connor danced in to whip it back into place. 'No. No. No,' he said. 'This is a lesson in pleasure, remember?'

Her eyes dare not search out Simon's, not while she was so crudely open to him. But as her sex throbbed and she waited for the ultimate prize, she realised she wanted this. To have three men explore her with their eyes. Until this gem of an assignment had popped into her head and allowed her to enter St Peter's, her sex life had coasted along, mundane but satisfactory. The priests had changed all that. Each time a priest touched her, made love to her, Faren was swept along on a tide of ecstasy, and now, with her legs parted wide, her sex open to the men, she waited. A stroke of a finger touched her softness. She slid her bottom forward on the chair, pushing closer to the source of pleasure. A finger dipped and rotated until dew coated her and settled beneath her bottom, squelching between flesh and leather, as she wiggled to convey where she wanted those busy fingers to touch next.

'Want to lick her juice, Patrick?'

Taking up the invitation, Father O'Connor pushed Mullahy aside. He dropped to his knees. 'I feel like I'm at prayer.' He giggled.

Peering down at Patrick O'Connor's sparsely covered crown as he licked her vulva with long, industrious strokes, Faren sighed, her legs strained and trembling. She watched Simon eye the action. She could not help but smile. Simon appeared so good, so pure and dedicated, that his participation in this sexual sport staggered her. Subconsciously she had earmarked him for some virginal pedestal, and to discover he was but a replica of every sex-hungry guy she had ever met made her desire him even more. She wanted Simon and she was going to have him. He smiled at her and her desire for him began to build again. She settled back, closing her eyes, giving herself over to the sensations centred in her sex as Father O'Connor's tongue slipped inside her and his nose flattened against her clitoris. With his free hand he burrowed beneath her; it was not an easy task, but he was not at all deterred from his target. The finger snaked along, seeking her second opening and, without warning, cruelly thrust inside. Faren stiffened at the intrusion, clenching at the finger in her tight opening and his tongue in her cunt. Then with one sudden move Patrick jerked back, and the feel of his tongue as it slid from her made her shiver. Her behind shot off the chair, effectively pushing his finger further into her rectum, and she screamed, only to have the sound cut off by a hand across her mouth. She could smell herself on the priest's fingers, and she calmed, relaxing further as he withdrew his finger from her second opening. Then he caught her fleshy globes in both hands, fingers digging in to take her weight, and slowly eased her back into the chair, an effortless operation, with her bottom sliding in the dampness, the leather slick with Patrick's saliva.

'It's about time you paid me the same compliment.' As

Faren shot Patrick a perplexed look, he stood and arched towards her, his engorged penis quavering, the skin so tight that it seemed to Faren he was ready to burst. 'Your mouth this time. There's nothing like some skilful mouth music.' He quickly knelt before her, taking her ankles to set her feet on the floor. He pulled her off the chair until she was kneeling. Face to face with him, Faren studied his lustful expression, wondering what his parishioners would say if they could see him now. The priest's mouth glistened with her dew, smelt of her dampness. His dark eyes filled with desire. And as she assessed him, he smiled. 'Would you like to taste yourself, my dear?' And he crushed her to him and kissed her, squashing her nose against his cheek and her sensitive breasts against his hairy chest. She could barely breathe, and, when he eased back a fraction, she breathed deeply through her nose, inhaling her own scent, her lips tasting of her own body. An intoxicating mixture.

When Patrick released her, Faren eagerly bent to take him in her mouth, and as her soft lips touched him, he groaned, falling back on his heels, then lowering himself to the floor as her mouth followed him. She had not realised how close he was. He shuddered as her mouth took all of him. Her eyes opened wide as the first hot squirt hit the back of her throat, followed by another and another until his come filled her mouth. She swallowed. One final shudder, and Patrick lay limp on the floor, his eyes closed, an expression of such contentment on his face that it filled Faren with a renewed sense of power and elation.

She got to her feet, stumbled over the prone figure and headed for Simon. Tonight she had allowed them all to use her. And now she wanted Simon. She watched him follow her progress across the room. Then she dipped her gaze to his penis that pulsated and strained towards her. She felt weak in the knees. At last he would be hers. At last she would feel him inside her. All evening, the true realisation of just how much she wanted him had remained on the periphery, but now, smiling, she reached for him.

'Father Murray? Simon?' Simon started at the voice, and Faren froze, glancing towards the door as the first tentative knock sounded. The rapping grew in intensity. 'Simon, are you all right?'

Simon leapt to his feet and started towards the door, and Faren cursed softly at the slumping of his shoulders and quickly diminishing erection. The untimely interruption had doused what she was about to sample.

'What the hell could that woman possibly want?' Tom Mullahy, unwittingly echoing Faren's thoughts, rounded on Simon, his breath hissing, and Faren was somewhat mollified to learn the intrusion was just as disturbing to the men.

Simon gritted his teeth. 'What is it, Mrs Cheaters?' he called. His erection deflated completely as he spoke. The two senior priests were experiencing the same lessening desire; Faren watched their penises shrivel before her eyes.

'I thought I heard you groan. Did you hurt yourself?'

'Holy hell!' Tom Mullahy hissed. 'Get rid of her!' He jerked his thumb at the door.

'You may get off to bed now, Mrs Cheaters,' Simon said.

'But what was that noise?' The door handle rattled.

Galvanised into action, the four occupants grappled for cover, each wheezing a grateful relief as the door refused to budge. 'For God's sake!' Father Mullahy muttered.

'Your door is locked.'

'Mrs Cheaters, will you please leave,' said Simon.

Faren pictured the woman bristling on the far side of the door. Time ticked by, and she listened to the rustle of the woman's skirts. Mullahy heard it, too, because he said, 'Christ! Don't tell me she's got a key.'

'Blast!' The muttered oath came from Father O'Connor. He wiped spittle from his chin with a shaky hand.

'It's Father Mullahy, Mrs Cheaters,' Tom said, unaware of how ridiculous he looked as he marched half-naked to the door. He had kept his tunic on, which came only to his waist, and his white butt was on show. 'There is no need for concern. Just us boys getting together.' If his voice was meant to soothe, it left Faren cold; she heard the hard edge to it.

A stunned apology filtered through the sturdy oak door, then, 'Goodnight.' And the sound of receding footsteps.

'Pour us a whisky, there's a good girl.' Father Mullahy waved a hand towards a corner cabinet as he struggled into his trousers.

Naked, Faren cruised the room, glorying in the opportunity to flaunt her figure. Maybe this would make Simon's cock grow.

'Just as well the door was locked.' Father Mullahy collapsed into a chair and drew his fingers down his face.

'Contrary to popular belief, a man does have a judicious brain prior to sex.'

The priest grinned. 'Speak for yourself, Simon.' Mullahy took the snifter from Faren and gulped down the fortifying liquid. He coughed. 'Another please, my dear.'

She sashayed away to show off her curves. She had unfinished business. Behind her came the crackle of cloth. Was Simon dressing? She could only surmise what else might have happened if the housekeeper had opted to mind her own business rather than sniff round her employer's office. Then again, the woman had made it clear on numerous occasions that she considered Father Murray her business. If it hadn't been for Mrs Cheaters, the sexual treats may have lingered on for another hour or two, although, studying each priest in turn, Faren noted their exhaustion. She was sure Simon had not yet come; his tongue and his fingers had teased and pleasured her, but there was still the thick rod between his legs. She smiled. She would guarantee that he had some life left in him yet.

'We'll leave you now, young lady.' Father Mullahy heaved himself from the chair then plonked his empty glass down on the desk. He lifted it again and sat it on a notepad. He patted her on the head as one would an obedient and faithful pet. She supposed that was exactly what she had portrayed herself as tonight. 'We trust you have gained a great deal of pleasure this evening, my dear.' Mullahy cocked his head. 'Have we proved to you how enjoyable sex is with the right partner?'

She nodded. 'Great sex.' Did he really think he was the perfect partner? If there was less to lose, she might just tell him he lacked a certain polish.

'Splendid!' He rubbed his palms together. 'Now, we might need to call you another night. Depends on our commitments, of course.'

'My diary is free,' Patrick interjected.

'Well, we will see, Father.' Focusing on Faren once again, Tom Mullahy added, 'We want to ensure your decision is the correct one. We came up with this performance as the surest means we know of to prevent you making a huge mistake. You do see it's for your own good, don't you, Miss Lonsdale?'

'Of course, Father.' She dipped her head to conceal the triumph she felt must surely show in her eyes.

'And you will gain so much.' The priest babbled on in an effort to justify the night's deed.

Oh, yes, I will, Faren thought to herself, keeping her gaze lowered while she envisaged her revelation as the lead story in a future issue of *Splash!* She checked the urge to race back to her room and write up her notes. 'Thank you, Father,' she said politely.

'We will leave you now. Think over this night, young lady.' At the door Tom Mullahy glanced back. 'Gluttony is a deadly sin, Father Murray.' The door closed, cutting off Mullahy's guffaw.

'Come here.' Simon's voice floated to her, tender and yet sexy, luring her to him.

When she had shuffled closer he reached out, his finger trailing her cheek. Then he cupped her chin. She flung her arms round his neck, pressing her body into his, unable to deny the surge of longing she felt as she lifted her face to his. As lips touched lips, the kiss deepened, his soft, pussy-scented tongue delving into her mouth, tickling her tongue. His hand cupped her breast as he pulled away from her. 'Still aroused, Faren?' Simon crooned, thumbing her erect nipple. When she cried out, he eased the pressure to a bearable stroke. Then his hand slipped along her abdomen, pausing to explore the roundness of a hip, before veering inwards to caress the silkiness of her skin, expert in his touch. Her breathing quickened and she felt she would scream for want of him. She parted her legs to invite him in. When he fingered her sex, she sighed. So many orgasms this evening, and still Faren hungered for more. She leaned into his shoulder, losing herself in Simon's fondling. Her senses ablaze, wanting more, she pushed against him and began to grind herself on his hand. Her fingers clawed through his hair, and as each beautiful, excruciating sensation buoyed at his touch, his fingers dancing in and out of her sex, she moaned, the indirect pressure on her clitoris more than she could bear.

'Do you want to come now? Tell me what you want, Faren.'

'I want you.'

'My fingers? Do you want my fingers inside you? Or this?' He pushed hard against her and withdrew his fingers. 'Tell me, Faren!'

'I want you, Simon. Oh, how much I want you!' She gasped; she was hot and ready, waiting to receive him.

'Say it, Faren! Tell me what you want.'

'I want your thick, hard cock inside my cunt! Plundering me. Please, Father Murray, push your cock inside me.'

The use of his title seemed to drive him wild, for he ground himself against her, groaning, and she shivered, feeling his heat on her belly. He bent his knees, aligning his body with hers, and she moaned as his rigid penis scraped her tender clitoris, her legs quivering as he cupped her buttocks and lifted her to take him. With her legs coiled round his waist she bore down, her flesh expanding to accommodate his width, sucking him in. Once impaled, she rested for a moment, the stem of him flush with her opening. Their breaths heaving, they gazed into each other's eyes. Simon's signal was a gentle kneading of her fleshy cheeks, and she responded, clutching his neck and lifting her body. She felt Simon synchronise with her movements while he took her weight, assisting the rise from him, then letting her sink back down on to his rigid shaft. Faren's satiny sheath gripped him until his groans sounded loud in her ear, his breath shifting wisps of her hair. When her legs began to quiver, she pressed her body into him and he met the thrust and held her there as powerful spasms rocked her. Before her orgasm receded, she felt him jerk, and then he was thrusting hard into her, bringing his own climax on.

The tangible reminder of tonight was there between her legs. A glow of warmth still lingered in her sex. Faren smiled and tapped the pen against her teeth. Tonight, there would be no need to haul out her magazines. She felt totally sated. She leaned back in her chair, tilting it so that only two wooden legs touched the floor. More than ever, on this night she blessed her shorthand skills as her hand darted across the page. Not only would she be done in a fraction of the time but there would be no reason to hide these notes. She pictured the furore that would result if they were discovered and legible. A keg of dynamite waiting for a match. Senior priests would be defrocked. And the novices? They could plead their innocence, heaping blame for the entire débâcle on senior members of the clergy. Faren champed on the end of her pen, frowning as she gazed at the white sliver of a magazine that protruded from her case. Since securing a key for her room, she had ceased to lock her suitcase. She could have sworn that the magazine had been stuffed back in between a few odds and sods she had left there. She shook away her paranoia and settled down to the task in hand, scratching across the page, reliving each delicious moment with Simon.

Nearly half an hour later she stood up and fired her pen across her desk. Fingers interlocked, she reached high above her head, emitting a primitive sound that added to her pleasure as the pull of her muscles gloried in the stretch. She yawned. A long and eventful night, she mused, satisfied she had remembered everything and recorded it in the diligent manner in which she tackled every task. She ambled over to the bed. So inviting, she thought, as she flopped down and began to unfasten her gown. Then a single rap sounded on her door. She groaned, dragged herself upright and rolled off the bed. 'Who is it?'

'Faren, open up.'

He sounded displeased. And that was a mild assessment. She sighed. 'No.'

'Come on, Faren.'

'What do you want, Karl?'

'I can't talk out here. I won't keep you long. You have my word.'

Well, he sounded reasonable enough. Now.

Chapter Thirteen

Karl Sterling was displeased. In fact, he would go as far as to say he was bloody furious. This evening he had expected to be entertained by Faren. For some reason she had been granted an afternoon free of lectures, and Karl recalled the simmering resentment among the men when she failed to show. Already it appeared that she was receiving special dispensation, and as Karl had watched the hopeful glances of the young men rapidly turn into scowls, he understood Faren's absence from class did not go down too well. Like Karl himself, the men looked forward to seeing her, to feasting their eyes on her, imagining, no doubt, what her soft pink lips could do to them. Yes, he had definitely felt an aching void, being deprived of her sprite-like presence today. But clinging to the promise of the night had kept him going. Then, tonight, when news of her summons to Simon's office filtered through, he had spent time in useless pacing, unable to settle on even the most mundane of tasks. He had sweated and churned, and when Edmonds poked his nose in, Karl had snarled and sent him on his way. The mysterious summons disturbed him more than he cared to admit. It came too early in the proceedings for student assessment. So what did Simon want? And the meeting had been anything but brief. The uncertainty also came from Karl's knowledge of his superior, a man who was anything but verbose. What the hell had detained her?

Sexual release was only part of what he wanted. For that alone, he could go to the confessional. Faren was intelligent and sweet and vivacious, and her soft body lured him. She was addictive, and he needed more. Earlier, his curiosity had sent him along to Simon's office, but before he could put an ear to the door, the housekeeper fronted up. Guarding her precious Murray, as always. What Murray saw in the plump body left Karl somewhat perplexed. But each to his own, he thought.

'What is it, Karl? Honestly, I'm exhausted.' Faren opened the door in what to Karl seemed reluctant invitation.

'Hi.' He wanted to take her in his arms. 'I missed you,' he said, and stepped into the room.

'You missed me?' He saw surprise in her eyes.

Why the hell had he let loose with that sentiment? This woman shared his views on human nature; only if he offered a challenge would she be interested. 'What did Murray want?' he asked.

She shrugged. 'Nothing.'

'You're lying.'

'Well, of course I'm lying. I'd hardly be called to his office for "nothing"!'

'Snappy, aren't we? Was it really that bad?' He took a hurried step towards her as an unwelcome thought came to mind. 'Were you asked to leave?'

'No.'

When he placed his hands on her shoulders and drew her into him, she tried to pull away. 'What's wrong?' he asked softly.

'I'm tired, Karl.'

'You do want to continue our little trysts?' Until that

moment Karl had been unaware of how much he relied on her eager participation. Something could happen without her, of course, but it was the enthusiastic and uninhibited young lady he wanted. 'Or are you playing some game with me?' If so, Karl vowed, she would not gain the upper hand. For a moment he had gone soft, telling her he had missed her, acting like some romantic suitor instead of a man in control.

'No game. And yes to your first question. But not tonight.'

Relief locked in with disappointment. 'You're exhausted. Get off to bed now.' He kissed the tip of her nose. Why was he acting like a whipped dog, ready to slink away?

He was already at the door when she called him back. 'Why did you come?'

'Isn't it obvious?' He grinned ruefully as she glanced down at his groin, his full arousal clearly evident. When his smile failed to trigger one in return, he suspected there was more to Faren's mood than the tiredness she claimed. 'He didn't ask you to leave?'

'Who?' Her heavy lids lowered further. 'Simon?'

'So, it's "Simon" now?'

She ignored that. 'I told you, no, he didn't ask me to leave. I wondered that, too, and I so much want to stay.'

'Good.' He felt immense relief. 'The second matter I wanted to discuss with you.' He raked his hand through his thick hair. How would she take this? He fortified himself with a deep breath. If, a few nights ago, he could have seen himself behaving like a buck on the eve of his first date, he would have laughed. Get a grip on yourself, man! You are being bloody ridiculous. You escaped the outside world because of the games men and women play. In here there is no veneer of love. No deceit. Only pure lust, plain and simple, touches us. But no woman had ever burrowed beneath his skin before.

'Yes?' Her small enquiry seemed to take so much effort. Her pale lids were closing. She swayed.

Karl jumped forward and grabbed her. He scooped her into his arms and carried her over to the bed. 'Do you want me to undress you, Faren?' he asked, setting her down on top of the quilt. God knows he wanted to; his hands burned with the need to run his fingers over every delicious square inch of her.

'Thank you for the offer. Not tonight.' Her lips twitched. 'This must cost you.'

'Little one, you don't know the half of it.' And he shifted his bulge so that it rested more comfortably against his belly. He smiled. Kissed her brow. 'We'll talk tomorrow.'

'Did you see her?' Drew Edmonds approached from the west wing to accost Karl.

'You doubt my power?'

'Of course not.' Drew fidgeted with his collar.

Karl's lips quirked, amused that the priest's eagerness for sex had escalated since the initiation in the shower. Ever conscious of the need for discretion, he quickly opened his door and herded Edmonds in. 'Make it quick. I'm tired,' Karl said, an echo of Faren's words. Not too tired to jerk off, once he was rid of the nuisance that seemed to hound him ever since he had allowed Edmonds to share Faren.

'She's not about to be chucked out, is she?'

'Not to my knowledge.' Let the boy sweat, Karl decided, eager to regain his cruel streak after having unsettled himself by coming over all sentimental with Faren just now.

If it were not for the man's twitching – first tugging at his collar and then patting down his short hair – Karl would have turned his back and left Edmonds to see himself out. Instead, with a knowing smile, his gaze dropped to the priest's lower region, not at all surprised to discover the thick erection. You are out of luck tonight, my boy. While in a sexual frenzy with a woman, Karl had been prepared to work in unison with the young priest, but alone, now that he had satisfied his curiosity, a man's body held no desire for him. 'Off you go, Edmonds. Bedtime.' Flustered, half expecting a sexual tryst no doubt, which was what all the fidgeting was about, Edmonds blanched at being unceremoniously dismissed. Karl said maliciously, 'It'll have to be a hand job tonight, old boy.' The bright flush that swept over Edmonds' face was sweet reward indeed.

Less than fifteen minutes later, Karl was stretched out on his bed, mulling over thoughts that refused to go away. When he had barged in on Faren, she had seemed on edge. Her claim to exhaustion, he was willing to accept. She was almost asleep on her feet and incapable of partaking in a night of pleasure. Suddenly, he tensed. If that damn Murray had touched her! No, he would not have the guts. And besides, Madam Cheaters would guard her interest. He chuckled to himself and relaxed back on the mattress, one elbow crooked behind his head.

Banishing Murray from his mind, Karl took a small bottle from beneath his pillow, popped the lid and dribbled oil into his palm. His large hand grasped his erection. He stroked himself, the lubricant making his touch slippery and sensuous like a woman's sheath. Calling to mind Faren's lithe body, Karl luxuriated in the vision, as his hand moved lightly along his shaft. His caresses were distracted; now and then he paused to push his little finger into the centre of his balls as he thought of Faren in the shower, water streaming over her ripe breasts. Suds poised on the silken points and thick in her pubic hair and, later, her moist centre opening for him. It was almost as though he could smell her, and he clutched himself more firmly, his hand action embracing a definite rhythm as his mind's eye showed the scented wet bush that had boldly been presented to him when he had surprised her in the bathroom. Just seeing Faren's embarrassment at being caught masturbating had been an aphrodisiac, and his penis had responded, swiftly becoming engorged and aching. Reliving the vivid sensations, Karl's prick throbbed, and his hand increased its pace, the sound slick and wet and erotic. His grip tightened. The petals of her sex had opened, a tantalising invitation to any man. She had been a little afraid that night, but not of him, for she had already accepted his overtures. Ah, yes, she had liked having her pussy licked. And sucked.

Karl's deep groan broke through the images; his hand whipped back and forth and he thrashed about on his bed, squeezing his shaft almost painfully as he thought about the moment when he had finally taken her. Tonight, his visual reliving of the erotic encounters assisted him far more than any fantasy involving a mystery woman or a movie star. Having possessed Faren, all of those other fantasies had lost their appeal. Breathing deeply – in reality inhaling the odour of hot candle wax, the stale air of his room, the leakage of his own semen – he could detect Faren's scent. That sweet essence, the hint of perspiration as her arousal grew, the slick, sweaty sheen that coated every inch of her skin, and – most seductive, most intoxicating of all – the moistness that gathered in the valley between her thighs. He moaned loudly, his hips arching off the mattress, and worked his hand rhythmically, feeling his sperm mount, readying to spray. His hand moved faster, faster, feeling the tightness in his neck as he strained towards his climax, his heart hammering, then his whole body stiffened, and he spurted out over his belly. Jet after hot jet, dribbling down to catch in his pubic hair. He slowed the pace, gave one last squeeze of his cock. The semen quickly turned cool and sticky on his warm belly. Then his body relaxed and he released his hold on his limp prick. He turned on to his side, curling his legs as his soft snake curled contentedly in slumber.

* * *

As she trooped through the dining room, Faren nodded to several of the novices she recognised as classmates. She weaved her way to the table she shared with, among others, Karl and Drew. Was it just her imagination, or were all its occupants staring at her? With eyes focused straight ahead, she greeted them.

'You're staying, Faren?' a novice asked. 'Father Murray didn't turf you out?'

'I'm here, aren't I?' At his dejected expression she silently cursed her sarcasm, though it had been delivered mildly. She spoke more gently, aware that they were all interested in her summons. 'Just a report on how I am settling in.' She avoided Karl's gaze.

The morning galloped along; prayers, meditation, demolishing breakfast and light chatter. Refreshed after an uninterrupted night's sleep, Faren pondered the purpose of Karl's late night visit. Her lips quirked. Apart from the obvious. Too sleepy last night to take it in, on awakening she remembered how concerned, how caring, Karl had been. Now she sweated a little guilt on recalling the night-time play in Simon's office. She felt almost as if she were cheating on Karl, which was ludicrous. She owed the priest nothing. But a small voice niggled. Without him she would not have successfully realised her mission. And there was Drew. But, she figured, only with Karl's adept tutoring had the young priest become the sexual animal unleashed upon her. So yes, she owed her thanks to Karl, not least for the amazing pleasure he gave her at every opportunity, the heightened awareness of each other, the sexual tension that had crackled between them for weeks. Memories warmed her and her eyes cut to his. The chemistry was still there.

'Later,' Karl mouthed.

She flushed and ducked her head to prevent every man at the table from guessing the emotions rocketing through her. Before entering the seminary, she had welcomed sex, indulging two or three times a week, but

175

now her body craved it every night. Preferably several times a night. One climax was no longer sufficient to appease her love-hungry body. Mundane lectures or tasks did little to divert Faren's mind, which in turn sent signals to her pleasure points and then the whole business started all over again. Only in her language class did she drag her practical mind from her sexual memories.

Lost in wicked thoughts again, she was dragged back to reality when Karl touched her sleeve, lightly, fleetingly. Punishment by the High Council was meted out to anyone ignoring prayers, and fear of early banishment made her swing her attention to the podium. Banishment? That would never do. And why not? Faren asked herself, as the senior priest's voice droned on. She could leave at any time. Tucked up in her room were scrolls of notes and, though she was reluctant to admit it, all she needed for her report.

'We'll be missed in class,' she murmured a short time later as Karl nipped her earlobe.

'That worries you?' It did. More than she could say. He continued to take tiny nips, and she trembled, the arousal that surged so easily these days engulfing her. He pushed her back on the bed, his fingers riding along her quivering thigh beneath her cassock. 'A quickie,' Karl said. 'I'll have you back in class so fast you won't even know you've had one.'

She pouted. 'What's the use of that?' But she felt the heat between her legs; a quickie would do very nicely.

Today he wore a black waist-length tunic and black trousers, and his arousal, the hunger that was always there, was blatantly clear. When she reached out for him, he ducked back, his breath almost a hiss. 'Give me a minute, or I'll explode. And I want to do that inside you.' Time was against them. No time to undress. Faren felt there was something very wanton about making love half-clothed. Like doing it with your boyfriend while your parents were in the garden.

Karl released his stiff cock, and the sight of it poking out of his trousers sent shivers along her spine. It looked so crude, almost alien, against the backdrop of dark fabric. Her arousal soared. Grasping himself, he guided his erection to her face. Flicking her tongue over the angry tip, she supped the drop of fluid that oozed there, then tongued along the ridge, strengthening her strokes each time he groaned. He pushed her skirt above her waist, and then, in one quick movement, he straddled her, his penis skimming her belly. He took the crotch of her briefs and tugged it aside, baring her sex. With two fingers he pushed his cock down until its heavy length was touching her flesh. She caught her breath, fixed on every beat of his pulsating member. When he lifted himself, she began to protest, only to utter a sigh when his cock nudged her. He rocked back and forth, each time splaying her wider, preparing her for his width. She wriggled, a silent signal that begged for more as she opened up for him. Strong fingers burrowed between the quilt and her behind, and he lifted her, then, pulling her down on him, thrust into her. Invasion was sweet. Karl squeezed the globes of her buttocks, increasing her pleasure, though nothing could surpass the powerful thrust of his cock as it slid effortlessly in her moist channel. As her muscles squeezed his shaft, Karl's harsh groan came uncomfortably loud in her ear. She lifted her legs and, taking her arms from round his neck, placed them about her knees and rocked, opening herself for deeper penetration. The slapping of flesh, the feel of it, spurred Faren quickly to the edge. She left hold of her legs to straighten them, needing the extra tension to milk each sensation for as long as she could. When Karl dropped from his elbows to cover her with his full weight, and ground his pelvis to apply friction to her clitoris, she came. She came in one long gush that threatened to end too soon, until Karl lunged again and again, inciting her pleasure to sweep on. Caught up in her climax, she felt the tension in Karl and knew he was going to come. And then his body shook and his mouth was smothering hers, his cock moving faster, his breath heaving loud and hot in her ear. He shuddered and he came hard and fast inside her, her sex contracting to grip and suck more of him.

Finally he grew limp and rolled from her. Faren felt a moment of loss, wanting desperately the intimacy of staying joined. But as their breathing calmed to a steady rate, and the reality of the world crept in, she recalled, with a snaking unease, that this was the first time they had dared to flout daytime rules.

'Before we go, I've got something for you,' Karl said, tucking his penis back inside his trousers. 'Something to make you think about me all day.' From his back pocket he withdrew a smooth, white oval attached to a string. Faren frowned. Whatever she might have guessed he had for her, it wasn't an egg. Sensing her disappointment, he laughed. 'You'll love this, little one. And it will love you. Believe me.' He sat back down beside her and gently parted her legs. 'Still so wet from our loving,' he murmured. He prised open the swollen lips and inserted the love egg, ensuring the string dangled. It promptly stuck to the damp slit and, satisfied, he pushed her legs together. As her vagina clamped the love toy, Faren gasped. Karl's hand slid between her thighs. His thumb rotated on her clitoris, then pushed in like a button switch until it met the hardness of the egg, stimulating her G-spot. She knew she was on the verge of her second orgasm. He wasted no time, keeping pressure and friction on her bud until she shuddered, exploding into her second, glorious release. When she was still at last, he chuckled, and playfully patted her damp fur. 'That's so you can think of me all day.'

'Well, spill, my girl! It all sounded terribly interesting on the phone.'

Faren tumbled into the luxurious passenger seat and yanked the door shut. Martine had wasted little time in responding to her request to meet; the little hint Faren had woven into the conversation was enough to have her boss cancel her appointment to have her legs waxed.

'Don't slam my door!'

'Sorry. Sorry,' Faren muttered, rearing up off the seat as the love egg jiggled and lodged near the mouth of her vagina. There was something so wicked, so sensuous, in feeding on secret ripples that were impossible to control, while conducting a conversation with one's employer.

Martine's elegantly shod foot depressed the accelerator, easing the BMW into the traffic. They headed towards the ocean. 'Never mind, we'll be there in a minute. Tell me then. I want to see your face!'

Faren laughed. The sheer joy of being out in the fresh air had her sinking into her seat, head thrown back, exposing her face to the sun. Then, to trigger the love toy, she wiggled her backside, and sighed as a delicious sensation waved through her. The stroll on the shore they would take held more promise; she might even come while looking innocently into Martine's eyes. She waited until the BMW was safely parked before she opened her eyes again.

'Shoot.'

Faren smiled. 'I've got proof.' While dressing this morning Faren made her decision to pass more information on to her editor. She had debated with herself, long and hard. Lord knew she wanted to keep quiet. Anything so she could remain at St Peter's, where the sea of young men consistently aroused her. However, the editor of *Splash!* was no fool. If Faren failed to be seen doing something, Martine's suspicious little mind would kick in. And she would demand results.

'Oh, Faren, you had proof last week.' Martine groaned, resting her brow on the steering wheel.

'Last week I had proof that a little hanky panky went

on amongst the ranks. Now, there's more. Ah ha, so now I've got your attention, Miss Danson,' Faren said when her boss slowly raised her head to look at her. 'Karl Sterling came up with an idea.'

When Karl had approached her at the end of their second lecture, Faren found herself seeking the support of the nearest wall. Propped against the granite, she listened, open-mouthed, to his plan. 'So, what do you think?' he asked, looking mighty pleased with himself.

Her mouth closed on a difficult swallow. Her eyes blazed. 'You want me to invite a friend in here?'

His palm came up to cover her mouth briefly, a silent warning that her reaction was too fierce and too loud, while he glanced about to see if they were being observed. 'Sounds good, huh?'

'You want someone else – someone I know – to join us?'

'That's right.' Karl cocked a brow. 'Why the surprise?'

'Oh, boy, don't label this a surprise. A shock is more like it.' And the cunning bastard had had this on his mind this morning. His body had pleasured hers, and yet not a word of the bombshell he was now exploding.

'Why a shock?'

Yes, why? she thought. You gave me a love egg and asked me to think of you, that's why. She had been nothing short of surprised at nearly every turn since the day she followed the wizened little priest up the stairs to her cell. Overtures she had geared herself to use had been unnecessary. From the first, Karl had played unwittingly into her hands. Dazed now, she shook her head. 'I don't believe this.'

He prised her from the wall where she seemed to have taken root. 'Come on, we'll talk on the way to class.' He stayed close by – as close as propriety allowed – and she was glad of that for she felt shaken. 'You can't be surprised,' he went on. 'Shocked, I mean.'

180

'Why can't I?' she snarled. Now she strode out, matching her steps to his, and felt the love egg moving inside, giving her pleasure, even as she wanted to bear down on it and expel Karl's betrayal.

'I thought you'd like the idea.'

'Maybe I will if you give me time to get used to it.' She brushed angrily in front of him, but his long strides did not allow her to outstep him.

'Have you got a friend you'd like to ask? Someone totally discreet, of course. Any holier-than-thou sort who would derive pleasure from squealing is out.'

She shot him a derisive glare. 'I'm not stupid, but I'm beginning to wonder about you.'

When he grabbed her elbow she was brought to an immediate halt. She cried out. 'Never, ever, underestimate me, little one,' Karl said quietly. He released her as quickly as he had lashed out and, though her flesh burned with his handprint, she stifled the desire to rub away the sting.

'I understand your concern,' she said sarcastically. He wanted to enjoy the clandestine encounters while holding on to his vocation. 'You took a risk with me, Karl.'

'Let's just say I'm a good judge of character.'

She wanted to smile. 'And you're prepared to take another risk to feed your colossal appetite?'

'If you want to put it that way, then yes.' They stopped outside a lecture room.

Names rolled through her mind. She nodded. 'I'd like some time to think about it before I approach anyone.'

'Of course,' he conceded. 'There is no room for error here. And some advice; test the ground first.'

That conversation was over two hours ago, and still she felt the injustice of it all. 'And then we went into lectures.' Faren watched her editor's fingers curl and uncurl about the wheel. When Martine finally turned and faced her,

her eyes shimmered with a dangerous light. After several moments under stiff scrutiny, Faren shifted in her seat.

'Shall we walk?' Martine suggested. This time Faren used her hip as leverage to close the door. Martine used her central locking mechanism, activated the car alarm with a chirp, and followed her. She slipped out of her stilettos and skidded down the bank, laughing. 'If I'd known I was going to play hooky today I'd have worn sandals. And by the way, for someone who said it would be difficult to get out, you're doing okay,' Martine commented, fighting with her hair. 'I'll be a bloody mess when I get back to town!'

Hot sand sifted through Faren's bare toes. 'Enjoy the sea breeze, Martine,' said Faren, gasping in the salty air as they walked towards the breakers and being reminded of her priest's defection with every step.

'Breeze? A hurricane more like it!' Martine grumbled.

'Well, I'm going to enjoy it. Simon has given me an hour off every afternoon.'

'Oh, aren't we the teacher's pet?' Martine teased.

'I have no idea why.'

Her boss regarded her intently, and Faren felt her cheeks redden. 'You've kept me in suspense long enough. So tell me. Then I intend to probe that other morsel of news.'

'As I said, I have proof.'

'Yes?' The woman's brown eyes gleamed, and Faren tossed round in her mind just how much she should reveal. Suddenly, she knew. Martine wanted everything. Every minute detail. And the mere thought of what Faren might divulge was enough to arouse her. 'Come on, Faren, don't be coy. Details! When you write up this piece there will be details.'

'Oh, no, I won't be putting all I know into copy. You wouldn't be able to print it.' That stopped Martine worrying about her hairstyle. Faren smiled.

'Really?' Martine asked eagerly. 'Christ, it must be dynamite.'

They were near the tideline now, and the pounding breakers drowned Faren's reply. She shook her foot to dislodge sand that had worked its way between her toes, feeling the little invader shift sensuously inside her as she did so.

'It's all masturbation, right?' And at Faren's sly smile, Martine shrieked. 'Oh, no! With each other? This is more than dynamite. It's nuclear bomb stuff! For Christ's sake, Faren, tell me!'

'Where to start? You know already that Father Karl teased me until I felt I would go crazy with wanting him.' But that he pleasured her beneath a perfect Sydney sky until she was driven wild with ecstasy; that was more difficult to confess.

'For God's sake, Faren. We're open-minded, twentieth-century women. We can talk about sex, can't we?'

With Martine's dark, penetrating gaze demanding all, Faren surrendered, realising her only option was to respond to her editor's entreaty. She dragged in a deep breath. 'OK. I've been ravished by the most delectable priests imaginable.' And some not so delectable she thought, when Father Mullahy came to mind. There, it was out now, and she heaved a sigh of relief. Each revelation should come easier now.

'Priests? Plural?'

'That's right. I'm going to tell you what happened, Martine,' Faren offered, 'then we'll get to Karl's most recent request.'

They halted near a crop of boulders, and both women sat, pulling their skirts high up along their golden thighs to take advantage of the sun. Faren propped herself up on her elbows, her breasts thrust forward, then she drew her legs up to enhance her pleasure. And began. 'There's Karl. And Drew, and Simon.'

'Father Murray?' Martine forgot about keeping her hair in place. 'The prim and proper guy?'

'That's the one.' Faren laughed, able only to see one inquisitive eye as Martine gazed between tangled strands. It was so nice to see Martine Danson dishevelled. 'Father Prim-and-Proper. But he's so nice.' She raked her own windswept hair from her eyes and secured it behind her ears so that she could gauge her editor's expression when the next mind-grenade hit. 'Then there's Father O'Connor and Father Mullahy.'

'Holy cow! Who in God's heaven are O'Connor and Mullahy?'

Chapter Fourteen

The powerful editor at the helm of *Splash!* magazine had always seemed unshakeable to Faren, dealing with copy on such diverse subjects as world famine and fraud, infidelity and despair. She thought never to see the day when anything that went on in the world would strike her boss with such potent fervour. Martine remained speechless, so Faren said, 'Thought you would enjoy the tale.'

Finally Martine exclaimed, 'Oh, my God, it's incredible.'

'And now Karl wants me to ask a friend to join him. Us. It knocked me for six, I tell you.' She lay back on the heated outcrop so that the pull of her muscles stretched provocatively through the length of her. She stifled a cry of pleasure – she was not about to share everything – as the love egg lifted with the stretch. Then, because her companion was silent for so long, Faren shifted her head to bring her into focus. 'I have one or two friends uninhibited enough to enjoy this situation. Though I think it would be unwise to let them know that the men are priests, at least until the last minute.'

'Oh, no, you don't!' Martine sat bolt upright and Faren

was startled when her shoulder was grabbed and she was pinned back down, her head taking a knock.

'You think it's too dangerous? It's the first thing that hit me,' she said nonchalantly, gazing into the woman's eyes. She had no intention of confessing to her boss that the first emotion to hit had been a flash of jealousy. Jealousy that Karl should want someone else. How could he be tired of her already?

'What I mean is, I'm the friend you will introduce.'

'What?' Faren's voice constricted in her throat. 'You?'

Martine's smile was sly. 'Of course. It's the logical solution.' But it was more than that; Faren could see it in her expression. 'Besides, why not? You want to have all the fun.'

Faren shook her head. She levered to sit up, but the small hand, still curled about her shoulder, held her down. 'And what could be safer? This way we'll be keeping it in the family, so to speak,' Martine said.

'Makes sense, I guess.' But how would she feel if Karl wanted to make love to them simultaneously? Would she be embarrassed, stripped bare in front of her editor? Despite the heat of the day, she felt a chill creeping along her spine. Could she do it? A strange tingle accompanied the thought of being with a woman. Faren gazed out to sea; the breakers that relentlessly pummelled the shore the only sound between them. What would it be like to touch a woman? This stylish, attractive woman?

Then Martine said, 'Now, don't tell me you'd be uncomfortable with my presence. No need to be. And it might be one-to-one. Though from what you've related, I somehow think your Father Karl has something far more ambitious in mind.' Martine paused. 'So, you'll tell him tonight?'

Faren was piqued that her editor made no attempt to hide her uncomely eagerness. Apparently the snap decision to volunteer was made as soon as Karl's proposition was revealed. 'I'll tell him.' Then she added, 'If I see him, that is.'

Martine smiled. 'Oh, you'll see him, all right. Bet my dandy job on it.'

The subject needed to be raised and, no matter how much she wanted to remain silent, Faren knew it was unethical to do so. She stood up, callously dismissing the dart of pleasure the jolted love egg gave her as she moved. She shielded her eyes to look at her boss. 'I thought you would pull me out. After all, I have the scoop. It's more than obvious how priests cope with celibacy. They –'

'Yeah, they don't,' Martine interrupted.

Puzzled, Faren ventured, 'So, why aren't you calling a halt? I have all the material I need.' She desperately wanted to recall those words, but it was too late. She told herself she need not worry; any intention she felt Martine might have of cancelling the assignment would be squashed, at least while an opportunity existed for a slice of the pleasure.

'One thing still puzzles me. OK. They use you.' Faren smarted at the idea but she let the older woman roll on unchecked. 'But what did they do when you weren't around? Oh, yes, the usual, of course. We suspected as much. But from what you've reported so far, it's all too pat. A man of the calibre of your Father Karl needs a woman.'

'So, I hang round and dig up more?'

'Naturally. I wouldn't dream of pulling you off this case until I have my little taste of heaven.'

Faren scowled. Enough. She needed to be alone with her thoughts. Not that thinking was going to change anything. Her editor wanted in, and Karl wanted another woman, so, no matter what she thought, it was destined to happen. Quickly she glanced at her watch. Despite a free half-hour looming before her, Faren decided to move. 'I'm off.'

Martine said, 'I have to get back as well. I'll give you a ride.'

Snatching at the opportunity she had wished for only moments before, Faren declined. 'I could use the walk.'

'Ring me when Father Karl arranges things. God, that sounds sexy. A priest.' Martine affected a shiver in her shoulders. 'I'll have to know the how and when. Don't forget now,' she called back over her shoulder.

'I doubt Karl would let me forget.' Hands clenched at her sides, Faren muttered, 'Nor you.' She watched Martine trudge back along the shore, taupe stilettos swinging by her side.

Several minutes later, when the BMW had sped off in a flash of red, Faren turned away. Head bowed, she waded through the fringe of water that brushed her toes. Without Martine and her demands, the beach held more appeal, she thought, squishing a string of seaweed with her big toe. It was only when a shadow overtook hers that she realised that she was not alone. She whirled round. 'Father Murray.'

'Sorry. I didn't mean to startle you.' His frank gaze held hers. 'Thought I'd walk to the next cove. Coming?'

'I'd like that, but I don't have the time.' Yes, she would very much like to be alone with Simon again. To hell with Karl. But as long as the love egg continued to make its presence known, she found it difficult to forget. Already her knickers felt damp, and she hoped Simon was going to do something about it.

He waited until she started towards him and, when she was near, he said, 'I'm granting you the time. Come on. There's a cave up here I'd like you to see. Or perhaps you know of it?'

She shook her head. Though she had lived in the city for several years and visited its beaches often, her steps always traced the tideline. Unlike most Sydney-siders – who were only happy when burnt to a crisp in the relentless sun – Faren visited the ocean to swim.

'Are you happy with us?' Simon asked, gazing ahead as though he preferred to view where he was headed, rather than look at her.

Faren took time to reflect, weighing happy against content. Surely to be content and satisfied in body did not automatically equate with happiness? She shrugged, wanting to delay her answer, hoping Simon was holding his breath. But if he was anxious for her reply, he made little show of it. 'Yes. I am happy.' And Faren realised the sentiment matched exactly how she felt. 'Lectures are invigorating,' she offered, feeling a swell of pride as she thought of her progress in ancient languages. And the nights are unbelievably erotic, she thought. What more could she ask? 'Nothing,' she murmured unwittingly to her mind's question.

'What?' Simon stopped and reached for her hand.

She turned and faced him. Her eyes swept from the tousled sandy hair to the toes that clutched at rubber thongs. Today he wore a minuscule bathing suit. It was black and silky and hugged his lean hips. It also hugged his bulge, which seemed to swell beneath her gaze. She lifted her eyes to his. For several seconds they stared at one another, then he turned inland, scattering a host of noisy gulls as he approached them. She chugged after him, her legs feeling weak and watery as the image of his bunched sex played tantalisingly through her mind. The love egg pressed heavily at the mouth of her sex, adding to her arousal. With each step, the swollen lips were stimulated. Then suddenly her footsteps seemed to lighten as she studied the strong contours of Simon's buttocks at each stride and the ripple of muscles as each leg drove forward. Faren's heart pounded, echoing in her throat, not altogether because of the pace of her gait. As her thighs brushed together they wreaked havoc; the love toy that seemed to pulse inside her ensured she thought of Karl, but then the previous night's memory of Simon's touch, and the unspoken promise of his presence, now

189

pushed the younger priest from her mind. And she knew just where she wanted Simon to touch again.

The cave was cleverly hidden behind jutting rock, its surface eroded by weather and time. Simon hunkered and then vanished. He called her name. She dropped on all fours to crawl in after him, felt the love egg heavy as it pressed near her opening and spread her lips. She sucked air through her teeth, then slipped her hand under her skirt. Her fingers slid beneath the elastic and she groped for the string. Her dew had caused the tail of the toy to be stuck. She peeled it away, shivering as it tugged at her. Quickly she hid the toy behind a rock, hoping she could get back to it before some child thought he had discovered treasure. Again, Simon's impatient command floated out of the cave. She scrambled in after him.

Once in, she sat back on her heels, brushed pulverised shell from her palms and scanned the cave. It smelled of damp silt and seaweed. 'Simon, this is great!' She bounded to her feet, absently swatted shell from her knees and turned to check out the cavern.

'I bet you figured dark and scary.'

'Oh, yes. And spiders and nasties.'

He laughed. 'Do you consider me one of the nasties?'

She lifted her chin, seeming to consider the question as she weighed every nuance of his smiling eyes, his twitching mouth. 'Prove otherwise.'

He produced a small amber vial. 'Challenge accepted.'

'Now, just where did you hide that, Father Murray?' She chuckled and made a show of glancing at the only piece of apparel he wore. It was as if her eyes caressed him, for he stirred beneath the narrow strip of silk. He reached out and touched her hair, brushing it aside, and his hand stroked along her jaw to her throat. She shivered.

'Come on. One relaxing massage for one uptight novice.' He was already tugging her further into the cave and, when her damp feet touched the cool, dry floor, she realised why. Wordlessly, he moved closer. He slipped one strap of her sundress from her shoulder, then bent and kissed the bare flesh, before sliding the narrow band down along her arms. His lips trailed along the satin softness of her throat, nudging beneath her proud chin to travel along her jaw. When he reached her earlobe – pausing to suck the tender flesh – her head dropped back, her moan guttural and intense. Her head was tilted in an invitation to her throat, and Simon's searching mouth kissed and sucked, giving swift nips here and there. His hand tugged her shoulder strap from where it rested on her sun-kissed skin, tugged it lower, and freed her breast. 'About that massage,' he said huskily, and he dragged her to the cavern floor.

She peered up at him and watched the thin oil pour from the bottle into his cupped hand, where it slurped, wet and seductive, as he rubbed his palms together. Inside she trembled, eager for the priest's touch. Her nipples were hard and aching in agonising anticipation of how that flesh-warmed oil would feel. She thought he was going to kiss her breast, but instead he took her cotton bodice in his teeth and tugged it down, easing her dress over her hips and down her legs, with little input from her, until he had it free of her body. He tossed it aside. The crotch of her panties was damp and she knew he could smell her. She wondered if he would peel them from her in the same seductive manner. Simon ignored them, and instead, his hands slipped easily across her ribs and up over her breasts, the frangipani-scented oil smooth and provocative as his fingers journeyed to the base of her throat and back down again over her breasts. Then he rolled her gently over. He straddled her and she felt the weight of his penis rest in the crack of her behind. His hands slid over each shoulder and down her arms, coming back up to massage the tight muscles of her neck, until Faren felt relaxed and special, worthy of his efforts. The heady fragrance of the oil on her heated skin filled her nostrils as it glided over bumps and planes, so slick, so smooth, and Faren's arousal soared, so that she longed for a more intimate touch. Then suddenly, as though that was enough of the light promise, Simon's touch firmed and he dipped to stroke the sides of her breasts then moved back up to tease along her spine once more. Thumbs and fingers rubbed sure and hard now, and his cock bumped rhythmically against her buttocks, her body moving with the momentum of the massage, her breasts pushing into the sand. He continued to stroke her until both his palms swept beneath her and his fingers burrowed into the sand to seek her nipples. She gasped as his fingers oiled each tip, fondling them to sensitive heights until she cried out, her pleasure reverberating through the chamber.

Simon flipped her over and stared at her breasts. She watched his deep swallow as his thumb brushed the sand-coated nipples. She moaned, and he lowered his head to nip at her throat before moving to the sweet skin of her breast. He suckled her mercilessly and she cried out as his tongue pushed the throbbing tip back, then sucked it back out again. Faren arched into him, urging her nipple further into his mouth, whimpering as she thrashed on the soft bed of the cave. Time and again Simon raised his head, coming up for air to kiss the tip of her nose or the corner of her mouth, running his tongue between her lips and into her mouth, before he slipped out to lap his way to the thrusting nipple once more. Her restless hips scooped a bowl in the sandy floor and she seemed to sink further away from the greedy mouth. Frustrated, Faren rested one shaky hand behind her lover's head, urging it closer to the distended nipple. In the cavern's stillness she listened to her own breathing – much more ragged than Simon's – but while half-crazy with the pleasurable sensations, she realised she was taking, giving nothing to him. But he moaned loudly as his mouth left her breast, and he kissed his way to her navel, his tongue dipping to tease and moisten the tiny hollow. When he blew gently, and the warmth of his breath dried the wet he had deposited in the seductive cup, she cried out in pleasure. 'Like that, do you?' he asked, and she felt his smile on her skin. Without waiting for a reply, Simon licked long strokes in an ever-widening arc across her tight belly, then blew gently; she knew the torture was deliberate in his slow journey to her secret place. Simon ripped at her panties, tugging them down over her knees. Then his fingers moved upwards again to burrow in her fur. She sighed as his fingers tickled and played, gently tugged to pull the skin and teased her clitoris with a stimulation that was maddening yet insufficient to bring her to exquisite release. In blatant invitation she spread her legs wide, and his finger crept down, skirted the stiff bud and inserted itself into her wet opening. With care, he probed inside her, then withdrew to play with the swollen lips, flicking on them while his mouth moved to her pelt and nuzzled, inhaling in one exaggerated breath the fragrant essence of her womanhood.

Faren's hand crept to the waistband of his swimsuit, but he veered away. She was puzzled at the slight. 'Your turn first,' Simon said huskily.

Her hand brushed through the sparse, pale hair on his chest, taking up the thin sheen of his perspiration. She inhaled deeply, savouring the sweet scent of desire. 'I need to touch you.'

'Soon.' Once again Simon's mouth sought her sex, his teeth nipping at the puffy lips, while he penetrated her with two fingers, driving and probing. Leisurely he explored her, and just when Faren thought she would scream with frustration, he thrust his tongue inside her and his thumb claimed that hard, aching nub. Then his knees shuffled either side of her as he moved away, but only for a moment, long enough to kneel between her parted thighs. He lifted her thighs, heavy and relaxed with passion, on to his shoulders and pressed his face into her moist pussy, his tongue dipping into her dark sheath then out to flick teasingly across the bud. With her heels pressed hard into Simon's back, Faren imprisoned his head, forcing him closer, wanting him to eat her, feeling his saliva seep between her buttocks and along her spine. Her legs taut and shaky, she reared suddenly, threatening to topple Simon, but his grip tightened, his nails digging into her behind as he strove to keep hold of her slippery flesh. With the beginnings of her climax, Faren pointed her toes, clenched her muscles, driving the sweet sensation to its pinnacle. Tremors racked her and she cried out, adding to the sensations that swept through her body but were centred at the very core of her, and then, as the energy of her climax faded, she collapsed, legs dangling uselessly over Simon's shoulders. Once every tingle had ebbed from her, Faren was aware of Simon lowering her to the ground, where he bent briefly to sup of her. When he lifted his head, his lips were glistening with her dew.

'Exhausted, sweetheart?' he asked. 'Not too exhausted for this, I hope?'

Faren lifted her gaze to find Simon's penis hovering near her face, wavering just below her dilating nostrils, as though daring her to take advantage and inhale his musky scent more fully. As he squatted over her, his cock was pressed against her nose, his balls squished against her mouth. Before she could put her tongue out, he moved away from her and flipped over on to his back, his penis aiming proudly at the ceiling, pointing to where blue slivers of sky shafted through rock.

Somehow Faren summoned the energy to push her body up; she dusted silt from her hands and knelt beside Simon. Her hair drifted across his naked belly, and she felt his stomach muscles contract beneath her splayed palm before she swished her hair about his erection. He groaned, digging his hands either side of him in a useless effort to grab hold of something firm. When she took him in her hands, she cupped the pulsating shaft and gently squeezed. It was thick and as hard as the rock that stood around them as the haven for their love play. She let him throb in her hands. Her fingers circled him as she pressed firmly round his stem before trailing up to the helmet of his sex, relishing the feel of the soft, silky tip of him. Each time she squeezed, Simon bit into his bottom lip, and on each squeeze, the tiny drop of fluid grew. She dipped her tongue to the slit and the fairy touch incited him, his body jerking, his cock prodding her mouth. Forcibly she shoved him back on to the sandy floor. Control was hers now. Simon was completely at her mercy, just as, minutes before, she was at his. The unspoken challenge showed in the tension of her limbs. The second time, she grabbed him roughly, and held him as her teeth grazed the head. The sudden wariness in his eyes imbued her with a tremendous sense of power. He is so vulnerable like this, she thought, and even though Simon communicated the intense pleasure derived from the sensation of her wet mouth on his cock, he was, perhaps – like men every-where – a little unsure of her teeth. His vulnerability excited Faren even more, and she felt the damp stickiness between her thighs. What would he do if I bit into his plum? she wondered, as a sadistic urge gripped her, fleetingly, before sanity reigned. If Faren were to shatter his trust in her, never again would he allow his cock to be encased in her mouth. Flicking her tongue along his organ, she paused to feel the throb of him, and cupped his testicles in her warm palms. She delighted in the tightness of the sac, in the smallness of the balls that seemed to shoot about as if they wanted to escape her rhythmic jiggling. Then she dipped her head, her mouth open to take him in, her fingers leaving the soft flesh of his balls to move round the base of his shaft and aid him in the right direction. She moved her head steadily up and down, sucking softly at first, then with as much suction as she could muster, pausing now and then to flick her tongue on the velvet plum, fighting to maintain the rhythm as Simon groaned and bucked beneath her. Simon's uncontrollable excitement encouraged and spurred his torturer on, and, as she felt his cock pulsate beneath her tongue, she opened her mouth wide, gently poking and prodding his balls until they, too, were encased in the warmth of her mouth. With a hand pressed to his stomach, Faren felt the rigid muscles fighting for control in a grand effort to stem his desire and hold back his climax.

Withdrawing his genitals from her mouth, Faren sat back on her heels. She relaxed her jaw and let her hand wander along the quivering shaft, pressing lightly with her fingertips. As soon as Faren observed a slight calming in Simon's breathing pattern, she dipped her head, letting her tongue lick round the swollen ridge, with cat-like satisfaction, noting the ragged panting of the man at her mercy. The reason women enjoy performing fellatio, she mused. Total power. The ultimate aphrodisiac. Oh, yes, Father Murray, in this position you are sapped of all power. The control is mine. This thought shafted a longing low in her belly, and she decided she did not wish to suck him off; today she wanted him to come inside her, where she would feel the release of his excitement. This was what power was all about. Bending another to one's will.

The warm air of the cave dried the moistness on his cock, and Faren spit on to her hand and rubbed it along his shaft. At the touch of lubrication, Simon went wild, animal-like noises emitting from deep in his throat as his fingers clawed vainly for a tangible hold and found none in his shifting bed of sand. He opened his eyes, a man in a tight sexual daze. And as Faren hooked a leg back over to sit astride him, Simon reached out to grab her swaying breasts. Lubricated with seeping love juice, they both gloried in the wetness round her buttocks, round the tops of Simon's thighs where she sat. Now she slid higher, spreading a trail of dew until she was poised above the straining cock. She lowered herself, picturing the spread lips ringing his cock, sucking him in, then reached for his balls, feeling the bunched rigidity of his desire. She gave them a light squeeze as she moved herself along his length, slowly at first, then, with Simon's hands splayed beneath her buttocks, she felt him lift her and hesitate before raising his hips and impaling her to the hilt. They found a rhythm, both of them grunting, sweat sheening on their naked bodies, her flesh slapping against his while her lovely priest writhed beneath her. She sustained the pace, until his hands left her hips and covered each oiled breast, slipping easily over them, and then she slowed, gasping. When he snagged her nipples between finger and thumb, he pinched them, and her cry comprised both pleasure and pain as relentless pressure was applied to each peak. She bent to kiss him and he caught her bottom lip and nibbled on it. Once released, Faren moved down his chest, blowing with deliberation on his skin, enjoying the deep groans each time her breath fanned his chest. Uncertain as to whether or not he liked his nipple sucked, she went ahead anyway, her lips closing round the pale disk, her tongue flicking the point of his nipple. It felt like a hard bead beneath the softness of her tongue, and Faren relished the taste of him, relished the sound of him as he moaned. She felt Simon flex inside her and, as he lifted his hips to link completely with her again, she began to ride him once more, thumping down on him, feeling the dampness where they joined, the spread of her lips at the base of his shaft. The teasing was over, and, sensing her lover's impending climax, Faren searched for her own, grinding her pubic bone to his, stimulating her clitoris, igniting waves and spasms that began deep within her and flowed over the whole of her. Her contractions grasped the cock that was creating such delicious torture and triggered Simon's own release. Just as she felt him come, Faren reached behind her and pushed her index finger into the base of his shaft, as though this would help his seed to rise and add further to Simon's enjoyment. Together they sang out, Faren reaching the highest of peaks, her legs shaking, feeling his legs trembling as he shuddered deep inside her.

In sheer exhaustion, she collapsed on top of him. Her cheek stuck to his chest. She breathed in the smell of salt and sex, frangipani essence and sweat, a heady mix that triggered a small contraction, and one that she knew Simon felt, because he groaned and flexed inside her. As the last pulse settled round her, idly she twirled her finger round Simon's perfect nipple. He groaned, and his penis remained predictably unresponsive. She smiled smugly to herself. Simon Murray was sated. For the moment.

Chapter Fifteen

Karl watched her from an upstairs window as she hunched into the wind, her dress sticking fast against every curve of her body. How he wanted her! In all his sexual encounters, he had never wanted a woman as much as he wanted this one. Which was why he had suggested she find a third party to join the nocturnal trysts. There was no place in his life for one woman and the only manner in which he could dilute his lust for this one was to spread it around many. In the confessional he took his turn at being relieved, but that was the crux of the matter: relief. No more than that. His colleagues survived the celibate dictum by being sucked off, their cocks stuck through a crude hole in the wall of the confessional box. Part of the absolution of parishioners' sins. He laughed harshly. What a joke! Invented to appease man's natural urge. The natural right to orgasm in someone's – other than their own – hands. Karl needed more. He needed to touch the malleable flesh of a woman, to stroke and kindle her fire, to have her respond to him as a man. While he delighted in each tongue that probed the eye of his cock, in the lips that circled his flesh, sucked him dry and then swallowed his come as

199

he knelt in the confessional, still there remained something cardinal that Karl himself failed to define: his need to bring fulfilment to a sensual woman. He was an arrogant beast, powerful and immoral, so why then did he – egotistic animal – care about a woman's needs in the sexual act?

Near the ringed garden-bed he watched Faren pause. She squatted to smell a profusion of scarlet impatiens, and Karl smiled, immediately thinking of the love egg that he had placed inside her that morning. The strength of her thighs as they took her full weight would ensure that the toy moved to her opening, and he thought of how her sex would now be straining to hold it inside her. His cock began to stir, his heartbeats to quicken. 'Christ!' he swore, aloud. He had to halt these emotional responses of his. That was the foremost reason he had suggested she introduce a friend. Already acting out of character, it was not in his nature to ask anyone – least of all a sexual partner – to produce another playmate. Proud and entirely resourceful, Karl was capable of producing his own partners. His purpose was to inflict pain on Faren. Not physical pain – that she would dispassionately cope with – but emotional pain; he wanted to hurt her emotionally. All in the name of armour. If left to the natural way of emotions and sensations, as inconceivable as it may have seemed in the beginning, the two lovers might come to mean more to each other than was wise. So, Karl admitted ruefully, by forcing Faren to produce a friend, he would be telling her, albeit subliminally, that there was no future for emotions in their love play.

Karl moved quickly along to the library. He had no wish for Faren to discover him skulking in his room, awaiting her return. Once seated in the furthermost corner, alone at the study table, Karl felt the stirring of an erection. Earlier, he had successfully quelled the signal that had shot right to his cock, but now, amidst the serenity of the book-lined room, a vision of Faren forced its way into his mind, and his curled serpent responded to its call. He yanked a volume towards him and stared unseeingly at the black text, trying to tempt his focus. But it was too late for that. His arousal escalated to a throbbing ache and the rigidity became more pronounced between his thighs. He tossed the book aside. What he had to do was to appease his aching body.

But for his tightly bunched arousal, Karl would have sprinted to the church. Good, he thought, entering quietly; no priest. However, on their knees in front of the altar, two young ladies paid homage. Karl's mouth twitched. He was in luck. Dispassionately, he watched one worshipper draw the sign of the cross and rise. 'Sally,' he called.

The girls gave startled cries. The pretty redhead, bolder than her friend, peered into the shadows. 'Father,' Sally said, sashaying over to the priest.

'Any sins to confess today?' Karl asked, his heartbeat thundering in his ears as he watched Sally thrust her pert little breasts towards him for optimum temptation. As her naughty little tongue snaked out and slid along her top lip, Karl's erection throbbed, his trousers cutting across the sensitive flesh. With the folds of his cassock, his arousal was adequately covered, unimportant though that was. Sally and her friend Jean knew the score, and were only too eager to service him.

The redhead's eyes gleamed. 'I'm sure I could think of something, Father Karl,' she demurred. Then she grinned and turned to her friend. 'What about you, Jean? Any sin you want to confess?' They shared a conspiratorial laugh.

A second check showed the confessional to be free, and Karl lifted the black curtain that draped across the rear of the box, while Sally entered from the aisle. In recent years, some ingenious priest had designed an accommodating hole in the plywood partition, a hole large enough to allow the most endowed of men to thrust his cock through to the other side. The circumference of

201

the cavity was lined with midnight blue velvet to deflect painful injury to a man's treasure by any rogue splinters or rough edges left from the cutout. On the other side where the sinners sat, a black veil of cloth obscured the hole. Only those in the know ever pulled the slip-cord at the side to reveal the secret behind. Now, as he heard a shuffle in the booth, Karl gazed through the latticed frame that separated priest from parishioner, and saw that Sally had opted to be first. Who wished to pleasure him first was unimportant, as long as he had some clever hands sliding over his throbbing member.

'Ready, Father Karl,' Sally whispered.

At last, he thought, heaving a grateful sigh as he lifted the voluminous folds that tangled with his legs, and then unzipped his pants to let his cock spring free. With it stuck through the hole, Karl found it more comfortable to kneel, whereas others might have squatted. It all depended on getting the right height. He heard the giggling. He closed his eyes, the sensation of waiting for the touch of magic fingers and soft lips devastatingly erotic. Like being blindfolded, not knowing where and what might touch.

The cock-hole – as it was aptly known to the privileged men of St Peter's – was a marvellous, if primitive, invention. It was not to be derided, for it had saved many a young priest's sanity. And the sanity of those not so young. But Karl, confident that he could improve on the unsophisticated operation, was already hatching plans in his mind of a more practical enterprise, that of a secret door through which to slip an eager young woman to the unused room known as the priest's hole. Here a man and woman could fully enjoy each other's bodies. Fellatio was a firm favourite of his, but there were times when he wanted to sink his hard penis into a warm woman. Until then, this hole was an exciting substitute.

Expert hands were fluttering along the length of him, tickling just beneath the sensitive ridge, so that he sucked on his lip to prevent himself from calling out. With his cock on one side of the wall, and the rest of him on the other, he seemed detached from the sensual strokes on his most sensitive part, and yet all the pleasure focused there. Rocked by the sudden sexual blast when feminine fingers gripped him, this time Karl neglected to stifle his groan.

'Forgive me, Father, for I have sinned.'

Sally giggled, but even that silly noise failed to sever his fierce and pleasurable concentration. With her hand still working him, Sally touched her tongue to the head and moistened the whole silky helmet, making him shudder. Then the softness was gone, and cool air caressed him, quickly drying the wetness deposited by Sally's tongue. The air seemed to tighten his skin, adding further pressure and sensation to his engorged penis. 'Talk to me,' he said huskily. Nothing fazed Sally, and Karl pictured her nonchalant shrug. A proven expert at fellatio, he suspected she pleasured all the priests. She set out to please him.

'You are rock hard. And warm,' Sally said. 'No. Hot. That's what you are, Father. Burning hot. Ready for me. And though it's a mite dark in here, I can just see the bubble on the slit of your cock. Shall I lick it off for you, Father?'

Karl hissed in his breath. 'Jesus!'

'Would you like me to lick your cock?'

He groaned loudly in response to Sally's rhetorical question, while continuing to move within the aperture in the wall, but there was nothing tangible round his penis, nothing sheathing it. Sally could not take him in her mouth while she was talking to him, but she could touch him. 'Touch me!' he commanded. And Karl jerked as cool fingers danced along his throbbing prick.

'I like your smell,' Sally said. 'It's sexy.' He heard her sniff. 'Musky.' All the while, nimble fingers slipped along his rod.

Breathing hard, Karl spread his thighs wide and reached round and pressed a finger just behind his balls, moaning loudly at the intensified sensation that added to his pleasure as Sally's hand pumped him. 'Are you wet for me?' he asked, his voice strained, as he felt the wetness of her luscious mouth replace her fingers and close firmly round him. 'Are you?' It was impossible for her to answer him, he knew; her mouth was full of cock.

Seconds later, when Karl exploded into the soft mouth, he felt his seed coat the young woman's tongue, imagined his come shooting down the back of her throat. This image incited another incredible burst, and another, until every shuddering spasm was spent. Finally, his orgasm fading, he gulped air into his heaving lungs. His head flopped forward against the wall. Stupid woman, thought Karl, listening to the giggle that was more suited to a teenager than the woman in her twenties he knew Sally to be. A few moments later he summoned the scrap of energy needed to pull away so that his penis slithered out of the hole. He sat back on his heels.

Conscious of a small voice calling him, Karl looked up, and saw the pretty face, with its smattering of carroty freckles, peering through the lattice. 'Do you want to watch me, Father?' Her nose was twitching and he knew she was sniffing the scent of sex.

He said, 'Get Jean.' At that, Sally pouted, and, conscious that she wanted his attention on her alone, he added, 'I want to watch you together.' There was nothing more infinitely erotic than watching two women having hot, lusty sex, Karl thought, as he tucked his cock back into his trousers.

The dark curtain slid aside and Sally's friend joined her in the small booth. Though only one person at a time entered to confess sins, there was adequate space to house two petite women such as Sally and Jean. He watched Sally slip her hand beneath her friend's mini skirt and imagined it groping through the girl's scented bush. He was able to see Jean spread her legs in the standing position, but her pussy was hidden from view, the disappearing hand perhaps more erotic than seeing her naked. The piston action that moved the hem of the girl's skirt, accompanied by soft gasps and a sweet smell which melded with the fragrance already in the air, made Karl wish he could finger the succulent flesh himself. But the partition made that desire impossible. Resigned to his role as spectator, he was settling himself for the show when his watch beeped.

Hefting himself to his feet, he swore. 'Time's up, girls.' Amidst the groans and curses of the women, Karl chuckled. They loved performing. Every time he watched them, he became aware that it was no trumped-up desire for his benefit and that the intense ardour generated in that booth was solely between the participants. 'You might get lucky next time,' he called over his shoulder at the scowling faces. He laughed, his prick snuggled and content, as he strode from the church.

It was over an hour later that Karl found the chance to accost his superior in his office. He ploughed right in. 'Simon, I need your permission to refurbish the room next to the confessional.' After leaving the cramped quarters of the confessional, Karl had begun to fume, thinking again of his plans, plans brought on by his feelings of degradation at having to insert his penis through the cock-hole in the cubicle partition. Never before had he felt this way. Normally, with most of his body on one side, while his erection protruded on the other, he found the game stimulating and highly erotic. The feeling pervaded but one was apart from it, somehow. Lately he had become preoccupied with notions of setting up a room with equipment that would show his fellow priests enjoying their fantasies. If it had been at all possible, he would have gone ahead without Simon's consent, but the volume of noise that would undoubtedly resound throughout the church during renovation would attract his superior's attention, if not immediately, then at least at some stage during its construction. Still, Karl realised now that he need not have feared the vetoing of his plans. Murray enjoyed the pleasures of the flesh just as much as he did.

There was the squeak of leather as Simon leaned back in his chair. 'You are telling me the priest's hole is lacking in its ability to satisfy our men?' he asked, distractedly scratching his chin.

Karl shook his head, knowing Simon referred to the hole in the confessional, not the small adjoining room. Whenever discussion became necessary it served as an adequate code. 'I don't mean that at all. It's satisfactory.'

'What is the problem then?'

'Why settle for "satisfactory" when we could have "highly pleasurable"?' Karl shifted in his seat, leant insolently over the desk and faced Simon squarely. 'I have an idea that will double the list of applicants for St Peter's.' He smiled, riling Simon right on cue, unable to resist needling the usually placid priest.

'For God's sake, man, we don't want to double it! The Vatican has already faxed me on the unusually high waiting list. They wanted me to confess St Peter's little secret – their phrase – so every other seminary could implement it!' At the end of his speech, Simon fired his pen across the desk. Both men watched it slide across the polished surface and topple to the floor.

'Knew you'd bite, old man,' Karl said lazily, relaxing back in the chair. Crossing his legs at the ankle, he surveyed Murray with a grin. How he loved to stir! 'It's not my intention to encourage any more young bucks to wheedle their way into St Peter's.'

'Some hint of what we're up to must have leaked out. Any more, and we'll have Bishop Latterly snooping round.' Simon's annoyance at being deliberately fired up by one of his minions was echoed by the tight set of his jaw, and Karl laughed. 'We can't have that. You can kiss our little gratification programme goodbye. Since its inception, there have been zero defections. It's the only way to compensate our men, and it's about time this was widely recognised.'

While Simon preached his little sermon, Karl mentally zipped through his own. He had never seriously believed Murray's opposition; he dealt with his guilt and then got on with the pleasure. Now it boiled down to available funds. Getting back to his original spiel, Karl explained. 'A room. A special room,' he emphasised, relinquishing his air of relaxation. 'Any number of your flock would be happy to volunteer their carpentry skills,' he argued, pleased to see the priest's eyes glinting with the possibility of acquiring free labour. Which in turn exempted him from having to account for the expenditure.

Simon chuckled. 'Got to hand it to you, Sterling. But –' he added, '– what about materials?'

'Already thought of that. Joe Melbury down the road. More than once the man has offered to make a donation of prime timber to St Peter's. And it's not that we'll need all that much.'

Simon nodded, admiration clear in his voice as he spoke. 'Looks like you have it all worked out, Sterling.'

'The priest's hole can be extended into the storeroom beyond. It will give us a tidy enough room. Sufficient for a few props.'

'And they will be what?'

'Anything we like. Anything to enhance pleasure. For the women as well, of course. Mirrors, definitely. They are always a big hit.' Karl gave a lazy smile.

Simon gazed back at him, obviously pondering a point. 'Right. Permission to go ahead.'

Karl got to his feet. He wanted to laugh out loud but wisely checked himself. Once he was at the door, Simon's command stopped him. 'Yes?' he said, looking back over his shoulder.

'These props. You'll make sure they are unrecognisable to the workers?'

'Grant me with some sense, Simon, please.'

'Karl, I don't have to tell you how careful we must be.'

'No, you don't.' So why the hell was the man doing just that? Murray had been humping the Cheaters woman for months, and he was not the only one who would suffer, should this leak. Since Faren had joined the Order and filled his thoughts – and his bed – Karl was not about to risk losing her.

'One other thing, Karl.' Yet again Simon called a halt to Karl's departure. 'Women. Where are we going to find them?'

'Leave it to me.'

'Did you manage it? You know,' he said, as she frowned. Karl's gambit was badly received, and, amused, he watched her flush. He sensed her confusion. She's wondering why she's not enough for me, he thought, holding Faren's gaze until she had no option but to look away. 'I'll come to your room.' At her brisk acquiescence, Karl felt his tension drain away. He had expected more of a fight.

Following in her wake, his lips twitching as he watched the sway of her hips, he thought: God, if any of the senior priests knew what Faren's rear did to the St Peter's contingent, they would have her out of here before those twin moons could corrupt any more priests. Away from where novices could feast and follow like panting dogs. Karl mused now at Simon's negligence, his lack of judgement, in failing to isolate Faren for his exclusive use. Maybe, Karl thought with a quiet snigger, the Cheaters woman was keeping Simon so tied up that he had no time to appreciate Faren's wares. Simon's loss, my gain, he affirmed with a smirk, as he reached her door.

Knowing it would be unlocked, that Faren had entered

only moments ahead of him, he turned the handle and slipped inside, closing the door gently behind him. She was fiddling with an assortment of glass and plastic paraphernalia that cluttered her dresser. OK, he thought, if this is the way you want to play it. He said, 'When is she coming?'

'Karl!' Faren whipped round, slamming a small bottle down on to the dresser top.

He shrugged. 'It didn't seem to me as though you wanted small talk. So, if this is disturbing you, let's get it over with. Then we can get on with what we both really want.' He watched the stubborn little chin lift a fraction in that haughty action that made her so adorable to him. You are a worthy partner, little one, Karl mused. And if this were the real world, we would make a hell of an act. But any sentiments down that road were detrimental to what they shared here. And this was why he had to show Faren there were no exclusive rights to him. 'Would you care to answer my question?'

Faren lifted her head and he noticed the fighting glint in her eyes. 'You asked me if I could get someone. You gave no instructions as to when and how.'

'Ah. You are one of those inept females who need a distinct line to follow or else you get lost?' Karl shook his head. 'Uh-uh. I think not, my dear.'

Suddenly her Douay Bible sailed through the air and whacked his left shoulder, its rigid corner grazing the side of his neck before it landed on the floor with a thump. 'Such disrespect, Faren,' he grunted, rubbing his neck. Before he had time to gauge what assault she might try next, she flew at him, lips drawn back in a snarl, claws ready to ravage. He grabbed her wrists. He thought he could stop the small teeth that attempted to bite him by spreading her arms, keeping her body from touching his, but he was too late; a sharp prick punctured his thumb. 'Why, you little wildcat!' he roared. He yanked her arms above her head.

As her struggles became weaker, Karl's mouth sought hers, first with animal lust, then with gentleness. Her response was immediate, as Karl had known it would be. He groaned as she pressed her body into his, her belly rubbing seductively against his rigid cock. He brushed her lips with his, then pushed the black fabric of her cassock down over one shoulder, kissing along her collarbone, and pausing to feel the rapid pulse beat against his lips. He kneaded her breast out of its cup and freed the nipple, squeezed it between finger and thumb until she moaned. With his hand riding up her skirt, he caressed her thighs, smiling at the realisation that at last she wore no panties. But his fingers were busy now, playing about in her velvet sex, reaping her dew. She was already endeavouring to ride his hand when he stopped her and held her away. His finger popped out. He held it up so that both of them could see the glistening wetness. 'Very wet, my dear,' he said, his voice husky. He brought his finger to his nose and inhaled deeply.

Once he had dropped to his knees, he pushed her cassock up to bare her breasts, and kissed along her ribcage and down over her hips. The scent of her was different. More than soap and female. And then he knew. Grabbing her by the arms he shook her. 'Tell me which priest you were with today. You were, weren't you?' Yelling at her, he saw a flash of guilt in her expression.

'It's none of your business!' Faren struggled, tried to manoeuvre those sharp teeth again, but Karl was too quick and grabbed her by her elbow.

'Which priest have you had now? And if I am not mistaken, which I know bloody well I'm not, how long ago did you have him?' Karl's breath rasped through his teeth as he shook her. Christ! How could she do this to him? Part of Karl's anguish came from the fact that he had omitted to detect it on her during dinner. They had come straight from the dining room, so it had happened before then. In the midst of his wrath Faren's courage fuelled his desire as he watched her eyes narrow, her lips set. 'Who, Faren?' He gritted his teeth. Drew Edmonds had taken her, so why this feeling of betrayal now? Was it Edmonds, doing a little sniffing on his own? No, he very much doubted that; these days the spineless creature spent a lot of time in Mary's side altar, lighting candles and praying for his soul. So, who? he wondered.

Faren looked him square on when she said, 'Simon. I was with Simon.'

'Murray!' She could not have winded him more if she had aimed a punch to the gut, and he suspected she would love to do just that. 'I don't believe you.'

Faren glared, wrenching free of him because his grip had loosened on hearing Murray had taken his girl. 'Believe what you want, Karl Sterling! And what's it to you, anyway?'

Yes, he wondered, what was it to him? He did not have the monopoly on her, and he had shared her willingly with Edmonds. So why did he balk at Murray? Because Murray was of a different calibre, and the senior priest's eyes had always feasted firmly on Rosemary Cheaters. Now it seemed those blinkers were lifted and he had found Faren. 'Where did he fuck you?' he asked, gripping her upper arms and shaking her. Karl found it difficult to devise times during the day to ravish Faren. Eyes were everywhere. But Simon Murray, in his position of seniority, would find it effortless.

'Do you mean where, as in locale? Or where, as in relation to which orifice?' Faren said with feigned innocence as she prised herself loose.

'Don't be crude, Faren, it doesn't suit you.' He moved towards her again but she held her ground.

'And how do you know what suits me? You don't know me, Karl, no matter what you think. You've used me. Like you want to use me now.'

'And don't you just love it!' Karl shucked his robe then reached for his belt, pulling it smoothly through the loops

211

of his trousers. The rasp of his zip was loud. 'Touch me,' he demanded, and she hesitated. 'Touch me,' he said softly. She obeyed him, and his penis sprang to life, throbbing and straining so hard that it seemed he might burst. He kissed her bare shoulder and inhaled a hint of frangipani. She smelled of the sea and the sand; he knew where she had lain. As his lips brushed her throat, Karl's fingers combed through the damp curls between her thighs, releasing the exotic, sexual fragrance. 'Like that, do you?' he asked as Faren relaxed into him, pushing her mound against his hand. Karl felt the ache in his loins as he bore her to the floor. Then he was tearing at her clothes.

When Faren was naked he parted her legs with his knee, then straddled her. He needed her so badly he could barely think, and was about to plunge in when he remembered; he hesitated, his shaft quavering at her damp entrance. 'The love egg. Better remove it.' He rained wet kisses over her face as he backed away from her, his hand fiddling in her dampness in its search for the string.

'It's out,' she said.

For long moments their eyes held, then he swallowed painfully in an attempt to obliterate visions of twining bodies on the shore, of grit clinging to sweat-soaked skin. He shook his head, denying the smarting behind his eyes, the lump in his throat. He lined up his prick, heavy and aching, with the soft, sweet target and plunged in with one long stroke. He groaned as Faren sighed in his ear. 'OK?' he asked between lunges, loving the slap of their sweaty flesh, their undulating bellies, his darker fleece and her paler one mating in the friction of their passion. 'I mean –' Karl said as she gazed back '– is your back being rubbed raw on the floor?'

'No. No.' She grunted and arched fiercely into him. 'Now shut up and keep going!'

Her sex squeezed his cock, the exquisite sensations

wiping the smile from his face. Each time she clenched him, he groaned. He continued his thrusts, feeling and loving the heat that sheathed him, the wetness that clung. He bucked when he felt Faren's fingers creep round and explore the cleft of his backside, moaned when she moved further along to press the sensitive spot at the base of his rod. God! This woman knew how to handle him. 'Christ, what are you doing to me?' he growled, but as the sensation began to overtake him the pressure withdrew and her hands climbed to his shoulders. Karl could think of better places for those skilful fingers.

With strength Karl was only partially aware of, Faren toppled him, and suddenly she was straddling his hips. 'Now I've got you,' she said, and, to prove her point, her muscles clenched him, waging their knowing torture, winning this sexual war, as she slowly moved along his length, almost letting go of his cock.

He reared, aiming for his target, but she was just out of reach, teasing, tormenting him. He ached for her. He wanted to embed his cock inside her and never come out. When Faren moved closer to his tip, he gripped himself, making contact with her cunt, stroking along her channel, nudging her clitoris. She groaned and moved her hips, and Karl felt her softness against his shaft. But he needed to be fully sheathed, so he lunged, and his throbbing cock was immediately sucked into her tunnel. She was hot and tight, and he raised his hands to cover her breasts and squeezed, leaving finger marks in the smooth globes. With Faren on top, Karl felt restricted, though he could rotate his hips. As she whimpered, he dropped one hand to seek her clitoris, burrowing through his pubic hair and hers to where he found the hard nub and rolled it between his fingers until she cried out. Her gyration on his hand became more frantic until there was no leeway left for stimulation. He let her own movements bring her to climax. Karl bucked beneath Faren as he felt the clutch of her pussy round his shaft, and, wanting his own release, he lunged, then withdrew. When she held him steady with one hand and pounded down on to him, the force of her hot sex spreading and encompassing him was more than he could bear, and he cried out. Sexual sounds heightened his pleasure and the bouncing, the slick sounds, and the pumping of his cock, drew his climax on. Any hope of prolonging it to please Faren once more was long gone as he tensed, then shuddered deep inside her.

Chapter Sixteen

*F*aren buried her face in his hair, rocking her lower body until Karl eased open his legs. Once insinuated there, she began squeezing his limp penis between her thighs, smiling when he groaned loudly in her ear. The scent of their recent coupling was a heady stimulant, and Faren ground against him, certain that his penis would respond. Karl, unfortunately, was bushed, managing only a half-hearted jerk upwards. She sighed and snuggled into him, a finger drifting lazily over his nipple.

'Come to me, tonight,' Karl whispered, his breath tickling her throat, his fingers playing along her spine. 'I need to be with you. Stay with me.'

She sat up smartly. 'It's far too dangerous, Karl.' But something pleasurable coiled inside her. Was her priest mellowing? Was there something more than lust? But if there was something special between them, then why was he demanding a *ménage à trois*? So he could attain more pleasure? They had formed such a tryst with Father Drew, but this time Karl wanted another woman. It would take the focus from her – something which she found difficult to come to terms with – although just now he had sounded as though he cared.

As if Karl realised he was in danger of throwing off his cavalier attitude as easily as he shed his priestly robes, he pushed Faren aside and leapt to his feet. He paced to the door, presenting his back to her. Her eyes swept the line of his tight, sleek buttocks and her insatiable need stirred at the sight of him, so that she itched to take hold of each tight moon.

Faren stood up and went to him, her fingers gripping his hips, her teeth grazing the sweetly scented skin of his back where sweat vied with his own unique smell. She fell to her knees, and felt the clench of his behind beneath her lips as she scraped her teeth across the taut skin, her right hand reaching to the front, seeking his half-erect penis. She smiled as she felt him grow stiff in her palm. All the while Faren nipped, moving nearer to the cleft that divided his buttocks, sticking out her tongue as she approached her mark. When her fingers prised him open, Karl's body relaxed and her tongue slipped in, the thin line of dark hair brushing her lips. Without hesitation she tongued along the cleft, skimming the tight rose, which twitched each time she touched it. She halted long enough to gasp, 'Bend over, Karl. Let me see all of you.' When he did so, she released his cock, now stiff and rock-hard as ever, to play with his testicles which she glimpsed from behind. She played her thumb over the fine dusting of hair. Faren's heart was pounding; the thrill of seeing him so intimately open to her sent shivers down her spine, as if it were days, instead of minutes, since her last orgasm. She parted her thighs so that the air teased her skin, imagining Karl's tongue sliding along her slit. Now Faren's deep-throated groan mingled with her lover's, despite her knowing the only touch she felt existed in her mind's eye. Expertly she continued to massage him, tonguing the back of his thighs and the tight skin of his buttocks.

Suddenly Karl wrenched away and she glanced up, wide-eyed, as he turned to face her. It seemed all Karl wanted was to touch her face, to kiss her, which he did, so sweetly. He stroked one breast as he deepened his kiss, and she parted her lips, and felt his tongue slide inside. She sighed as he pressed his body into hers. She felt his breath warm in her ear when he spoke. 'I'm going to taste your sweet skin. Lick you until you beg for mercy, stick my tongue inside you.' He rained kisses along her throat, rocking back and forth, letting his penis lightly touch her belly. 'But first I want to kiss you from head to toe.' By the time he reached her feet, Faren was whimpering; her skin was damp and tingly. 'Now that I've gorged on your toes, I'll tongue my way back up until I find the treasure. And I shall nibble there until you come.' Faren groaned, Karl's words having ignited the warmth between her thighs into a fierce blaze, the images he so skilfully wove with his cunning words and his busy mouth making her throb in anticipation.

Faren stretched out on the floor to allow Karl to fulfil his promise. His tongue flicked along every fold, every crevice, probing her sex until she writhed and clawed. Just when she felt she might come, Karl's exploring tongue slowed and became sensually inquisitive. A light flick here, feather touch there. She relaxed into him, the softer side of her priest prominent, as he caressed and suckled, his hands tender on her belly, on her breasts, her ribs, his gentle fingers stretched to encircle her nipples. Quivering, she neared her climax, the thought of her release right there against his mouth an added aphrodisiac that spun fire into her loins.

Then suddenly Karl clasped her waist and swung her round so that she straddled him. 'Fuck me, little one.'

She thought it impossible to blossom still further, but, with his coarse word, it was as if some electrical pulse crackled through her, distending her already swollen sex. Deft movements had her lifting her rear to poise above him in a tease, tormenting them both before she sank down on to his cock. As she welcomed him inside her, she cherished the width and length of him, listened to the hiss of air being sucked through his teeth, and smiled in quiet endorsement of her feminine power. She watched Karl's expression, knowing he was looking down to where his sex disappeared inside hers. With practised ease she held herself halfway along his cock to give him a better view before she slid down again. He groaned like a man in pain, and she realised how very erotic it was to watch the actions of sex, damp curls tangled so they appeared as one. And as she slipped up and down upon the tumescent flesh, sometimes wild, sometimes tame, into Faren's mind swirled a vision so vivid that she caught her breath; that of another woman straddling her man. She would not share him with Martine! 'Damn you, Sterling,' she gritted, each word punctuated with a downward drive as she landed at the base of his prick. 'You asked for it. Now you're going to get it.' If he heard her, he made no sign. Only deep groans slipped from his half-opened mouth.

The moment she lifted one leg over him to hop off, his cock slid out of her. The priest's eyes flew open. He gripped her thigh. But she was merely changing position, wanting him to watch her from behind, and Karl sighed as soon as she took hold of his sticky cock and guided it back inside her. Then she cheekily scratched the crimped flesh of his balls until he jerked his hips, begging her to ride him again. The primitive animal sounds coming from her lover suggested that he was near his climax, and that for once his concentration focused solely on his own gratification. With each grunt he rose to meet her. Beneath her palms she felt his hard thighs tremble. Quickly she removed her right hand and her fingers homed in on her clitoris. She rubbed along the small shaft, craving further stimulation so she could explode in unison with Karl's climax. Her teeth clamped her bottom lip and she tasted blood. Then, just as she felt him shudder inside her, she clenched her muscles, urging her own pleasure to expand and encompass the whole of her. Encouraged by the intensity of her release, she felt Karl jerk beneath her in several wild spasms. She felt the tension flow from his limbs, his thighs losing their rigidity, seeming to relax in an instant. Then he was still.

With her palms on his knees she flopped forward, knowing that the curve of her spine and her rounded bottom would present Karl with an enticing view. She felt his hands come up to caress her smooth globes before a probing, inquisitive finger explored the underside of her pussy, and she smiled against his thighs. 'Still want someone else along, Karl?' she said, unable to keep the smugness from her tone.

Karl's reply was nothing more than a growl as he clasped her round the waist, and lifted her as he stood. She shrieked when he flopped back on to the bed, dragging her with him. While Karl dozed, she relaxed with the comforting steady rise and fall of his chest. His penis came to life before he did, and Faren squirmed against him, knowing the exact moment he became conscious of his own arousal. He began nibbling her ear, then sucking the lobe into his mouth, before pushing it out again with his tongue and blowing gently. She trembled, craving the foreplay, knowing she could suffer his brand of teasing all night. But then he stretched down to pluck something from the floor, nearly toppling her until his arm shot out, steadying her. At the strange noise she turned, looking over her shoulder, watching him peel the foil top from a pot of yoghurt she had left standing in a bowl of iced water. 'That's my midnight snack, Karl!' she grumbled.

Without a word he pulled himself out from beneath her. Lounging against the bed he announced, 'You're my midnight snack, sweetheart. Get on all fours.'

With Karl's prodding, Faren took up the position of moments before, arching her back so the underside of her sex was plainly on view. She watched him dip a finger into the tub of creamy yoghurt and hold it up for her to see. She felt the insistent throbbing again, knew she was wet and had no need of yoghurt or anything else to lubricate her.

Karl hopped back on the bed and knelt behind her, between her legs, while she waited for the creamy finger to penetrate her. She felt her buttocks being prised open and then felt the coolness of his finger trail down the crease. She shivered; it was a delicious sensation, foreign yet highly pleasurable. Karl's finger began to nudge the small opening, not getting very far, and she gasped and pulled away. 'Hold still. You'll like this,' Karl promised, his finger continuing to nuzzle the puckered ring.

Despite her lover's assurance, Faren was far from sure that she would; it was something forbidden for her, though very natural for many men. Especially the men at St Peter's, she mused. They appeared to enjoy it, but it was beyond her comprehension. Although, if she could bear the pain, she would have another experience to notch up. Could she muster up enthusiasm for it, so Karl would continue? She bit her lip when a wet finger pressed the tight ring and barely entered her before withdrawing. She knew Karl must have dipped his finger in the yoghurt tub again, because on his next try it slid in with comparative ease. When it withdrew, she cried out, feeling the pain more then than when it had entered her. Feeling the nudge of his finger again she gritted her teeth; it felt thicker than before, and she realised it was because he had penetrated her further this time. Apparently Karl was attuned to her response and sensed when she became used to the intrusion, because he began gradual in-and-out movements. She groaned, beginning to find some pleasure in the thrusting motion, though still a little fearful of this exotic loveplay. When he withdrew his finger completely, she sighed. More balm was slapped on her behind and rubbed into her crease. Ready to drown in the cool, silky pleasure, she suddenly felt something large butting her and she knew it was the head of his cock. She tensed. Surely Karl did not believe he could enter her there? He started to grunt, the mattress dipping beneath her knees as he nudged her back and forth, holding her tightly by the hips, his penis still aimed at her anus. She felt her muscles beginning to tense again, the image of such a large part of him wanting entry overtaking every other thought. Firm fingers gripped her hips, held her steady, and, feeling the tension of his hard thighs against her buttocks, Faren realised he was through with waiting. Willing herself to relax, to accept him, she heard him grunt as he surged forward and entered her. She screamed. He was panting, and grateful that he held himself still so this small passage could accustom itself to the thick and lengthy intrusion, she felt him quiver against her thighs.

'Do you like this, sweetheart?' Karl asked as he slowly moved out and then back into her again.

'I don't know,' she gasped, feeling each brush of his thick bush when he butted up against her. But as Karl's thrusts found an acceptable pace, she realised she was rapidly adapting to this strange invasion, backing on to him when his cock threatened to leave her. He reached round then to finger her clitoris and her whole sex began to tingle; she knew she would climax if he continued the stimulation. She met his thrusts and Karl's fingers moved more rapidly on her clitoris, pressing hard and fast every time he buried his cock into her. His breathing was ragged and matched hers. When his grunts became more guttural and she realised he was about to come, she urged her own climax on, wanting to experience this because of the strangeness of it all. Pressure on her bud was released as Karl used his hands to hold her hips, his hard thighs shaking against her buttocks as he came, his shudders rocking the bed. He seemed to go on forever, and then Faren's climax was triggered and she groaned at the intensity of the sensations that swept through her. The weight on her arms made them shake, her knees unsteady, and when Karl collapsed on top of her, she, too, fell flat on the bed.

Rosemary sat astride him and his spent penis slithered out and curled against the dampness of her sex. It felt comfortable, there in the stickiness. 'Good girl,' he said drowsily.

'You were with her today, weren't you?'

Simon opened his eyes and gazed at the rolls of pale flesh ringing the familiar body, its pallor so out of place in a city that thronged with sun-bronzed bodies. When she had come to him with the revelation of Faren's stashed magazines, he knew Rosemary expected him to expel the young woman. The fact that Faren owned magazines that showed stiff pricks and pink pussies had turned him on, his own prick stiffening when he envisaged Faren pleasuring herself while she gazed at the lewd photos. Rosemary should thank the young woman, he thought, smiling; she had, after all, reaped the benefits.

'And don't bother to lie. I can smell her on you.'

'Why should I lie?' If she were looking for a fight, he would deny her the satisfaction. But still he hoped that would be an end to it. 'You've had a bee in your bonnet about Miss Lonsdale ever since she arrived.'

'Simon, you don't need her. What can her body give you that mine can't?'

Fed up, totally sick of her need to possess, he lashed out. 'A host of sensations that you can't arouse in me!' And was immediately contrite when tears brimmed in his lover's eyes. 'Oh, Rosemary, forgive me.' He gathered the shaking woman in his arms. 'I don't want to hurt you. Leave Faren Lonsdale out of it, eh? I care about you. We have been good for each other. Let's keep it that way.' As tears continued to streak the woman's pallid face, Simon added, 'I don't care about Faren Lonsdale.' And had to look away for fear she would see the lie in his eyes. His lies, he told himself, were to protect St

Peter's. A jealous woman could vent great harm on the seminary.

'Make love to me again, Simon,' his lover pleaded as she lightly touched his cheek.

He nursed little desire for Rosemary these days but he knew, as a chill raced along his spine, that if he wanted to remain in his senior post at St Peter's, he would continue to service her. Perhaps it was time to pass Rosemary on to one of the younger priests. As long as there was someone, she would be happy, and he cared for her well-being. The priests had no cause to be picky, as long as they had somewhere to shove their cocks. Simon knew – as did a small number of his associates on the High Council – that a fair proportion of seminarians indulged in self-gratification, with a select group having access to the confessional, and, as long as they did penance, their souls would be saved. Like his colleagues, Simon turned a blind eye to the transgressions; it was the simplest way of keeping novices happy and in the priesthood. And the very reason St Peter's had acquired a long waiting list. Though it was never openly acknowledged, delicate matters such as this had a way of being transmitted across the miles.

'Do you want to stick it in me, Simon? I'm so hot for you,' Rosemary said, lifting her ample backside.

'First, let me pleasure you my way,' Simon said as he gently pushed her back on to the bed. Rosemary needed no urging to spread her legs, and Simon bent over her, before using his thumbs to prise open the swollen lips. The clitoris was distended, and he pulled back the hood, flicking his tongue out to touch the shiny red bead. With Rosemary squirming beneath his face, Simon found it difficult to concentrate stimulus right where it was most needed, but his tongue laboured the length of her fragrant pussy until she arched into him, and he sucked her bead into his mouth. He sucked on it as he would her nipple, and, when she rewarded him with a yell, he pulled away from her, now using two fingers to plunder her while his thumb vigorously massaged her clitoris. He knew her climax was upon her when she looked dazedly up at him, her hands gripping the rumpled coverlet, her legs shaking. Allowing her scant time to recover, Simon fell back, hauling Rosemary with him until she was astride him. He guided his prick to the damp triangle, brushing lightly through the curls before feeling the sticky lips part in welcome, awaiting a thicker penetration. He teased, and entered Rosemary with only the tip of his member, amused by her fierce concentration as he slipped his hands beneath her buttocks to take her weight. Closing his eyes, he thrust upwards, burying himself in his lover's sheath. He let his mind's eye serve sweet Faren to him so that he could perform as expected and observe the peace – as well as his position – at St Peter's. So it was Faren's honeyed sex that caressed his, Faren who possessed him. Close to exploding, he pulled out. Each jet seemed to gush forever, and it was Faren's belly he splattered, Faren who received his seed.

Sometime later Simon stirred and grimaced as he moved his cramped leg. After the mutual pleasuring, he must have drifted off, carrying Faren's image with him. His lover was stretched out alongside him, her greedy hands playing with his prick. 'Go to bed, Rosemary. I'm tired.' He pushed her hand from his groin. 'I couldn't get another erection tonight if I tried.'

'Father, you want me to . . .er, look after Mrs Cheaters?'

'That's right.' The boy is brimful of guilt, thought Simon.

'But –'

Simon watched as a trembling Father Drew flopped down in the chair in front of his desk. Contrary to his mood last night, Simon had found sleep difficult. The problem of his lover haunted him. He had chosen Edmonds because of a belief, a sixth sense almost, that

Sterling had corrupted him. But in reality he did not care a damn which priest took his place with Rosemary, just as long as somebody did. 'No buts about it, Edmonds. Most of you have to make do with male apertures.' He paused, noting the young priest's tell-tale flush. 'Agree to this or miss out on an exciting new scheme. Karl Sterling's idea. And you know how ingenious he is.' Though Simon stayed well away from the room adjacent to the confessional, he suspected that what the arrogant Sterling planned would surpass every priest's dreams. And best of all, it was a painless method of ridding himself of Rosemary's attentions, which he should have spurned from the very first. He had entered his vocation a devout young man, wanting only to serve God and willing to sacrifice earthly pleasures, and look what he had become. But unlike others not of his church, he could ask for absolution.

Chapter Seventeen

*I*f she so choose, Faren could leave St Peter's. Her two-and-a-half months here had transformed her into a highly sensual woman. She needed no more motivation than that to stay. What she would do about it as yet loomed unclear. Her editor wanted in on the action, which in itself supported her cause. While mulling over her options, Faren hurried to the shower block. Deliberately she sought to infiltrate the priests' time. The briskness of her walk made her concentrate on the throbbing between her legs, and she sucked in her breath. Already the crotch of her panties was damp. These days she needed very little stimulation to reach a climax, and the sooner she closeted herself with the priests, the better.

She pushed open the heavy swing-door and headed for the bank of showerheads lined against the far wall. A soft murmur of voices stirred the air. Peering through the steam, she spied four naked bodies standing beneath the pelting jets. Oblivious to the presence of their voyeur, they continued to soap long, lean limbs, to shampoo their hair, to touch between their thighs. Hearing soft moans to her right, Faren's gaze swept over and registered two figures on the floor. The sight of men making love was hardly new to her but somehow – naively so, she realised now – she had not expected it to happen in the showers. But why not? In this ideal environment the temptation would be far greater than elsewhere; they could not help but be aroused. For Faren, the mating couple proved riveting to watch, and she sucked in a breath. Because her viewing position was side-on, the pose offered sensual advantages; she could see the thick cock pumping, actually disappearing, inside the man's body. Eyes wide, Faren's hand went to her throat. Her breasts were heavy and sore and an ache low in her belly intensified with each stroke of the disappearing cock. The distended head appeared two or three times, but mostly it remained clutched in the tight passage, the stem of the penis all she could see. Her knees threatened to buckle, and she swallowed hard. Between her thighs her dew felt slightly sticky; all feeling was centred in her sex. Someone cried out, drawing Faren's attention from the copulating pair to a young man masturbating, his hand vigorously pumping his cock. A man in the stages of shampooing his pubic hair stilled in the midst of white froth. He dropped his hand and Faren got a wonderful view of his sinuous snake, which, even as her gaze lingered, grew fat and straight. On the periphery of her vision she saw three erect cocks pointed at her and knew it was time to divest herself of her clothing. If her own arousal had been less, Faren would have gloried in teasing as every man swung round to watch, but to deny the intense physical ache between her thighs was to spite desire.

A blond giant stepped from the shower and within the space of a heartbeat he was beside her. He allowed her no time to remove her panties before he shoved one finger at her crotch and pushed the cotton into her slit. Faren groaned as it grazed her sensitive lips, and he moved his finger several times, keeping up the friction. Arching into him, she used her right hand on his shoulder to push him to his knees. The priest appeared to read her desire, for he was already tugging her panties down, and she stepped out of them, anxious to have him touch her. His long thick fingers eased her swollen lips apart, his elbows prodding open her legs. His busy thumb teased her clitoris and a raspy tongue streaked over the tight skin of her belly. She was trying to ride the priest's hand when a finger penetrated her, and then another, and she sighed as the bulk widened her, craving more. With a jerk of her hips Faren hinted for him to move and he laughed, teasing her with his stillness, until she ground against him. Then he bent to inhale her perfume, nuzzling her curls as though certain her sexual scent was enhanced by his play with her.

Just as she felt like screaming her frustration, two naked priests advanced on Faren. They then lifted her, before gently laying her on the tiles. Each arm was kissed, each leg caressed. And everywhere in between. Lips clung to her sensitive nipples, fingers probed her sex. Her hand was grabbed and placed around a thick penis, while another penis entered her. A rhythm took hold and tongues licked and mouths nibbled. Someone gave her an upside-down kiss, all that was possible with the thrusting priest on top. An illusional thousand hands caressed her. Then the cock withdrew and Faren felt air where once there was warmth. She ached. Deep in her sex, she ached. Frustrated because her impending orgasm was arrested, she cursed, and was suddenly flipped over on to her belly, grabbed by the waist, and hauled up on all fours. Her bottom reared in blatant solicitation. Every inch of her tensed: her scalp prickled, waiting for the cock to fill her, and she sighed when at last it sank inside her. With her whole body blazing where they touched, licked and suckled, and now with the wild penetration of the priest behind her, Faren sobbed. As her climax neared, she pushed back to envelop the thrusting rod more fully, feeling the light scratch of his bush against her behind. Her knees bumped and scraped on the tiles, but she was uncaring of the graze, wanting only to burst asunder in ecstasy. Her rider grasped her buttocks, fingers digging into soft flesh, while her jerking body tugged backwards so he could grind into her. As Faren's body responded to the fierce stimulation, tentacles of pleasure gripped low down in her belly, spreading warmth throughout her sex, and her contractions clamped her partner's shaft so that he, too, came shuddering inside her as she cried out, his thighs shaking against hers until he collapsed and she buckled beneath his weight.

When Faren felt him slide out of her, she wriggled out from under him. Moments later, her heart pounding, she propped herself up only to be swept away and on to someone's lap. Strong arms lifted her, lined her up with the rigid cock and guided her down. Clamped together, unmoving, she listened to the priest's laboured breathing, felt it filtering through her hair as his hands crept round and squeezed her tender breasts. With each brush of his thumb against her nipple, Faren groaned, squirming in his lap, needing the gentle stimulation on her bud. When he squeezed her nipple between thumb and forefinger, she cried out, her hips rising from his lap in an endeavour to escape the cruel pinch on the sensitive tip of her breast. But the stinging nip of his fingers became harder, dug deeper into the rosy flesh until she thought she might climax this way, without direct friction on her clitoris. Feeling the need to tense her limbs and urge the impending sensations on, they were suddenly snatched away from her when, each side of Faren, a man grasped her forearms, lifting her so that her cunt unsheathed the pulsating rod. They bore her away towards Jonathan, a novice known to Faren only because they shared a psychology class. Jonathan's hand was already ringing his erection, steadying it to receive her. The priests then plunged her down and the thickness of a shaft opened her once more. Almost immediately one priest got down on his knees before her, his hand reaching out to fluff the curls of her bush before delving into her pussy. Despite the sultry atmosphere, Faren shivered, a tingle radiating through each sensitive inch of her skin. A large hand caressed her belly, while the thumb applied consistent pressure to her clitoris. She shuddered with delight, her bottom pressing hard down on the novice's lap. The only pleasure she felt she could give Jonathan was to squeeze his cock, and she did so, recognising his enjoyment when he groaned loudly in her ear. Faren closed her eyes, surrendered to the sensations and erotic stimulus of being controlled by three priests. As her second orgasm peaked, Faren heard her partner's muffled cry, felt his fingers dig into her breasts as he climaxed; his lap quivered, jiggling her, spurring her climax to string out, and her sex convulsed round him.

Faren stirred, peering through her lashes. She bolted upright. 'Karl! What do you want?'

'Stupid question, Faren,' he said, stroking the bulge in his pants.

Her fingers slid through her hair as her gaze shifted. Someone had put her to bed. Delirious and sated after countless orgasms, two priests – dressed, she recalled – had half dragged, half carried her to her room. Drunk on sex, Faren had fallen into a deep slumber. Now Karl was here. She flicked him a wary glance, found his eyes slitted, as if silently accusing. Did he know? 'What do you want, Karl? It's late.'

'It's early,' he contradicted. 'And as to what I want, well, it seems you are quite blind. My cock, for the benefit of your blindness, is itching to burrow deep inside you.'

If Faren thought herself done for the night, the heat that flared between her legs at Karl's words disclaimed the notion. She knew it was impossible, but already it seemed she was moist with wanting of him. 'You shouldn't be here.'

Karl, as though sensing her need, stalked over to her and planted a wet kiss on her mouth. 'Come with me.' His fingers clutched her wrist and he dragged her up. 'Better slip something on,' he said, his dark eyes devouring her scantily clad form. 'It's more exciting to start off dressed.'

'What is it?' Faren shrugged into a skirt and cotton sweatshirt and tottered across the room while trying to shove her feet into slip-ons.

'You'll see.'

With Karl dragging her through the dimly lit corridors, Faren had time to take stock of the fact that he was actually holding her hand. Tonight he didn't care that they might be seen by fellow priests. So what had changed? She bumped into him when he stopped outside a black-curtained booth. 'The confessional?'

'Sometime I'll let you see in there. You're curious enough to want to know how I got on before you arrived, I reckon. Well, I'm willing to tell you. But first I've got a surprise.' He turned to a dark, panelled door set about a foot away from the confessional. 'You first.'

Crinkling her brow, Faren wondered what surprise lurked behind this door, then noted with quiet smugness the protuberance beneath Karl's fly. The brass knob twisted quietly and she stepped inside. She gasped, unprepared for the tableau that met her, inhaling the strong scent of incense and burning candles. Through the haze, candlelight illuminated several figures – perhaps a dozen in all – and though they were naked, she assumed all to be priests. A lone female with her back towards the door stood in Faren's immediate sight, wearing scarlet leather jackboots and what Faren now realised were flesh-coloured briefs, the silk embedded in the crease. It was little more than a G-string with two soft globes on blatant show. Sweeping her gaze along the sun-tanned spine to the ebony hair, Faren felt her throat go dry. She shook her head, refusing to believe her eyes. Then, as though sensing dazed eyes upon her, the woman turned.

Martine Danson sauntered towards her with a feline smile, her pale-tipped breasts swaying provocatively, while Faren's mind formed a dozen questions. She grabbed Faren's shaking hand. 'Hello, Faren.' Long nails pressed deep into the soft inner flesh of her wrist. 'You can't be surprised,' she said.

Before Faren could speak, a naked Father Murray loped up, his manhood jiggling. A hand rested on Martine's bare shoulder, his other hand already groping the dainty breast. With his palm, he pushed it high, then leaned over to flick his tongue across the nipple. She watched Martine shiver. 'You kept this beautiful creature a secret from me, Faren,' Simon admonished. 'Now I'm going to have to punish you.' His grin suggested he would derive much pleasure in meting out the chosen punishment. 'I'm sure I can come up with something.'

So much for thinking I had captured Simon's affections, Faren thought. 'Martine. Nice to see you,' she said, fighting the urge to grit her teeth. 'What are you doing here?'

'Ladies. Ladies. This isn't a garden tea party. Catch up later.' Simon turned to invite Karl into the fold. 'Martine, I don't believe you have met Father Karl. Faren has been keeping him all to herself, I'm afraid.'

Relieved when Martine unfurled her fingers to take Karl's hand, Faren stepped back, scrubbing her wrist against her mouth, using her lips to soothe the imprint left by the woman's claws. She glared at her editor, and felt further incensed when Martine pressed close to Karl. She squeezed between them. 'Martine. A quick word.' And before either man could protest she propelled Martine towards the nearest corner. 'What the hell are you doing here? How did you get in?' Faren hissed.

Where moments before the editor was all sweetness and charm, now her dark eyes narrowed. 'You chose to ignore my warning, young lady, so I took matters into my own hands. Very clever too, if I do say so myself,' Martine said, as she did a mock polish of her nails on the swell of one breast.

The action ensured that Faren followed the woman's movements, and at the sight of the perfectly shaped breasts with their cheeky pink tips, Faren's breath caught in her throat. She clenched her hands, fighting against the sudden urge to feel silken skin. She glanced back up. 'Why?'

'Just keep your lips buttoned. I'm enjoying it here and so are you.'

'How did you do it?' Faren clenched her teeth.

'Details! Who cares? I ran into Father Murray in town, although I didn't know his name then, of course. So I introduced myself. Friend and employer of your lovely new novice, I said.'

Faren's shoulders sagged. 'You didn't tell him anything, did you?'

'Christ, credit me with some brains. One thing led to another.' Martine shrugged.

If Simon had not bounded up at that moment Faren swore she would have garrotted her editor. With an apologetic smile he herded Martine away.

'What do you know about her?' Faren fired her question at Karl, as, naked, he appeared beside her.

Lazily his dark gaze joined hers in a sweep of the gloriously proportioned woman who cruised the room with Simon. 'Not as much as I'd like to know.' And when she rewarded him with a light pinch, he laughed. 'You want to play rough, then let's get going.'

He marched her into the centre of the room and, having swallowed the worst of her shock over Martine, Faren opened her eyes to what was happening. Several men, mouths slack, hovered on the periphery of a heart-shaped bed decked out in red satin. In the centre was sprawled Martine. Simon straddled her, looking towards the soles of her feet, and was rubbing a thick liquid into the backs of her thighs and up over her buttocks, ensuring his fingers stayed well clear of the cleft.

Faren edged closer, the woman's moans and the scent of sex heavy in the air. 'What is that stuff he's massaging into her?' she whispered to Karl, not taking her eyes from the sight of Simon's jutting manhood, which swayed in time with his strokes. She squeezed her thighs together, feeling the pressure on her sex generate warmth and moistness. Her mouth went dry, as if she were the one the priest caressed.

'Semen.' At her disbelieving gasp, Karl nodded. 'His, of course.'

She watched as Simon hefted his leg and faced the other way before lifting the woman about the waist until she was on all fours, her upturned pussy presented invitingly. In response to a call from Simon, a young man held out a steaming white towel that dangled from a pair of tongs. Once the towel was in Simon's hands he juggled it, whistling, until he dropped it across Martine's backside. She yelped, and would have collapsed on the bed had the priest not held her. While she shook, whimpering, Simon moulded the towel to the contours of her buttocks and cleansed her, patting to remove the dried come from her skin. The helpful priest then held a bowl of soapy water for Simon, who washed his hands diligently before touching his lover again. When he raised the towel, Martine's skin was raw, glowing from the heat it had endured and from its scrubbing. Now he prised open her cheeks, murmuring his appreciation and keeping them splayed as his thumbs massaged inwards, each time moving closer to the small rose of flesh. When one of the spectators passed Simon a long object and a small pot, Faren raised herself on her toes to see more clearly. She watched while the priest dipped his fingers into the pot and then slapped a dollop of cream round the orifice, and, without any further preparation or warning, deftly plunged the dildo into his partner's rectum. Martine yelped, almost shooting up off the bed, squirming in a futile endeavour to escape the torturous prop. Faren flinched, as if it were her own small passage the meaty-looking toy had penetrated.

Stooping to whisper in her ear, Karl squeezed her hand. 'She loves it. And so will you.'

Sensing her sacrifice was next, Faren's body trembled. How could anyone believe that to be pleasurable? She could not bear to have that fat, ugly toy inside her. She would refuse. Her gaze crept to Karl again, but his attention was fixed on the writhing body in the middle of the bed. Martine's moans, the rocking of her body, touched her audience; there was not a single limp penis in the room. Some tilted sideways and others pointed up to the ceiling, but every one of them – including her priest's, she thought, as she felt a pang in her chest – was as stiff as the semen-soaked red satin. Faren slid her hand to Karl, the tips of her fingers twirling the thatch of tight curls before trailing upwards to glide over the tip of his penis and anoint the drop of fluid round the velvet plum. She pumped her thumb on the slit until he groaned and pressed his body into hers. How Faren loved the power! She glanced round at the men, hardly able to think of them as priests, stripped as they were of their regalia, and smiled secretly as she watched hands working their own pricks, or that of their neighbour. The chapel will be a blaze of candlelight when these sinners crowd in there tonight, Faren thought. She recalled her musing during mass this morning, when she had glanced around at the pious assembly and thought of how hypocritical the priests were, indulging in pleasures of the flesh and ungodly acts.

'We'll soon have some pussies in here for that sorry lot,' Karl whispered, cutting into her reverie.

A scream rent the air and Faren turned quickly back to the rocking couple on the bed. Simon had slipped a condom on and penetrated Martine where once the dildo had. His right hand stroked along her slit with the love toy. The strokes calmed the woman, and Faren wondered if she would allow herself to be penetrated that way tonight. She may not have a choice. It seemed as soon as Martine had settled into a comfortable rhythm that the priest withdrew, rolled a fresh rubber on himself and this time entered her vagina, tossing the dildo aside. Faren shifted restlessly, scraping her inner thighs, squeezing, endeavouring to wring pleasure from each squeeze.

Karl's hand crept up under her skirt and she sighed when he foraged through the damp curls, seeking to please her. She lifted one leg slightly, making access easier, and sucked in her breath when he found the treasure. His touch was gentle, playing lightly along her crack, reaping her dew. When his fingers withdrew, he raised them to her face so that she could see the shiny surface before he pushed first one, then the other, into her mouth until she sucked, tasting herself. It was slightly bitter, but she sucked his fingers clean and when she was done, Karl began tearing at her clothes. Once she was stripped, he edged behind her, rocking his body against her, the length of his penis nestling along the split of her behind. With strong arms he lifted her off her feet, slid her back down slowly, sensuously, the hardness of his shaft hot and heavy on her skin. She wanted to watch the couple – the sounds emanating from the bed were a frenzy of erotic emotions that touched her – but she also wanted Karl. She turned into him and he lifted her once more, before, this time, settling her against his erection. Twining her legs about his waist, she crossed her ankles to grip more firmly. She wiggled to position herself, felt his hand clasp his shaft as he pulled back to allow room to rub the pulsating weapon between her swollen lips. After several delicious strokes, he guided his penis to her entrance. When she sank down on his hardness their sighs, like their bodies, combined. Her head resting on

Karl's chest, they remained unmoving, apart from the clench of Faren's sex that corresponded faithfully with the growing sounds from the rutting couple behind her. Then her priest began a slow rhythm, a tempo which gradually built and intensified as men all around them reached climax with guttural groans, yells of triumph and sweet curses. As a burgeoning tightness spread through her sex, Faren's pace doubled, helped along by Karl's manoeuvring and his well aimed thrusts. She wanted to come, and yet she wanted more time like this. The feel of his thrusting penis was a source of exquisite pleasure. Her breathing became laboured, and Karl's was an echo of hers, ending with an excited grunt every time she thudded down and her sex swallowed his. Suddenly her legs stiffened and she gripped the priest more fiercely than before, his thrusting cock sustaining the motion. Reaching her peak, Faren ground against him, saw the tightness in his jaw before shudders racked him. Arms tightly about his neck, the thud of her heart against his, Faren continued to clutch until her orgasm ebbed and she was left with warm, tingly sensations. She protested weakly when he unhooked her legs and slid her off of him. When her toes touched the floor she gave a final sigh and turned from him, her pussy still tingling, and while she watched the couple on the bed, Karl toyed with her breasts, only now it was a distracted fondling.

While Faren had been lost in her own pleasure, her back turned, someone had secured Martine's spread-eagled limbs with rosary beads which had been fed through metal rings positioned at each end of the bed. A lumbar roll was pushed beneath her to thrust Martine's pelvis forward. A priest placed a crucifix between her heaving breasts, then drew it down in a straight line through her thick bush. He jiggled it between the lips of her sex and dipped inside. He left it protruding from her cunt. Faren gasped. Such sacrilege! Someone handed Simon a sable mitten and he paused only long enough to don it. He leaned in to stroke his lover's breasts in long, slow circles, the pace mesmerising to watch as he trailed the ribs, over the hipbones, across the taut belly. The woman's body quivered each time the mitten skimmed a particularly erogenous spot, and Faren thought she heard her purr like a satisfied kitten. Then Simon pulled the crucifix out from Martine's sex and licked it, before throwing it aside. He backed up and aimed his cock at his partner's entrance before sighing loudly as he sank inside. As she watched his cock plunging in and out, Faren's legs grew weak, the lips of her sex feeling swollen and sticky again, sensations kindling into flames. She groped behind her and fondled Karl, delighted to feel him stir in her palm. However caught up she was in the scene before her, however erotic it was to observe Simon pleasuring Martine, Faren ached to be in the midst of it. To feel. To have the soft fur inch across her skin, along her thighs and behind her knees, to have it caress her hard nipples, the swell of her breasts.

Without a second thought, Faren tore from Karl's embrace and leapt on to the bed. Simon's tempo did not falter as Faren's weight dipped the mattress beneath his knees. He flashed her an encouraging smile. Completely unaware of the intimate spectacle her upturned bottom presented to the intrigued audience, she crawled towards him. No sense or strategy mapped out, she was alongside the priest when someone grasped her ankle. Simon reached out to tweak her nipple but missed as she was whipped away. Angrily she turned to see Karl. 'Leave me alone!' she shouted.

'In a minute. First you must allow Simon and Martine their pleasure. Then we'll join them.' Karl tugged her off the bed then guided her towards the back of the room, though she resisted all the way. 'Get this on,' he said, and he picked up a black bundle from a corner table and thrust it at her.

'Don't be dumb, Karl. I want to fuck without clothes!'

She stamped her foot, wondering what he was playing at, determined to get back to the lovers. Karl was equally determined to have his way, and he proceeded to dress her. 'Here, let me,' she grumbled. If she was to get dressed, she could do it in half the time Karl took. Stroking pliant leather, Faren began to smile as she thought of how often she had fancied dressing up like this. 'If you had told me I'd be wearing this in the first place, I wouldn't have complained,' she said sweetly, giving a little jump to wiggle her legs into the tight trousers.

Karl laughed. 'You are the most exasperating woman I have ever known!' He kissed her hard on the mouth, ran his hands over her curves, then, with two fingers, he probed for the metal tag of the zip that was partially concealed by her bush. Painstakingly he tucked her pubic hair in and away from the metal teeth as he slowly slid the zip up, grinning his appreciation when it pouched out over her breasts, then travelled to beneath her chin, where it ended.

As Karl had done moments before, Faren trailed her hands over her hips, shuddering at the pure sexual feel of the leather. The catsuit clung like a coating of crude oil, boldly displaying her womanly pout. Heads turned and mouths dropped open at the sight of her. So this is what it feels like to be desired by a roomful of men, she thought, savouring the moment before waltzing off towards the bed. All she needed now was a sleek Harley, complete with helmet. Engrossed in her fantasies, Faren had failed to hear the couple climax, but seeing them sprawled was evidence that they had; limbs were haphazardly entwined now that Martine was untied and the heady scent of spent passion was in the air. Though it body-hugged every cleft and curve, the catsuit proved pliable, and Faren easily crawled up on to the bed. Flipping over to sprawl on her back, she admired her sensuous figure in the ceiling mirror as she ran her palms over leather-clad hips and wondered what was going to happen next.

The mattress dipped as Karl crawled towards her. He quickly straddled her, his cock already seeping, pointing at her. Not until his hand flashed in front of her did Faren see the glint of steel, and she reacted by heaving herself up, trying to make sense of what Karl fisted in his hand. With a wink, his free hand pushing her back, he said, 'A surprise, little one. To see how much you trust me.'

Words stuck in her throat; her heartbeat quickened. She saw now that he held a scalpel, shiny and lethal. She began to shiver. 'Karl?'

The deadly instrument lowered, rested on her shoulder. Please God, he's not going to slit my throat, she thought. She licked dry lips. Then Karl sliced into the polished leather, lifted her arm, and followed the line of the sleeve with the barest of whispers. He tugged the sleeve off and held it beneath her nose so she could inhale the scent of fear and the newness of leather before he tossed the sleeve aside. The second sleeve followed suit and this time she swore she felt the blade skim her vulnerable underarm skin. Faren trembled as she gazed into his dark eyes. She watched Karl's mouth curl as he lowered the scalpel to her heaving breasts, and she knew he was enjoying this. With skill he quickly sliced two rings, and lifted the almost perfect circles of leather away from her body. Then he tugged her breasts and let them sit out against their black backdrop. Faren took a quick look at her reflection and saw two shivery mounds topped with strawberry nipples. Next, Karl traced the line at her groin, sadistically applying more pressure. As she dipped into the soft mattress the scalpel followed. She whimpered. Moistened her lips. The blade drew a line from thigh to knee, riding the rise down to her ankle, and the suit opened like a raw gash to reveal her quivering flesh. As Karl rendered the right leather-encased leg

240

as expertly as the left, Faren bit her lower lip, this time willing her body still. One slip. She dare not think. Her clammy skin made the leather cling to her. Her exotic perfume, fused with fresh sweat, was a heady brew. Then he started on her throat and loud gasps followed the heavy breathing from the crowd congregating round the bed. Faren began to shake, her fingers clawing the bed-covers on each side of her hips, but he was adept as with his first incision, and the blade flowed effortlessly down between the soft hillocks of her bare breasts to pause at her heaving belly.

Her gaze flew to his, and though no sound came from his smiling mouth, she sensed he hid a laugh, conscious of her trepidation, of the laceration one small slip could inflict. Adept as ever, Karl sliced. And then Faren felt the nick. She gasped. The knife continued on, now between the lips of her sex, and she held her breath. As the suit fell apart, he bent to kiss her vulnerable belly, suckling at the tiny injury. It took only seconds to be divested of the leather that now splayed about her in black tentacles, and, with one long exhalation, Faren relaxed back on the bed. Seconds later, Karl slid a finger through her bush, applying friction directly to her clitoris. His finger slipped up and down in the lubricated crack with ease, making a sloppy noise as he stimulated her. As Faren writhed on the bed, the crowding priests started to clap, the noise cutting short when Karl mounted her, and she reached to cling to him, needing the closeness after being on the heightened edge of fear. He nuzzled her throat and whispered, 'You were magnificent.' And in one sweat-slicked movement, he plunged deep inside her.

Until now fear and lust had remained unrelated, but as Karl pumped into her and she met every thrust with vigour, Faren's body siphoned off the remnants of those emotions, feeding on them to transport her to raptures previously unknown. Her head slipping over the coverlet as she thrashed, Faren spied grinning faces and did not care, not even when her vision cleared and one became the self-satisfied smile of her employer. Faren arched off the bed, and someone slipped a small cushion under her. She writhed until it was positioned beneath her buttocks. Karl's shaft penetrated her more deeply. He was performing long, slow strokes now, withdrawing his cock completely so that, with a small action, the tip of him touched her clitoris. It was like fire, but the brevity of touch was insufficient to sustain the greedy bud, so that the next time his cock came up to gently tease, she grabbed it and rubbed herself, perfecting a short but satisfying friction until she thought she might come. As her moans heightened and she began to squeeze his vulnerable tip, Karl quickly took hold of his cock and targeted it to her entrance, plunging into her wetness with ease. Faren was reaching down to rub her clitoris when she felt Karl's thumb there, such a delicious friction that she completely gave herself over to his skill. Then suddenly her legs tensed while Karl increased his tempo and he was shouting, long and triumphantly, as he came, and her pleasure joined his. Collapsed on top of her, his body was still joined with hers, and Faren gazed up at the ceiling and smiled at the reflection of his long, powerful body and beautiful, tight behind.

Karl's damp skin peeled away from Faren's as he rolled from her. She stuck out a finger and ran it along his penis. She brought it to her mouth and sucked, closing her eyes as though that would enhance its flavour.

Feeling a finger tracing the shape of her dark triangle, she stirred, looking up into Simon's eyes. He said, 'Come on, lazybones. It's you and Martine this time.'

Startled, Faren stared at the priest. 'Give us time to recharge our batteries.'

Breasts swaying, the older woman clambered on hands and knees towards her. Unsure as to whether she could do this, Faren felt a tingle of alarm. Never before had she fancied a woman, and to touch her editor, in the intimate way Simon suggested, was totally abhorrent to her. About to protest Faren bucked when lips clamped her nipple, crying out as a charge of sweet pleasure shot through her. The tenderness shocked her, the sensation unique, as delicate hands traced her breast while her nipple was expertly tongued, the difference between male and female loving so great that Faren wondered why she had never tried this before. It felt immoral somehow, but she found herself swept along on a new current of sensuality, unable to help herself. Of their own accord, Faren's legs flopped open to invite fingers to stroke the silken skin of her inner thighs. She sighed. Other fingers penetrated her but not Martine's, for hers continued to float over her hips, her ribs, finding all the little erogenous hollows and dips. It felt like a thick cock was embedded inside her now, probably three or four fingers, she thought, as no one was atop her. They pumped with frantic speed so that she moved up along the bed, while her sex sucked with its greedy hold.

'Sit on her face. Let her lick you,' someone encouraged.

It appeared Martine needed no further incentive, but the swiftness of the deed startled Faren. Before she had a chance to protest, Martine was astride her, and, without a pause, shuffled up until a dense black bush was poised above Faren's mouth. The scent and heat emanating from the woman above was sweet, an exotic promise of pleasure, and, with barely a hesitation, Faren's tongue snaked out to taste the bitter-sweet nectar. She ran her tongue along the wet length, feeling the quiver of Martine's excitement as she did so. More confident at each touch, her tongue began to probe, relishing the lush softness, the erotic contrast to hard male flesh. She felt Martine shifting above her to target her clitoris to receive the attention. Enjoying this unique pleasure, Faren tapped lightly with her tongue, supping the moistness surrounding the bud, and felt the woman's quivers increase. Faren shivered; it was extremely erotic to lick and suck someone's clitoris while knowing very well the immense pleasure it gave and loving the way her unknown partner was thumbing hers. Under the aggressive thumb, Faren's excitement mounted and, with her pinnacle near, her suckling of Martine's hard bud grew stronger, forcing the woman's pleasure to its peak. When suddenly the cry rang out, Faren bucked, pushing her sex hard against the thumb that rotated her small shaft, and she tumbled into her climax, uniting with Martine in ecstasy. Faren was conscious of soft curves that appeared to melt into hers before Martine rolled off of her. The strength draining from her limbs, she became aware of murmurs of approval in the room, and suddenly Faren realised that she never wanted to leave St Peter's, with its excitement and erotic riches.

Karl leaned over her, his rejuvenated member brushing her hip, and kissed her Martine-pollinated lips. Faren felt a sudden stab of jealousy – irrational, she knew – for what she wanted would never be. She wanted Karl to breathe her intimate scent exclusively, taste her to the exclusion of all others. She propped herself up on her elbows to survey the scene, needing a diversion from her jealousy. Priests had paired off and, though she was accustomed to man-to-man impaling, the sight continued to excite her. She reached out and clasped Karl's penis, idly drifting up and down its length. He thrust at her, conveying a message, and she smiled, wrapped her hand round him, and lightly squeezed the head to milk the fluid that oozed from the eye. She heard his sharp intake of breath, knew he was ready. Her tongue darted out, supped the bead, and another appeared; the taste was unlike feminine dew but was sharp, and pleasant in a completely different way.

'Turn round,' Karl said hoarsely. 'I want to take you from behind.' And Faren flipped over for him, on her knees, sticking her bottom in the air. 'Spread your knees.'

As soon as she opened up, she felt something twirl about her anus, and recoiled. 'Hang on! It's only a toy to intensify your pleasure. Look,' said Karl. As she glanced back he held up a slender, ivory vibrator, not much thicker than his finger, and she nodded. It looked far less lethal than the dildo Martine had endured. At first she tensed, and Karl slapped her on the bottom until she released her cheeks. 'Good girl. It'll pop in easier.' But she clenched again. He backed away from her and she wondered what he was doing now. As he fingered something cold and creamy round the puckered flesh, she relaxed her muscles. 'That's better.'

The plastic vibrator slipped effortlessly in, her snug passage closing around it. It was a strange intrusion, more so when the switch was flicked on and delicious waves of sensation flowed through her body. Then his cock was nuzzling her, searching for her opening, scraping her tender clitoris in its quest, causing Faren to yell her pleasure. Karl groaned when he found his mark, rocking back and forth several times before he plunged inside. Savouring the definite tempo as Karl's hard cock moved with her, the vibrator doing its teasing inside her second passage, Faren tensed her arms to pound back on to her lover. In this position she was unable to stimulate her clitoris, to receive the friction needed for her to climax. Karl held the vibrator in one hand and clutched her hip with the other. She glanced over to see what Simon was doing. He was busy with Martine's breasts, but as soon as he caught her gaze, he whispered something. Martine got up and moved out of Faren's sight, while Simon crept across the bed and positioned his head under Faren. He steadied her for a moment while he sucked one of her nipples into his mouth, forcing her to cry out with joy. Spurred on by her excitement, Karl's tempo increased, and Simon, still suckling, reached down and found the pleasure point between her thighs. She felt him rotate his fingertip on the sensitive protrusion, and she sucked in her breath, tensing, forcing the sensations on. All around the room men wailed and groaned in their own passion, inciting couples and larger groups to perform faster. Karl stepped up the motions of his thrusting cock, as well as the vibrator, managing with finger and thumb to flick the toy around to full speed while Simon kept up the friction. Weakened by the pleasure being wrung from her, just when she felt she could suffer no more, Faren's orgasm hit, and she clamped the invading forces. The duration and potency of the spasms that clutched Karl's cock shook even Faren, so that when he came, releasing an uncharacteristic yell, it was the most exciting sound Faren had ever heard. She must have clamped him with unbelievable power, because he continued to jerk inside her long after her orgasm faded.

In the soft afterglow of sex, Faren felt hands explore her. She looked up to see Simon. He was urging her to sit up but, feeling boneless, she lay there. 'No more,' she groaned.

Ignoring her plea, he slipped an arm beneath her and jerked her into his arms, then carried her over to a table. The cold surface on her behind injected new energy into her limp limbs. Surprised, she realised the tabletop was glass. 'Here, squat down,' Simon said.

The pleasure meted out tonight was beyond anything she could have fantasised on her own, that Faren happily agreed. Then she watched as Karl carried Martine over to the table and she, too, was instructed to squat. Now the two women faced each other. Faren could feel Martine's eyes on her, but she refused to return the scrutiny, admitting to herself that she still felt a vestige of embarrassment at having had the nerve to lick her employer so intimately. A scuffling noise gave Faren reason to glance down, and five or six men crawled beneath the table and then settled themselves below the glass. Eyes peered up, appreciative of the wonderful view. Faren cringed, instinctively closing her legs to shield her sex, only to have them thrust apart by Karl.

'Oh, no, you don't. This is a peep show. You're going to love showing every bit of your pussy as much as your audience is going to love ogling it.' After the first few moments of humiliation, Faren realised Karl was right. Knowing she was vulnerable and open to them like this, being examined in minute detail by several pairs of eyes sent shivers along her spine. This blatant, erotic display was immensely stimulating for her, and, needless to say, for the voyeurs. 'Show them how pink and pretty you are, girls. Imagine those fingers caressing you.'

Karl knew his carnal pleasures, Faren thought, as she picked up a harsh cry, and, glancing down, observed semen spray upwards and splatter, the milky substance smearing the glass. A young man she recognised as Philip – one of the first priests she had caught making love – pressed his nose against a clear patch of glass and licked, a parody of licking pussy, a sight that made her dew flow. Apparently Philip noticed, and his hand strayed to the tabletop, a finger waving until he found the slick aperture and plunged inside. Just as quickly he withdrew it and, fascinated, Faren watched the glistening finger retreat, find Philip's mouth, and slip inside. He sucked his finger, then noisily smacked his lips. Faren felt unbearable joy, the familiar ache, and wished Philip would touch her again.

After a bit of jostling, Simon crouched beneath the table, and, mimicking the younger priest, snaked his finger along to Martine's exposed cunt. The woman knew what was coming, because she threw Faren a triumphant smile. Faren did not care; Karl was the man she wanted. Let Martine have Simon. She already had him anyway. She suddenly felt pity for Rosemary, Simon's other lover. It wasn't me you had to worry about after all, old girl, Faren thought.

Firm fingers roamed her buttocks, prompting all

thoughts of the housekeeper to flee, prompting her to focus on her mounting arousal, and Faren glanced over her shoulder, catching the smile in Karl's eyes. She groaned and leant into him, feeling the weight of his shaft press her lower back as he anointed his fingers with her honey and played them along her slit. Hunkered for so long, her legs were beginning to ache and, with relief, she bounced, relishing both the ease in her cramped muscles and the friction the boomerang effect rewarded her clitoris. Busy fingers stroked her bud and she knew Karl sensed her impending release as he kept the tempo brisk, reaching round with his free hand to penetrate her with two fingers. She felt his cock nudge the slightly sweaty base of her spine, wanted to reach round to stroke and caress him, but what self-control she possessed dissipated and, instead, she tumbled into orgasmic release.

Moments later, exhausted, she rocked back on her heels only to be scooped up in Karl's arms. Suddenly she became aware of Martine's intense stare and how crudely her sex was displayed, and even while she stilled the reflex to clamp her thighs, Faren understood that they would barely shelter the puffy lips. Before she had time to feel uneasy at being so vulnerably open, Karl whipped her away and carried her to the far side of the room. He deposited her in a priest's lap and the young man immediately began to feel her breasts. She felt his stiff prick pressing into her spine. Then a black ribbon was placed across her eyes and tied securely behind her head. The immediate loss of sight plunged Faren into a mystifying void, and when plucked from the solidity of the man's naked thighs, she felt as though she were floating. Deprived of her sight, Faren's hearing and her sense of smell clicked into more sensitive mode. Breathy moans and deep-throated grunts were more audible, the acrid scent of musk and mingled sweat combined with pungent incense to form a sexual bouquet for her newly amplified senses.

Being lowered – it seemed too much like falling – Faren clutched Karl's shoulders, and then her backside touched warm, hairy flesh and her feet were placed either side of the man on a wooden chair. She had no idea whose body she sat upon, and suddenly, as the priest beneath her fingered her swollen lips, searching for her entrance it seemed unimportant. Perhaps he, too, was blindfolded, and the idea so aroused her that abruptly she felt an involuntary spasm. Lubricating his fingers in her slit, the man groaned, playing in her moistness before unknown hands clasped her waist, lifting her. When lowered again, Faren opened to the nudge of a hard cock, and as it sank inside her she nearly came, so potent was her arousal in her small dark world. As she felt her lips spread and rest at the base of his penis, hands she had been unaware of suddenly gripped her breasts, and she wondered why she had never before tried this most exciting of games. Her partner's cock throbbed more fiercely, and she knew she might never have experienced this sharpened sense if she had gazed upon his body. Her muscles squeezing him, the jockeying of her mystery lover instantaneously rewarded Faren, and she joined the frenzied bumping, intent on her pleasure. Because of enhanced feeling she understood that the man she rode was a stranger; his cock was bulkier and seemed longer than any she had so far sampled here at St Peter's. Straying hands, softer than those squeezing her breasts, scampered from the base of Faren's spine to her nape. Her flesh tingled. She focused on the heated coupling, concentrating mind and body on her own pleasure. The essence of her rose, strong and potent, as she bobbed to her own rhythm, leaning forward to stimulate her clitoris, interrupting the tempo only when she needed to grind upon him for more friction. With her level of excitement constantly sustained, Faren's climax dawned very quickly, and her head fell forward. She bit into the priest's shoulder, his moan of pleasure sending her to the pinnacle of her own euphoric release.

Almost as soon as she flopped down, strong arms plucked her away. Being whirled about in the darkness gave Faren a weird sensation of weightlessness, and when those arms folded her body, something scratchy yet fluffy, something light, teased her exposed sex. She shrieked, the sensation so intense and unexpected in her small, dark world. Her torturer laughed.

Chapter Eighteen

*B*y some small quirk, Faren refused to fret that it was
her editor who bestowed this pleasure, that whatever
Martine used was held and guided by her hand. Blocking
from her consciousness all rationale except the in-
dulgence of feathery caresses along the seam of her sex,
Faren quivered in the priest's arms, the only sound the
moans and grunts, the slap of sweat-soaked bodies, the
occasional shout when somebody came. Held in her
twilight world with its scent of sex, its sexual soundtrack,
Faren reached an explosive climax within minutes of
feeling the long, caring strokes on her slit. Rubbing
against the now idle plaything, her lower body shivered;
she wanted so much to stretch her legs, flex her muscles,
and prolong these pleasurable sensations. She sensed the
woman lean over her and heard, in her darkness, the
seductive linking of lips. A jolt to her stomach, as she
visualised her editor kissing Karl. Her man! Legs flung
out, her arms outstretched, Faren shoved the would-be
lovers apart. She tore at her blindfold.

Martine's peal of laughter raked along Faren's nerves.
'My, my. The little cat is jealous!'

'Let me down.' Faren squirmed in Karl's arms until he

set her feet on the floor. 'I'd like a moment alone, Martine, if you don't mind.' Without waiting for a reply, she gripped her editor's wrist and marched her over to a secluded corner. 'Why did you have to come here and ruin it all?' she hissed, dropping her hold on the woman.

In all her naked glory, the confident Martine preened, patting her sleek ebony hair so that she was as coiffeured as ever. Before Faren realised her intent, her boss stepped closer so that her nipples brushed hers. Feeling scorched where the hard peaks touched, Faren jumped back, reluctant to consciously admit the arousing effect of this woman's body.

'You chose to ignore my warning, Faren, and I told you I wanted in.' Martine shrugged. 'You made your feelings very clear to me that day, though you were probably unaware of it. So, when I realised you had no intention of smuggling me in, I made things happen.'

'You should have stayed out of it!'

'And let you have all the fun? How naive. Besides, I strongly suspect you won't do this story now,' Martine said, her eyes narrowing. 'Right on, huh, Faren?'

Over the woman's shoulder, Faren caught sight of Simon beckoning her, a valid excuse to take her leave. Not quite ready to have an in-depth chat with Martine on the subject, Faren stalked away.

'Want some loving, sweetheart?' Simon asked as soon as she reached him. He kissed her tenderly.

Faren sucked in her breath, amazed that Simon could make her feel this way when she wanted Karl so much. 'That's the best offer I've had all night,' she replied sweetly, taking his hand, determined to show that boss of hers. 'Let's do it in the confessional.'

'It's almost claustrophobic in there.'

'Good.'

Simon grinned down at her and tweaked her cheek as they brushed by a couple just entering the dimly lit room.

'Why, Faren,' the housekeeper gushed, clutching the

arm of the priest beside her, avoiding looking at Simon. 'Who would have thought to find you here.'

'Rosemary,' she greeted. Then she gazed up at Rosemary's partner. 'Father Drew. How's things?'

'Er, . . . fine, Faren.'

He reddened, while Faren's wilful gaze slid to the rapidly deflating bulge at his groin. Good, she thought, happy with the amount of power she wielded. Purposefully she reached out and took Simon's cock in her hand. Stiff, hard and throbbing. In the housekeeper's presence, Faren felt omnipotent. 'Well, see you later.' And she led Simon – as men have been led since time began – by his cock and out the door.

'You enjoyed that,' Simon remarked, his arm tightening across her shoulder.

'You could say that.'

'Is that the only reason my cock is now clutched in that dainty little hand?'

'What do you think?'

'I think you want it inside you.'

'Then what are we waiting for?'

As Simon had remarked, the confessional was small, but it hardly mattered. With their bodies aligned and aching to mate, Simon lifted Faren by her bottom and instinctively she twined her legs about him. With Simon taking all her weight, she lifted her rear just high enough for him to position his penis beneath her entrance, and she sank on to him with a long sigh.

'That's it, baby. We're good together,' he said, altering his posture, his shoulders braced against the wall.

'Oh, God, that's beautiful,' Faren moaned.

Simon kissed her brow. 'My sentiments exactly.' Then he began his thrusting, each time lifting her a little higher so that she could plunge down on to him with as much force as possible. His fingers burrowed between her buttocks, played along the cleft until her muscles tightened and imprisoned them there. 'Lift up just a little,'

Simon gasped, and when she did, his finger found the rose of her anus. 'Now ease down.'

She complied, tensing, envisioning the pain without lubrication, then gasped, clenching involuntarily as Simon's finger entered to the knuckle. Neither moved for several seconds until she was comfortable with the protuberance in the once-forbidden place. Then, slowly, Simon pressed as though striving to break through to the other tunnel. This, coupled with Faren's distended vagina, gave her the illusion of being filled to capacity with one enormous phallus. She began to move, slowly at first, groaning each time she sank on to the stiff tools that penetrated her two most secret places. His finger withdrew, and, shuddering, she arched her back, offering up her breasts so Simon could nibble on her nipples. Hot breath and roving hands, coupled with warm moistness, inflicted seductive fire to every inch of her body. He massaged all the little contours, the dips, cracks, and cavities until she trembled, her breath coming in shallow pants. Faren clung to his neck, marvelling at the strength and dexterity of him. Then she released her hold, wriggling to get a better grip with her legs. Inside her cunt, Simon's cock pulsed. Wickedly, she squeezed, knowing the effect it would have on him. He groaned, nuzzling her throat before choosing a tempo to suit his position.

Minutes later, with his hands at her waist, Simon slid his back down the wall until he crouched. Faren's toes curled in protest at the chilly floor. Then he tipped her back so that her body curved and he threatened to pop out of her. She saw that Simon knew just how far to go to ensure they stayed linked. Slowly, sliding his back up the wall this time, he stood upright. She wondered briefly what could possibly happen next, since they appeared to be limited in the confines of the cubicle. And as her head touched the floor, Simon's hard body leaning into her, she knew; he planned to give her one of those mind-blowing orgasms with a rush of blood to her head.

At first his strokes were slow, but as each plunge grew in strength, he, too, became more excited by the unusual position, his deep-throated grunts thrilling her, telling her of his enjoyment. She felt for her clitoris and used the tip of her finger to rotate the nub, picking up speed as Simon lunged into her. She was dizzy, the feeling of helplessness scaring her a little, then the dizziness blended with the excitement, sucking her up in a vortex of pleasurable sensations. Near the brink of orgasm, Faren relished the tingles that radiated from fingertip to toe tip, relished the heat, and the increased lubrication in her sex, along with the build up of pressure in her head. And when she came, passive in her inverted position, her climax produced the most startling of sensations that shuddered and convulsed her as never before, encompassing every sensitive inch of her, shooting her to the stars, seeming to last forever. Her cry of joy lodged in her throat while Simon's loud primeval sound strung out, followed, moments later, by his own climax.

Finally, Simon was quiet, and he hauled her upright into his embrace. Sobbing, she wound her arms tightly about his neck. 'Shush. You're okay. The dizziness will pass,' he said, brushing her hair back from her face.

'Oh, Simon,' she cried, nestling her tear-stained face into his shoulder. She could smell his sweat, the odour of their coupling on his skin. She sniffled and cuddled into him, secure in the comforting thump of his heart against hers.

He stroked her damp hair from her eyes, kissed her lids. 'An orgasm that way is always intense, sweetheart.'

Gulping down a sob, she shook her head. 'It's not that. Not just that.' With a fist she scrubbed her tears and looked at him through spiky lashes. 'I don't want to be a priest.' When he chuckled, she glared at him; how dare he make fun of her emotions! 'What?' she asked, aware of her suspicious tone.

'You're not telling me anything new, my dear. But you want to stay, don't you? With Karl. With me.' She nodded. 'Well then, I have a proposition for you.'

Back inside the love room, wearing a brilliant smile, Faren wove her way between writhing bodies, her hips brushing the bare buttocks of the priests, her eyes casing the room, searching for Karl. Searching for Martine. When she found Karl masturbating as he watched the young priest and his new partner, the housekeeper, pleasuring each other, Faren's shoulders sagged. He was squatting so that his stiff prick pointed at the couple, one arm stretched out behind him for balance, and Faren noted the strength of Karl's thighs, muscles straining as they held his weight and the stress of his movements. She wanted to reach out and touch his smooth penis, but to do so would surely interrupt his rhythm, and it was riveting to watch. To reveal her presence she ran her hands over his clenched buttocks, then gently grasped his balls. It was the only touch he needed, as, his head lolled back, he spurted on to the spoiled satin covering the bed. Faren dipped her fingers into the fresh come and drew them to her mouth. One by one she sucked on them, making lip-smacking noises so that Karl would open his eyes. When she had his attention – half-hearted though it was – she again dipped into his semen and repeated the performance. He groaned wildly once more, then, spent, he shuddered, his grunts quieter and slower.

Faren lifted her head for a kiss. She could feel his smile beneath her mouth. She pulled away. 'What's funny?' she demanded.

'Thought you'd find me enjoying Martine, didn't you?'

'So?'

One slender finger beneath her chin tipped her face to his. 'So, I like a bit of jealousy.' Then his eyes hardened. 'But what happened to you?'

Faren waved at the curls of smoke, the incense nearly burnt out. 'I had to get out. This atmosphere was giving me a headache.' She was uncertain whether he believed her or not, but at least he had missed her departure with Simon. After her recent show of jealously, somehow she doubted that he would appreciate it.

'There's your friend waving to you.' Karl nodded over her shoulder.

Turning, she cursed softly, but decided to have it out with her editor now. 'You were right earlier on, Martine,' Faren admitted, when she was face to face with her boss. 'I'm not going to write the exposé.'

'Oh? And just what is it you are going to do?'

'I'm staying at St Peter's.'

The woman's lips curled and she waved a hand at the passionate performances going on around them. 'After tonight, I can see why.' Faren heard the amusement in Martine's voice and began to seethe. 'But aren't you stretching it a bit, darling? I mean, a priest?'

She lifted her chin. 'Not a priest, Martine. Simon has offered me a job as sex tutor to the novices. In their vocation they come into contact with people who need support and advice, and having knowledge of erotic pleasures will add to their counselling skills. I'll have the best of both worlds. So yes, Martine, I'm staying.'

'Let's hope you won't get bored,' Martine grumbled.

But Faren glimpsed the light of envy that slashed through those eloquent eyes, and felt a surge of triumph that it was in fact she who had found the ultimate in careers. But Martine had always been good to her, so she said now, 'Friends, Martine?' The woman nodded. Satisfied, Faren was about to turn and rejoin the love party when she glanced up to see Karl striding towards them. She reached out and touched her editor's wrist. 'And this man is mine, Martine. No matter how many times you might come here, I advise you to remember that.' Then her lover was there and she let him fold her in his arms.

'I'll be seeing you,' Martine whispered before she brushed by, and, her beautiful bottom swaying, walked away.

Karl's forearms squeezed lightly across her breasts, the hairs tickling her. Faren sighed, sinking back into him, and his penis stirred against her. 'You're miffed she came here. But for all that, you like her.'

'I'll like her a lot more if you don't.'

Karl laughed. 'Done. And Faren?'

She smiled, turned to snuggle into him. She reached up and lightly touched his cheek. 'Yes, Karl?'

'I'll like Simon a lot more if you don't.'

She touched her fingertips to his lips. 'Done,' she whispered.

BLACK LACE NEW BOOKS

Published in July

ASKING FOR TROUBLE
Kristina Lloyd
£5.99

When Beth Bradshaw starts flirting with handsome Ilya, she becomes a player in a game based purely on sexual brinkmanship. The boundaries between fantasy and reality start to blur as their games take on an increasingly reckless element. When Ilya's murky past catches up with him, he's determined to involve Beth, who finds herself being drawn deeper into the seedy underbelly of Brighton where things, including Ilya, are far more dangerous than they seem. This is a hard-hitting story of sex and crime.

ISBN 0 352 33362 6

WICKED WORDS
A Black Lace Short Story Collection
Edited by Kerri Sharp
£5.99

Black Lace anthologies have proved to be extremely popular. Following on from the success of the *Pandora's Box* and *Sugar and Spice* compilations, *Wicked Words* takes the series in a dynamic new direction. This time the accent is on contemporary settings with a transgressive feel. The writing is fresh and upbeat in style and all the stories have strong characters and a sting in the tale. This is an ideal introduction to the Black Lace series.

ISBN 0 352 33363 4

Published in August

LIKE MOTHER, LIKE DAUGHTER

Georgina Brown
£5.99

Mother Liz and daughter Rachel are very alike, even down to sharing the same appetite for men. But while Rachel is keen on gaining sexual experience with older guys, her mother is busy seducing men half her age, including Rachel's boyfriend. Both women are proud and head-strong, and when a business conference takes them to the same location sexual rivalries surface and mother and daughter are primed for a head-on collision.

ISBN 0 352 33422 3

CONFESSIONAL

Judith Roycroft
£5.99

Faren Lonsdale is an ambitious young reporter. Her fascination with celibacy in the priesthood leads her to infiltrate St Peter's, a seminary for young men who are about to sacrifice earthly pleasures for a life of devotion and abstinence.

What she finds, however, is that the nocturnal shenanigans that take place in their cloistered world are anything but chaste. And the high proportion of good-looking young men makes her research all the more pleasurable.

ISBN 0 352 33421 5

To be published in September

OUT OF BOUNDS

Mandy Dickinson
£5.99

When Katie decides to start a new life in a French farmhouse left to her by her grandfather, she is horrified to find two men are squatting in her property. But her horror quickly becomes curiosity as she realises how attracted she is to them, and how much illicit pleasure she can have. When her ex-boyfriend shows up, it isn't long before everyone is questioning their sexuality.

ISBN 0 352 33431 2

A DANGEROUS GAME
Lucinda Carrington
£5.99

Doctor Jacey Muldaire knows what she wants from the men in her life: good sex and plenty of it. And it looks like she's going to get plenty of it while working in an elite private hospital in South America. But Jacey isn't all she pretends to be. A woman of many guises, she is in fact working for British Intelligence. Her femme fatale persona gives her access that other spies can't get to. Every day is full of risk and sexual adventure, and everyone around her is playing a dangerous game.

ISBN 0 352 33432 0

If you would like a complete list of plot summaries of Black Lace titles, or would like to receive information on other publications available, please send a stamped addressed envelope to:

Black Lace, Thames Wharf Studios,
Rainville Road, London W6 9HT

BLACK LACE BOOKLIST

All books are priced £4.99 unless another price is given.

Black Lace books with a contemporary setting

PALAZZO	Jan Smith ISBN 0 352 33156 9	☐
THE GALLERY	Fredrica Alleyn ISBN 0 352 33148 8	☐
AVENGING ANGELS	Roxanne Carr ISBN 0 352 33147 X	☐
COUNTRY MATTERS	Tesni Morgan ISBN 0 352 33174 7	☐
GINGER ROOT	Robyn Russell ISBN 0 352 33152 6	☐
DANGEROUS CONSEQUENCES	Pamela Rochford ISBN 0 352 33185 2	☐
THE NAME OF AN ANGEL £6.99	Laura Thornton ISBN 0 352 33205 0	☐
SILENT SEDUCTION	Tanya Bishop ISBN 0 352 33193 3	☐
BONDED	Fleur Reynolds ISBN 0 352 33192 5	☐
THE STRANGER	Portia Da Costa ISBN 0 352 33211 5	☐
CONTEST OF WILLS £5.99	Louisa Francis ISBN 0 352 33223 9	☐
THE SUCCUBUS £5.99	Zoe le Verdier ISBN 0 352 33230 1	☐
FEMININE WILES £7.99	Karina Moore ISBN 0 352 33235 2	☐
COOKING UP A STORM £7.99	Emma Holly ISBN 0 352 33258 1	☐
AN ACT OF LOVE £5.99	Ella Broussard ISBN 0 352 33240 9	☐
DRAWN TOGETHER £5.99	Robyn Russell ISBN 0 352 33269 7	☐
DRAMATIC AFFAIRS £5.99	Fredrica Alleyn ISBN 0 352 33289 1	☐

PANDORA'S BOX 3
£5.99

ISBN 0 352 33274 3

☐

Black Lace non-fiction

WOMEN, SEX AND
  ASTROLOGY
£5.99

Sarah Bartlett
ISBN 0 352 33262 X

☐

THE BLACK LACE BOOK OF
  WOMEN'S SEXUAL
  FANTASIES
£5.99

Ed. Kerri Sharp
ISBN 0 352 33346 4

☐

----------✂----------------------

Please send me the books I have ticked above.

Name ....

Address ....

....

....

.... Post Code ....

Send to: **Cash Sales, Black Lace Books, Thames Wharf Studios, Rainville Road, London W6 9HT.**

US customers: for prices and details of how to order books for delivery by mail, call 1-800-805-1083.

Please enclose a cheque or postal order, made payable to **Virgin Publishing Ltd**, to the value of the books you have ordered plus postage and packing costs as follows:

UK and BFPO – £1.00 for the first book, 50p for each subsequent book.

Overseas (including Republic of Ireland) – £2.00 for the first book, £1.00 for each subsequent book.

If you would prefer to pay by VISA, ACCESS/MASTER-CARD, DINERS CLUB, AMEX or SWITCH, please write your card number and expiry date here:

....

Please allow up to 28 days for delivery.

Signature ....

----------✂----------------------